# Noughties

*A novel*

## Ben Masters

**HOGARTH**

London  New York

Copyright © 2012 by Ben Masters

Published in the United States by Hogarth, an imprint of the Crown Publishing Group, a division of Random House, Inc., New York. Originally published in Great Britain by Hamish Hamilton, an imprint of Penguin Books Ltd, London.
www.crownpublishing.com

HOGARTH is a trademark of the Random House Group Limited, and the H colophon is a trademark of Random House, Inc.

Grateful acknowledgment is made to the following for permission to reprint previously published material:

Curtis Brown, Ltd: Excerpt from "Oxford," copyright © 1938 by W. H. Auden, renewed, from *Another Time* by W. H. Auden. Reprinted by permission of Curtis Brown, Ltd.

New Directions Publishing Corp.: Excerpts from "Marriage" by Gregory Corso, from *The Happy Birthday of Death*, copyright © 1960 by New Directions Publishing Corp. Reprinted by permission of New Directions Publishing Corp.

Library of Congress Cataloging-in-Publication Data is available upon request.

ISBN 978-0-307-95566-1
eISBN 978-0-307-95567-8

Printed in the United States of America

Jacket design by Ben Wiseman
Jacket retouching: Tal Goretsky
Jacket photographs: (table, glass) Tamara Staples, (matchbook, ashtray) David Bradley Photography, (cigarette on front cover) Maren Caruso
Endpapers art: Andre Thijssen
Author photograph: Angus Muir

10 9 8 7 6 5 4 3 2 1

First American Edition

*For my parents*

*With thanks to Georgia Garrett,*

*Simon Prosser,*

*and Zachary Wagman*

# CONTENTS

*And is that child happy with his box of lucky books,*

*And all the jokes of learning? Birds cannot grieve:*

*Wisdom is a beautiful bird; but to the wise*

*Often, often is it denied*

*To be beautiful or good.*

—W. H. AUDEN, "Oxford"

# Pub

"Ah mate."

This is how it begins. This is how it always begins. Four flat characters sitting round a table, with our pints of snakebite, our pints of diesel.

"Ah mate."

We contort our faces into gruesome grandeur, gurning with eloquence and verve: Scott with his question-mark nose, Jack with his inverted-comma eyebrows, Sanjay with his square-bracket ears. Nodding and grunting and twitching our legs, we clutch our carbonated weapons of mass destruction.

"Ah mate."

My name is Eliot Lamb. I'm the one with the fierce mane. Utterly fantastic it is: blond, wavy, thick, and full of spunk. You can tell I've gone to a lot of effort with the old creams and unguents, but it is a special occasion after all: it's our last night at university. I've even cultivated some designer stubble, sprinkled over my rosy face like Morse code, with all its dots and dashes. And if the code was readable it would go something like this: *There's a lot on my mind tonight, pal—oh such a lot—and things could get very messy.*

We are in the King's Arms, Oxford, rainy weekend eve, unfortunate travelers fumbling our way into the sticky crotch of a night on the lash.

"Ah mate."

This is the end, beautiful friend, the end. Our university finale; the last time we'll ever do this. The real world snaps viciously at our cracked-skin heels, groaning of jacket-and-tie, briefcase-headcase, hair-receding, tumble-dry mortality. I stare into the bottom of my pint glass and glimpse faint outlines of the infinite. I gaze into the abyss.

Sip, sip, chug: "Ahhhhhhhhhhhhhhhhhhhhhh"—four pressurized valves released and relieved, letting off steam.

"I needed that," blurts Jack, right on cue.

Scott: "Anyone else out tonight?"

(A droopy old man falters past. He wears the heady bonfires and dissident blossoms of the cool summer air, stirring fragrances of ale and tobacco.)

"I sent a loada texts" (that's me). My tripwire legs are vibrating beneath the table, compulsive and anxious. "Some of the girls are coming in a bit," I add judiciously. Rhyming nods of solemn approval. Jack traces his highrise quiff just to make sure it's still there.

Glug, glug, swallow.

The phone in my pocket chatters, clamping after my testicles with cancerous claw. I don't reach for it. It'll be Lucy.

She rang just before I came out, but I was a bit hesitant and evasive, needing to fix myself for the big night—picking the right shirt, nailing the hair, generally ogling the mirror in a you-talking-to-me-type fashion—and also being at an awkward place in my character development: I already have something pressing to face up to . . . something that needs to be dealt with, *tonight*. I do feel bad about Lucy though. She sounded, well, nervous; lost somehow. It was all the preambling that got in the way: *Where are you, are you on your own, please don't overreact to what I have to say.* I was running late and that was valuable time spent already. Only now I have the feeling that it was something important . . . must've been . . . I mean, we don't really talk on the phone anymore, and my promise to call her later seemed desperately inadequate. I should've just heard her out. But she was the last person I wanted to speak to, given my plans for tonight.

Maybe I'll send her a text in a bit.

She doesn't go here—Oxford, that is—not being the academic type. She'll be making a lot of appearances though, whether haunting from the margins or dancing resplendent across my imagination, and she's playing on my mind already.

"Ah mate."

The King's Arms is filled to spilling point. Students run rampant in red-cheeked naïveté. With military-front precision the place bares its insistent demographics: flowery thespians with lager for Yorick skulls; meathead rugby players (cauliflower-eared, broccoli-beard, potato-reared) floundering in homoeroticism; red-corduroyed socialites with upturned collars and likewise noses; bohemian Billies and Brionys, all scarves, hats, and paisley skirts; indie chics and glam gloss chicks; crushed-velvet Tory boys feigning agedness; pub golfers and fancy-dress bar crawlers; lads and ladettes, chavs and chavettes; and the locals, frowning at the whole motley spectacle. And then there's us: the noughties. We are quotidian calamities; unwitting lyricisms; veritable Wordsworths out on the razz, lugging twentieth-century regret on our backs.

How to convey the gang to you . . . Scott, Jack, and Sanjay . . . Well, I like to buttonhole people; fasten them in nice
and tight wherever I see fit and wait for the holes to sag. The
buttons begin to shuffle and slide, impatient with the restric-
tion. And then—the hold worn, no longer adequate—they
break free. Excuse the ready exchange of metaphors, but as
Augie March says, there is no accuracy or fineness of sup-
pression; if you hold one thing down you hold the adjoining. My style is to hold *everything* down, as firmly as possible,
and hope that only the most vigorous stuff rises.

So, there's Jack, still my best mate (I think) and clown
extraordinaire. Right now he's clenching a pint of Stella
and wearing a white-collared blue shirt (sleeves rolled, top
three buttons undone), flashing a hairless chest with each
flap of the loose collar, his shortish brown cut molded to
aerodynamic specifications. Next to Jack is Scott, rocking a
sprawl of auburn without styling gel (he's private school
and they don't really do hair product like us staties). Scott's
drinking Kronenbourg and chancing a pink shirt. He's bigger than the rest of us, being a college rower and rugby
player, but he has the softer disposition, his various insecurities taking the edge off his muscles. Jack and I have
affected occasional gym regimes ourselves, though we
never actually change shape or size, clinging to our coat-
hanger frames and the self-assuring consolation that "girls
don't like big men." They don't. Muscle freaks them out.
Still, we bought a barrel of protein shake at the start of our
second year, hoping it might prove the key tu the kind of
rapid muscle development we felt we deserved. I was
happy just mixing the potion in with a glass of milk after
each workout, while Jack all-out binged on the stuff, sprin-
kling it on his cornflakes, dipping crisps and chocolate
bars, pouring it into his bedside glass of water, even layer-

ing it on top of his toothpaste. Naturally our bodies stayed stubbornly put: no tightening of skin, no swell of veins, no progression in shirt size. Don't get me wrong, we're not runts or anything . . . just bothersomely average. And finally there's Sanjay (Stella), wearing his black Fred Perry with the white trimming. It's his "lucky" shirt, though I can't testify to the accuracy of the appellation. If it does attract the fairer sex it's certainly not working its voodoo tonight: our table is demonstrably cock heavy. Sanjay has a little blinking tic going on. Every now and then he is able to shake it off, but as soon as you remind him ("Hey, Sanj, I haven't seen you do the blink in ages") it returns ("Oh, for fuck sake" wink wink). You want to know what I'm wearing too? Black jeans, on the skinnier side of slim fit, and a blue and white check shirt. Stella.

We're over at the quiz machine, slurping our student loans and tossing shrapnel into the slot. Gather round . . .

**Q:** *In* **Brideshead Revisited,** *what is the name of Sebastian's teddy bear?*

**A: Paddington     B: Rupert**
**C: Aloysius       D: Baloo**

Drink while you think.

"C'mon, Eliot, you do English," says Jack.

"*Did* English. I'm finished now, ain't I?" I protest. "How the fuck should I know anyway?" Jack, a physicist, has always wondered what exactly it is that I *do* know—literature as an academic pursuit being entirely mysterious to him—and is looking at me doubtfully. The only social utility of my subject that he can make out is its occasional propensity for sparking progress on quiz machines, as well as select rounds of *University Challenge*. "But yeah," I add. "It's definitely Aloysius."

English: I've served three years. Pulling all-nighters over weekly essays, arguing indefensible points with unswerving commitment, and defying all common sense with consistent ill-logic, I've completed my subject. English. I'm nearly fluent now, mate. But what next? Back to Wellingborough I guess. (I feel it closing in like an obscene womb, pulling me into its suffocating folds . . .) And then what?

"Fuck yeah," shouts Jack, selecting the correct answer.

There goes my phone again. Lucy.


Why did I have to mention Lucy so early on? I promised myself that I wouldn't. It makes things so much harder than they already are. Perhaps that's why I was reluctant to talk to her earlier. Too late now—she's gone and hooked herself into the night's narrative. It's fitting, I suppose . . . she was with me at the start of this Oxford story, and now she's making her presence felt at its end.

Lucy was my secondary-school sweetheart. She's a year younger than me and therefore, in school terminology, falls under the ominous label of "The Year Below," such distinctions being vital in the zitty adolescent universe. We hooked up the summer before I went down to Oxford, three years ago now, and fast-tracked our way through the various steps of romantic training—an eight-week intensive in Sex Theory and Love Management.

I remember those early days vividly. She used to leave pieces of herself in the bed for me to commune with through the night: bittersweet surprises, proof of our love and decay. She'd douse the sheets in her secret smells, deftly scattering personal trimmings under the duvet and atop the pillow: long brown hairs like fragile question marks, arranging themselves into the broken outlines of a sketch; minute bits of skin like the baubles on a damp towel; all those mysterious stains and pools of our concentric love.

On my last night at home—my final night before the horror-movie transformation into lager-lube student—everything still felt so new. There we lay, fallen creatures. The fledgling months, ah—

"Same again, mate?" asks Jack tentatively. I tilt my glass and soberly evaluate the contents . . . nearly empty.

"Yeah, cheers." I drain the leftover. Jack's heading off to the bar.

Where was I? Yes, the fledgling months . . . they're the sweetest, are they not? Explorations into the unknown and no turning back. Discovering new creases and folds, hidden moles and scars, we marked up the cartography of each other's bodies. Our greedy hands learned to the touch, molding and impressing, leaving imprints for rediscovery to be fitted into again and again. We puzzled over our astonishing elasticity, pioneering to establish ourselves.

Oh Lucy . . .

Not that everything was so profound on my "farewell" night. There was, for instance, the sexed-up playlist singing instructively in the background with all its hints and prompts: Vandross, Marvin, Prince, Boyz II Men, Bazza White, Sade . . . which must have had her thinking how white and unsexy I was in comparison, and how small my— no, no, no! You can't say that kind of thing! All it had me thinking of, on the other hand, was my parents' vinyl collection, forcing involuntary images upon me that I just didn't need, that I just don't ever need, believe me: *I do not want to have sex with my mum. And Dad, put that away RIGHT NOW!* Luckily Lucy did not take the lyrics as a direct representation of my intentions ("You want to do what to my what?," "You're gonna spray your what all over my where?"), though there was considerable calamity when the iPod malfunctioned and switched of its own accord to *Reign in Blood* by American heavy-metal outfit Slayer (how'd that get on there?). I leaped from my bed to the thrashing riffs and commando-rolled across the floor, my buttocks flashing pale like two miniature moons, groping after the disobedient audio player. Eventually the sound track played itself out (coming in around the thirty-minute mark, which I have to admit was wildly ambitious on my part) and we snuggled down on the embarrassed bed.

Lucy peered up at me with inquiring eyes, her naked figure censored by the shelter of my side. Her dark brown hair, with its subtle sheen of ocher, fanned out over the pillow like an upended curtain tassel, and her heavy tan bolstered the already potent comedy of my fridge-white skin. I'm like a man wrapped in printer paper to look at in the buff. Weak-kneed from the cold scrutiny and paranoia that swallows you whole after orgasm, I was glad to be lying down.

"I don't want this summer to ever end," she whispered.

This was my cue. We'd begun our relationship under the promise to split come summer's end, when I would leave for Oxford. Not my idea. Lucy, with her extra year left at school, thought it gallantly realistic and (mistakenly) what I wanted to hear. But then we were ignorant of adult complication. I begrudgingly accepted our relationship's small print, secretly ambitious to violate this most restrictive clause. I didn't care about rocking up to uni an available man. I really didn't. I'd begun to revel in my not-for-sale status; in our private culture for two.

"But I guess it's time," she concluded, a lilt of martyrdom in her voice.

I would be leaving the next morning to become, as Fitzgerald's Gatsby puts it, "an Oxford man"—whatever that means. The ruffled bed was surrounded by boxes brimming with my stuff—books (battered Dickens, partially read Shakespeare, unthumbed Joyce, Eliot, Wordsworth, Keats, straight from the uni reading list), DVDs (*Partridge, Sopranos, Curb*), clothes (flimsy tees and skinny jeans), CDs (the Stones, Leonard Cohen, Talking Heads, some old-school hip-hop, Radiohead, Arctic Monkeys, D'Angelo). I stroked the top of Lucy's inside thigh—that part of a girl's body so exquisitely smooth and soft it feels like you're about to slip off the earth.

"Suppose we don't want to break up," I risked.

Her eyes widened as she pulled closer, and I felt a flutter of clichés coming over me.

"What do you mean?"

"I don't really want to end this."

"No, neither do I."

"Will you come visit me next week?"

"Of course."

I chewed on the inside corner of my mouth, creating that subtle metallic taste of silent concentration. I tried forecasting how the turn of the conversation might impact our futures, how it would actually unfold, but the vision was limited by the soft warmth of the body next to mine.

"Shall we just stay together then?" I asked.

Lucy has an adorable habit of nodding along in conversation, regardless of the content—a kind of ready agreeability—but this time it seemed thrillingly conscious: "Yes . . . I think we should," she said.

"Awesome," I said (a sublime note to end on, I thought).
"Great."

The wallpaper in this joint is waxy; smoke-stained from
times of yore. It's lumpy and tactile, like a golden-brown
resin caked over the top of dead insects: worm circles and
cockroach grids, the patterns of nausea. The furniture is
despairingly ad hoc: drippy tables and diverse races of
chairs rubbing up against each other; tall and thin, short
and fat, sunken, bony, flappy and slappy, and all else in
between. These death-row seats, those unholy pews, don't
so much nuzzle our buns as butt them away.

"It's proper muggy in here," says Jack with an air of con-
straint, like he's trying to dispel an unacknowledged awkwardness.

"Is it," I concur.

I've been dreading this night for three years now, all of
which have been spent looking the other way, hoping it
would never come. But it finally has, with its big hairy balls
dangling in my terrified face: the end of my student "career"
(don't you dare laugh!) as I pass into— no, can't say it . . .
*mustn't* say it.

Immediately to our right stands a harem of females,
pretty, but clearly underage. It's easier to sneak in on busy
nights like this. They're getting chatted up by some
smarmy postgrads who should know better. Trouble is,
they know they can't *do* any better, punching above their
weight and below the law.

"Been Pizza Express with the girls," yaps the head teenager, twirling her hair and fluttering her lids in response to
some tiresome questions-by-numbers, administered by the
overeducated elders. The front man of the latter is a gangly

specimen of the DPhil variety—a red-faced piece of lank—
and he plies the fairer sex with Smirnoff Ices and WKDs.
He's the type of bell-end who'll order a half pint and pay
for it by card.

"That's so cool," he says, an unfashionable turtleneck
irritating his shave-sore jugular. The girls look like nervous
peacocks, pastried over with gunky layers of makeup, debil-
itated by high heels and cling-film miniskirts. We grimace
at each other knowingly as these older hard-ons work their
desperate black magic. We roll our eyes and make obscene
gestures.

Ella, Abi, and Megan arrive and join us by the quiz
machine. My skin prickles and I can feel the color rising to
my face. I can't even look at Jack. "Evening ladies?" chirps
Abi with the habitual rising intonation, like she's asking a
question. We grin sheepishly (ever seen a sheep grin?). And
before you can shout that B: Joe Strummer (not D: Joe
Bummer) was the front man of The Clash, they've been
served. Fact: girls get served quicker than boys. They have
a preternatural ability to make barmen bend to their every
whim.

Guzzle, guzzle, chug.

Megan is pretty inconsequential as far as my narrative is
concerned, but Abi and Ella deserve mentionable spots in
the dramatis personae (Abi in the minor category, Ella in
the major). Abi is all makeup and short skirt—the kind of
girl who becomes increasingly fascinating in dark scenar-
ios, supplemented by copious booze—while Ella is more
inscrutable and weightier of soul. Ella's got her big-night
purple dress on and the matching heels to boot, which further compounds the sense of occasion. Our very last night?
It's hard to believe. Ella gives me a loaded look; just a glance,
yes, but rammed with so much history and heartbreak. The

minute glisten in the corner of her left eye is enough to spark a personal revolt. (A girl bearing a pitcher of Pimm's on her head squeezes past, granting me a second's relief.) If only I had the words and colors to paint the visionary dreariness of my feelings for Ella. But I don't. They are unknown to me. She means everything, and sometimes everything is too much . . . everything overwhelms and confuses, and what I need right now is distinction. There is such a crowding of thoughts, such an excess of emotions jostling inside of me, scrambling to get out. If only I had the words . . .

I dart my eyes away and sip my beer. I realize that I've got to face up to it all, but it still messes with me. And yes, I realize that now is the time to grow a pair. Whether or not I have the skills to do this is wide open. I feel like a puppy, poised and tense, watching the leaves flutter in the breeze as he learns the physics of the mysterious universe around him.

I know what the root of all this turmoil is though. It's the one thing I know for sure. I am unbearably aware of what I'm running from. Michaelmas term of my second year, when I was—

"Photo!" screams Abi, waving her flash new camera in the air, putting me off my stride. Everyone groans with fake weariness while sorting their hair and straightening their outfits. We're conceited little buggers. These'll be on the Internet tomorrow—mugshot.com—verifiable and incriminating.

"One two three?" Abi counts down, wishing she was in the huddle too. A right cheesy one, I can tell; all pouts, grins, and carefully cultivated embraces. We're pros at this stuff: the performance of a private life. Produced for all to have a gander, we make ourselves into mini-celebrities. We want everything to be known and we want to be bitten for it. But that's just how it feels, right now, so early in the century.

"Let's see, let's see," we shout, inspecting our handiwork. We piss-take Sanjay's half-shut eyes. Megan secretly rues her roundness and tastes a deep pang of dissatisfaction, suffering in silence. Minor characters, negotiating their self-loathing.

"Gross. Take another," demands Ella.

Now, we all know that people judge ensemble pieces entirely on their own performance, so it seems doubly ridiculous for Ella to complain when she is obviously the stunner of the cast. Nevertheless, she strolls over to a group of lads, tossing her wavy blonde hair over a bare shoulder (the hair and neck you yearn to touch and nuzzle), and asks one of them to do the honors.

"Sure."

Ella is an effortless ingratiator. Any one of these fellas would've clambered to push her button, simplified and softened by the measured attention. I remember my own initial encounter. It was the first night of university, a cocktail event in college, when the real world was but a drowning murmur far off in the distance. Lecherous second-years sharked about, scanning the fresh talent, mixing drips of Coke and lemonade into plastic storage boxes filled with cheap vodka and Bacardi. Ella and I waded our separate ways through the frantic mob of small-talkers (Hey what's your name where you from what you studying what's your name again?) to scoop our cups in the toxic vats. She caught my eye.

"This stuff tastes of arse," I said.

"Mine's not *that* good."

I laughed. I was terrified.

"Here, try some," she said.

Before passing the cup, she ventured an emboldened mouthful for herself, an elastic cord of saliva connecting the brim to her succulent lips as she pulled away. Stretched tight—tight as the chestline on her panting red boob tube—the string snapped, pinging with abandon into the drink. I took the cup and pressed my mouth against the lip-glossed rim, swigging her while she smiled at me. That drink, more than any (and there've been many), went straight to my head. It went charging, leaving dizzying shock waves in its wake . . .

We're ready for photo take-two. The girls turn on their pouts (they're hardwired for this shit), Jack points at Ella like a gimp, and Abi leans her head on my shoulder. I strategically fold my arms to make my biceps look bigger. Cheese.

"Would you rather sneeze every time you orgasm, or orgasm every time you sneeze?" asks Jack with considerable sincerity. He's saved this ice-breaker precisely for the moment the girls arrive, I'm sure of it. Abi loves these games more than anyone.

"Give me a break?" says Abi. "The latter? Of course? Firstly, you avoid the embarrassment of sneezing in the bloke's face every time you come? And secondly, who's gonna complain about bonus orgasms?"

"I can just picture you," says Jack, "dallying in wheat fields, staring at the sun, rolling around in the grass with no clothes on . . . probably lodging a feather up your nose . . ."

"But what if you want to protect the specialness of the orgasm?" interjects Ella, sweet and earnest. "Won't it lose all effect and . . . meaning?"

"What, you're just gonna sneeze up in the fella's grill?"

says Sanjay, the repulsiveness of such an outcome intelligible in the scorn of his voice.

"What if you've got severe allergies? You'd be buckling at the knees all day long!" says Megan.

"What if you're allergic to orgasms?" I add as a witty modification.

"That would suck cock?" declares Abi. The entire group nods in concurrence. We've all got one thing on our minds now . . . the one thing that's always on our minds . . .

Sex. It's astoundingly democratic and permissive here in the twenty-first century. At school you heard rumors of people at it all the time—Year 11s (always boys) banging awed Year 9s (always girls); ugly brothers and sisters making ugly sons and daughters in bushes on the council estate; sixth-formers settling into "serious" relationships and boning away on a more permanent basis . . . ragging with regularity. I use impassioned and degrading verbs intentionally, because that's what young sex is in the twenty-first century: a cold verb; a *doing* word. It's all about performance and tally . . . love rarely figures . . . doesn't even make a cameo. There is no meaning in the act beyond your shagging CV. And I meant "rumors" too, coz that's all sex was to me as my final school year came to an end: a rumor that had begun to preoccupy my mind with alarming tenacity. All its intrigue and unknowns, its supposed universality, had me a gibbering mess.

I was a conscientious non-fucker before I hooked up with Lucy. I could've got my end away multiple times (oh yeah, believe me), but I had standards. I wasn't going to give it all up for some get-around or industrious cock-monster. No—I wanted my first time to be pumped with meaning. That's why I was so keen to make it legit with

Lucy . . . so ready to resolve the panicking virgin's inner turmoil with some outer turmoil. I couldn't possibly arrive at university branded with virgin status—

"This is ridiculous," says Ella. "Shall we grab a table?"

"Good call," I say, snapping out of my reverie. I'm never going to get anywhere tonight if Lucy continues to steal my spotlight like this.

The place is heaving, but there's an unmanned table near the entrance. I slot myself in on the oak settle that backs up against the wall, with Ella and Sanj for accompaniment. Jack and Scott are darting around doing the old "Excuse me, mate, is anyone using this?" Sip . . . sip . . .

So yeah, my virginity (why not? It's a welcome distraction and we have got a long night ahead of us). I aimed to dispense with the big V-tag before starting at Oxford and made arrangements, accordingly, about two months prior. The whole affair was pulled off with clinical precision. Lucy and I met in the Wellingborough town center outside a crummy chain hotel, 8 p.m., a sticky July Friday, suggestively early in our relationship.

"Hey," I said, glowing red and pecking her on the cheek.

"Hiya," said Lucy, not glowing red, receiving the peck on the cheek.

I took her small overnight bag. I had gentlemanly aspirations.

I hadn't asked, but I was pretty sure she had done *it* before. She hadn't asked, but she was pretty sure I hadn't. Neither of us had asked, but we were almost certain that we were going to do *it* that night.

I felt like Dustin Hoffman in that film. You know, the one where he goes to the hotel to meet the older bird. Only I was meant to be the older one. I sure didn't feel like it. "Just do it," I advertised to myself (the image of Michael Jordan soaring in for a dunk seizing my concentration).

"Have you got a reservation?" asked the orange receptionist, with her heaving chest that sang of experience and boasted special moves and combos that I could never imagine.

"Yes . . . double room for Mr. Reservation please."

"Mr. Reservation?"

"Errrr, no, I said Mr. Lamb."

"Right . . . one second, please."

While she did whatever it was she did on her computer and rooted for our key, a hen party tramped into the lobby, clucking and crowing. They had just pulled up outside in a pink Playboy Bunny limo—those once exclusive chariots of statesmen and celebrities. They were a flabby lot, dressed in pink, plastic tiaras riding their heads. The cumulative sexual know-how of this orgy was climactic—something to which their specially made T-shirts bore testament: Deep-Throat Debbie, Katherine the Clunge, Tit-Wank Terri, Donkey-Punch Delilah, Fist Me Full of Fun Fran, The Head Mistress. I mused over the future marriage they were so eager to celebrate: would the golden couple be able to keep the nascent romance alive; maintain their lovers' dignity through thick and thicker; uphold the integrity of their intimacy? And on cold winter nights would they light a fire and open a book, passionately discuss their reading over a glass or two? Or would they wake up next week, in a few months, next year, on their fiftieth wedding anniversary, and roll over in abject horror?

What was I getting myself into?

Lucy looked at me and laughed. I took a deep gulp and smiled back.

"Oh dear," I said. The words melted in my throat. Lucy gripped my hand and we made our way to the prepared love-nest.

The room was no Cleopatra's boudoir, let me tell you. The brown raspy duvet was smudged with the kindness of strangers and the carpet was hard as concrete. In lieu of curtains hung feeble blinds, and our luxury view on the other side was the delivery vehicles' drop-off point. It was our very own anti-romance factory.

"Freedom, eh?" I said, trying to swallow the desperation in my voice. But we had come here to escape parental CCTV, and that much this shit-ole did achieve.

Sat on the breeze-block bed, we set about kissing and fumbling. Interestingly, we didn't hold a position for longer than five seconds, rolling and re-forming with hysterical energy. Don't get the wrong impression—I was well experienced and educated in the first three bases (figure *them* out for yourself). It was just that elusive fourth base—the deal clincher—that was absent from my repertoire. But all experience crumbles when you know you're going the whole hog—when you're promoted to the main stage. This might help explain our manic maneuvers: we wanted a bit of everything, and all at once. That's just part of the twenty-first-century condition though . . . isn't it?

I thought it best to stretch this thing out, what with the whole night before us—and paid for—so I directed our attention to the unplugged minibar instead. Two minutes later, Lucy was indulging in a lukewarm Smirnoff Ice and I was savoring a flat tin of Carlsberg.

And then we were at it again.

It pains me too much to recall every sordid detail . . . to retrace the event step by step. But if there was a halftime report it would've gone something like this:

"Hello sports fans and welcome to the Virgin Halftime Analysis with me, Corey Shucks, and Rod 'the Hitman' Nosh. Eliot's performance in the first half was perhaps as to be expected, Rod."

"That sure is right, Corey. At moments he seems content to make the usual rookie mistakes: frantic with the tempo, a bit too aggressive around the box, and occasionally struggling to keep himself up for it."

"You've hit the nail on the head there, Rod, but remember: Eliot isn't a big-game player. Let's get serious here, okay? At the end of the day, when you look at Eliot you've gotta like his intensity. Here's a young guy, not used to the big occasion—a perennial semifinalist, to be fair. You've gotta give him a lot of credit, going into a hostile environment and trying to come away with the win—something which, frankly, his franchise has never managed to do before. It's a game of two halves and the second is going to be huge. For me, if you can't get up for a big one like this there's something wrong with you."

"That's a great point, Corey. What are the areas to look out for in the second half?"

"Well, Rod, watch for Eliot to tone down some of his offense. For me, when he wraps around her he needs to be less grippy and grabby—he needs to stop attacking her like an indoor climbing wall. At the same time, if you're Eliot, you've gotta like the fact that she hasn't run out of there yet. She's sticking around and he needs to feed off that. I'm not being funny, but, for me, if you can't get up for a big one like this there's something wrong with you."

"Another great point."

"It may not be pretty, Rod, but he'll get the job done."

It was hard work, I'll tell you now . . . but yes, we got it done (a solid 6.5 or thereabouts). The intersubjective

dynamic pricked my curiosity. Or was it more intrasubjec-
tive? Well, no, actually. No, it wasn't. Disappointingly there
was no ontological mix-up . . . no blurring of being as the
Beat poets had led me to expect. It was far more carnal
Earl of Rochester than transcendent Keats. I don't think
Lucy would've put it like that, but there you have it. At all
points we were two very distinct people, slopping about in
our individual anatomies . . . our individual autonomies. I
was brutally aware of where I ended and she began. Zero
confusion on that front. But it was a relief, like when you
manage to use up all those stray five pences and coppers
that have been weighing down your wallet for so long; that
cozy feeling of "well, at least I don't have to worry about
that anymore."

The post-match bit I could handle. Snuggling and chatting I had down. I had prescribed some sophisticated conversation in preparation for this part of the night ("How
did that compare to your ex?," "Got any sexually transmit-
ted infections?"), but none of it seemed appropriate when
the moment came. Like contented springer spaniels we
rolled about in our own mess, riffing on fancy and autobi-
ography into the early hours. Lucy was tender and, as my
paranoia would have it, implicitly forgiving. She didn't tell
me about her dreams and hopes, because at that point I
don't think she really had any. But she watched me. She
wrapped me in a warm woolen stare. It was the beginning
of the summer and already I couldn't see how we would
ever call it off.

"Are you looking forward to uni?" she asked, staring past
me at the wall, pretending not to be bothered. Even then I
think she saw the obstacles that Oxford might present: different interests, diverging ambitions, alternative ways of

seeing the world . . . an inflated sense of self. I was far more idealistic about it at the time, or maybe just wilfully shortsighted.

"I guess. Why?"

"Just wondering."

"Cool."

"What are you thinking?"

What am I thinking of? What thinking? What? Such a disarming question, this one, the answer rarely ever worth knowing. I toyed with saying "How beautiful you are," but feared the cringe police would come tearing in, bent double with their contortions of squirm-armory, clamoring to throw up all over me.

"Nothing really. You?"

"Nothing."

"Cool."

There was comfort in our aimless words. There was true romance in our banality. It all made sense.

"Haven't you got something you want to tell me?"

I thought this one over carefully, rolling it about in my mushy head. At least five minutes passed in our unhurried embrace.

"I love you?"

"Oh, I love you too, Eliot!"

This pleased me. I don't like getting questions wrong. (Goes right back to Year 6 SATs.)

Lucy fell asleep first, as would become our standard. Her body looked for mine in its sleep with exploratory fidgets and experimental wiggles. When it found the warm contact of my wakeful limbs, I would crumple and curl around her like a benign Venus flytrap. I happily allowed her everything: her intermittent snoring, her bed-hogging antics, her ovenlike heat, her funny suckling noises, her bullying hair getting in my face. I allowed her everything, as I lay awake, collecting pins and needles in the arm lopped beneath her neck, right through till the beeps and grunts of the early-morning delivery trucks made her stir.

Jack has wandered off, probably rucking his way toward the bar, and the girls are ranting about some bitch in the year below, which I really can't be bothered with. My pint is almost nonexistent so I may as well follow.

"I think I'm gonna get another. Anyone?"

"I'm good, ta."

"No, cheers."

I'm up and off.

I need to stop delaying. Either confront Ella or ring Lucy and find out what the matter is . . .

And how about these dreams I've been having? I'm not even sure if they are dreams . . . hallucinations or visions might be nearer the mark. They've been with me for a while now. For example: I'm sitting in a café. A jet-black Americano, dark as the day I was born, steams its little heart out beneath my nose. An odd bustle, mindful of being hush, murmurs and meanders. I'm surrounded by academics with their squints and their dandruff, their Biros and ring binders.

I'm sitting in a café on Broad Street, opposite the Sheldonian Theater and its comic grotesqueries; those gurning statues of Monty Python stock. A chap to my left, like a monk in a suit, talks of the South African constitution; a ruddy old Irishman in the middle of the room raves at his seen-it-all-before interlocutor about terrorism and the Church; a bohemian tutor conducts a tutorial with two undergraduates on economics in the eighteenth-century sentimental novel. I take my place in this brain boggle with my *Essays of Elia* and thirteen-part *Prelude*.

I'm in a café, in a bookshop, the university's unofficial library and staff room. It smells of aspiration and intrigue. It sounds of niche interest and internal gossip. I've got my laptop out in front of me, whinnying and whirring, drafting yet another job application, trying to sound like I possess direction, trying not to sound like an arrogant prick. The flakes of a pain au raisin get about the keys and granules of brown sugar are embedded into my forearm. My stomach begins to hurt and I find myself doubling up.

"Alright mate." I look around but can't locate the voice. "Down here," it says. A pram has appeared to my left. "That's right . . . in here." I peer inside to find a baby grinning up at me. I try to scream but I've got nothing. Its body is the size of an eighteen-month-old perhaps, but its head is preposterously adult-sized. I look harder, almost falling off the edge of my chair: it has my face on it.

SMASH.

I jump at the unexpected sound of a slamming door: "Ian, stop being so *gray*," says the lady over from me to the ranting Irishman. "You could win an Oscar for such a wild performance!"

I stare incredulously at the mini portrait of myself, wrapped up in its abandoned pram. I can't see his body, hidden behind a soft white blanket, but I can make out the hump of his exaggerated baby's paunch.

"Do you mind? I'm a bit embarrassed about the old beer belly. That's what three years of *your* hard drinking has done to me, I tell myself, but I still don't like it." The baby reaches behind his head and pulls out a can of lager, whacks

it open, and takes a thirsty glug. "What can I say?" Its voice
is a perfect imitation of mine. "Helps us sleep though,
doesn't it?" His large head, transposed onto that toddler
body, impractically fills the pram. Facially he's identical,
though his hair seems a little thinner than mine and I can
make out some specks of premature gray. "What now? Is
it the hair? Well, you have put us through a lot. The question is: do you think you've been provident in peril?"

"I guess we're going to find out, aren't we?"

The babe lets out a small burp. From the mouths of.
"Excuse us. Well, let's just hope for some *success*, eh?"

I don't know what to say.

"Are you thinking about Lucy again?"

Startled surprised by the noise of the sound of her name
coming from the tiny little thing, I hit and knock the scald-
ing hot Americano all over me, myself, and I, but feel no
hurt pain. Curiouser and curiouser.

"Careful!" shouts the babe, steam effervescing from his
ears and nostrils in cartoon frenzy. "That hurts like hell!"

"Shit, I'm so sorry. I didn't get any on you, did I?"

The babe ignores my question, too busy writhing about.
And then he takes another swig.

"You make me feel like a sinner," I find myself crying.
"Is all of this justified?"

The babe simply stares.

"Why are you hogging my attention so?"

The babe looks at me, deadpan, knowing eyes. "Dreams,
innit."

I start to panic; the entire café has gone silent and is
watching. Nervously I begin packing my things away and
without acknowledging the babe I wander off into the
shop, searching for escape. The customers switch back on
and continue with their routines. I avoid looking behind as

I flank the enormous rows of bookshelves, narrowing and leaning down on me like a bizarre Fritz Lang set. I can hear a squeaking noise creeping up.

I turn to find the pram wheeling itself in pursuit. No one accompanies it: it's chasing me like some crazed M/F, driven by invisible forces. My heart is thumping and I long to wake up.

"It's a strange case, I know, but you can't hide from me, Mr.," says the babe, panting from all the exertion. "Anyway, why do you pun so much in your sleep? It's a bit over the top, isn't it?"

"I'm not punning—you are!"

"Exactly. I think you've read far too much, mate. It's hurting my eyes." The babe is squinting, struggling to keep me in focus. "I suppose you think this is all a bit of a riddle though, don't you?"

I find myself amassing the bibliography of my subconscious, frantically rushing between shelves and floors, not thinking about the selections: Oscar Wilde, Shakespeare, Martin Amis, Lewis Carroll, James Hogg, Anthony Burgess, Robert Louis Stevenson. Obvious when you think about it.

"Do you think they're going to help?"

"I don't know. I need answers from somewhere though."

"Good luck with that."


There's Jack—queuing, as I thought. He's seen me and is making room amongst the crowd.

"Ah mate."

We've already been served. Jack knows when to make the call. Wise. Experienced. It never takes long to refuel, what with Jack's pub/club know-how: he's from Manchester.

"Ella looks well fit tonight," he says. It must hurt him to acknowledge this, given the history, and it hurts me too, though he wouldn't know anything about that—yet. Hearing him come out with stuff like this makes my night's task even more difficult. Can it end in any way other than disaster for the two of us? I'm struggling to draft an alternative in this hurriedly planned script.

"Huh?"

"I'm messing! But seriously though . . ." We exchange rueful grins.

When I first met Jack, at the very beginning of our Freshers Week, I thought I had found myself. Not in a spiritual or metaphysical sense. Nah. As in I had found someone exactly like me. My principal criterion when electing new friends was music taste, and Jack caught my attention in the JCR at a welcome talk, that first afternoon, when he muttered "tune" to an old Smiths song that came on the radio (was it "This Charming Man"? No, let's go for "The Boy with a Thorn in His Side"). I immediately checked him over (vintage denim jacket, black skinny jeans, self-consciously cool hair) and made my move. "You a fan?"

"Fookin love um. From Manchester innit."

"Oh right, cool."

"Whereabouts you from?"

"Wellingborough?"

"State school?"

"Yeah. You?"

"Of course. Could tell from your accent."

"Cheers."

"No worries." We shared a look of mutual attraction. "What are you studying?" Jack asked.

"English?"

"Nice. You any good?"

"Urrrr . . . well, I like got an A I guess."

"I can't even write, me. Nah, we didn't have any pens at my school."

"Oh yeah? That's nothing. My school didn't have a roof."

"Roof? Fookin luxury one of them . . . my school didn't have buildings."

"Really? At my school we played football with a first-year's bladder . . . used a different one every break."

"We played catch with bricks."

"Hence no buildings?"

"Exactly."

We paused for a second, each searching for extra material but finding none.

"Eliot," I said, extending my hand to him.

"Jack," he said, giving it a solid shake. "Nice one."

Perhaps it's a shame that I have so readily sought out characters similar to myself. But there are two clear options available to the sniveling statie at an institution like Oxford: locate your compatriots and stick together with a resentful, snotty leer, or do that cringing dance we like to call "The Upward Mobility." I should know by now that things are far more complicated and nuanced than I allow—go for the particular over the general. But it's difficult. I'm still uncertain about how I even ended up in a place like this.

Maybe it's time for some of that Copperfield bullshit: It was my primary-school teacher, via my proud, puffed parents, who first put the grand idea of Oxford into my head. They returned home from the annual parents' evening at my school, up the lane, all suited-and-tied and whatever it is mums wear to these occasions. I was waiting with the eager need-to-know of a boy accustomed to doing well.

"So, what did she say?"

Dad smiled as he filled the flaky kettle, Mum looking on all goopy and warm.

"Mrs. Parker thinks you're the kind of kid who could end up at Oxford or Cambridge," he relayed, with a quick glance to gauge my reaction. This extraordinarily premature news registered with little-to-no referential meaning, yet I could tell it was a fucking good thing.

"Ah," I proffered in schoolboy wonder. The seed was planted.

We took a fidgety Saturday trip to Oxford not long after, with all the conventional stuffiness and aches of a family day out. You remember the ones: stately homes and landscape gardens; museums and galleries . . . all those hellholes that were anathema to your sucked thumb and anti-attention span; to your childhood mess and E-number erraticism.

I remember seeing the Radcliffe Camera for the first time, the photogenic library that is the city's centerpiece, poised in middle of cobbled square like bulbous tit and nipple, suckling the dreamy sky. Beleaguered, I had followed

Dad around Christ Church College and its capacious dining hall, tripping up over my shoelaces and tonguing the River Thames that oozed from my nostrils. Five centuries of roast dinner blended with fumes of polish and Dettol.

"One day, one day," Dad kept muttering, with a knowing nod of his head.

Gloomy blokes with comic beards and wooden titles stared down from the oak-paneled walls. I was bored out of my tree. While Dad divulged titbits of some illustrious history from the tourist pamphlet, I staged an imaginary war-to-end-all-wars between my G.I. Joe and a coalition of Boglins, WCW wrestlers, and Transformers, raging amidst the silverware and beneath the long tables, the anthem of my charmed youth. Soldiers fought for their lives in mires of English mustard while associative baddies abseiled down John Locke's portrait, making mayhem all over high table, splashing sherry and bleeding port in front of his wizened mug.

"One day."

My primary-school teacher's prophecy infused my plastic noggin. We used to write stories in her class and she seemed to really dig mine, mainly because they didn't end "And then I woke up. It was all a dream." She suggested books—*Cider with Rosie, My Family and Other Animals*—getting me hooked and dependent, frothing angrily at the mouth for my next fix. She told me to read *To Kill a Mockingbird*, but should wait a few years first, cautioning me that its adult themes might be a bit much. Naturally I went straight to the library and ragged it in two days, searching for glorious gang bangs and female things I couldn't get my mitts on just yet. It was hardly *Naked Lunch*.

Then Mum and Dad began to worry about the big "what next?" They couldn't afford to send me to private school but gave me the option all the same. Fat chance of that: all my mates were going to the local comprehensive and that was where I was going too. They needn't have worried. I wasn't going to get lost along the way. My destiny had been decreed.

I spent my seven years of secondary school hanging out by vending machines, rustling Monster Munch, gobbling Tootie Fruities, scouting for girls, and playing concrete football. While the kids at the pricey boys' school in town were building jet planes and learning first aid on top of Mount Snowdon, I was contorting myself into impossible positions to cop a feel of Emily Morris's boobs in Media Studies as she leaned forward, obligingly, so that I could learn the alien dimensions of her bra beneath the graffiti-scarred desk. Walking across the classroom, I'd shove my hands into the dry-tissue recesses of my pockets to disguise the throbbing bulge of my curiosity. At that age you never know when it might rear its grubby head. You have to be on constant red alert: marching into assembly in front of the entire year; in the sick room desperately pleading with the nurse ("No, I can't possibly go on"); in the swimming-pool changing rooms . . . oh god, please not in the changing rooms. Cocked, loaded, and ready to spit; but out of your hands . . . until you get home (a Ginsters pasty and strawberry milk shake from the garage along the way), approximately 4 p.m.

I enjoyed school. As my personal statement would have it: got stuck in with sports and a bit of music; got high grades; popular with my peers; liked by the teachers. "What a tosser," many might say. But then my school comprised perennial non-achievers: cigarette-butt-gobbing-unbuttoned-earring-jokesters. My best mate from home, Rob, could be said to belong squarely (or roundly, but what's the difference?) in this category. We were opposites: I could barely muster three kick-ups; he was the captain of the football team . . . that kind of thing. I liked Charles Dickens; he liked Pro Evo. I was a virgin; he shagged Janice Nutsford in Year 9. I got A grades; he failed General Studies. Yet we were inseparable, doing laps of the schoolyard at lunch, an established tag-team, talking about girls and planning legendary nights out. During the occasional break times when he'd go off to do mysterious things in the Design and Technology block, working on a project or some extracurricular (I never asked and didn't listen when he talked about it), I was utterly lost. I missed him. Sure he ribbed me relentlessly about my academic interests (though I did a pretty good job of hiding those, my mates being genuinely shocked when I bagged all the A*s) but I didn't care. I was off, secretly chasing bigger and better things.

And here I am just a few years on. I take a couple of swills from my pint and wonder how many times all the drink I've consumed at uni would fill the King's Arms.

"Mate, it's gonna be an emotional one, innit?" I say to Jack. We're hovering in the middle ground between the bar and our table.

"Less of that! I want to get appalling tonight!" says Jack—his usual boast—carefully stroking his quiff with the butt of his hand.

Sanjay fights his way over. His bushy black monobrow looks like a large caterpillar undulating across his forehead, his expression wavering between a frown and a smile. "Ah man, Megan looks *well* fit."

"Oi, less of that," we cry in unison.

"What? Ah, I guess."

The atmosphere is both somber and celebratory. The ignorant bliss of university life is coming to an end, but we still have a big one lined up. It's been a blow-by experience and I can't quite grasp what (if anything) has changed about me just yet.

"What time is it?" asks Scott, also strolling over, pint in hand.

"Eight thirty," I say, checking the watch that Lucy gave me for our one-year anniversary. I'd say "eight firty" and elongate the vowels to death if I was with my old school-mates back in Wellingborough. But I'm not. I'm in Oxford. So I say "eight thirty," crisp and clean. You should see me at home though. Woooooo, I'm an entirely different proposition: more of a lad; better to know; more fun to be around. I sparkle with earthy witticisms and fizz with mock put-downs and ball-breakers. I share carnal truths with the boys. I walk with a strut (a rhythmic loping sideways bowl). I'm garlicky and rambunctious. I call a spade a fucking spade and don't take no shit from no one. Ah, the double life of the boy done good; the double life of mind and mouth.

But like I said, besides Ella and Scott (a renegade Etonian who's crossed over to the dark side), I have tried to surround myself with mirror-image mates. We are Judes who would not be consigned to obscurity. We don't stand on these benches drunkenly railing the Latin creed at bloated dons and upper-class undergraduates. Nah. We are more likely to chant yob tunes and smack empty pint glasses upside down on our gelled heads. Maybe our attitude to it all is different: everyone goes to university now; you just kind of end up there. (So I guess I should feel extra pride about making it all the way up the ladder to Oxford rather than anywhere else, but I would never shout about it.) It's one of the defining features of our peculiar epoch, this further-study craze. We expect to go to university, and we're not even sure why. Generally speaking, intellectual curiosity and aptitude are irrelevant (not at Oxford, mind, but I don't resent people for going to Oxford, obviously. Why would I? I go there! No, here we just resent all the sex and booze that we assume every other student in the country is enjoying, and strain to replicate them on those rare nights when we don't have work to do). I know people who practically failed school but still wound up student clones. This is the age of entitlement: it's our prerogative and ain't no one gonna take it away from us.

Jack drops a penny in my drink, so I down it, because since time immemorial that's what you do when someone drops a penny in your drink. I drop the penny in Sanjay's drink and he downs his. Rules be rules.


Wellingborough. Trinity term lately over, and me and my old schoolmates sitting in the Tin Whistle bar, reconvening for our first university summer vac. Placable August weather. As much drunken carnage in the nighttime streets, as if all water had but newly retired from the face of the earth, and it would not be wonderful to meet a massive munter, forty feet wide or so, waddling like an elephantine lizard up to the bar.

Wellingborough. A place of no enterprise. Just a bustle of grim day-to-dayness and littered souls. (I am an Oxonian, but Wellingborough born—Wellingborough, that humdrum town—and go at things as I only know how . . .)

But it was on that first return, with a year of university under our slightly tighter belts, that I most acutely felt a divergence of experience. The worlds me and my mates now inhabited seemed radically different . . . or the world *I* inhabited. To make matters even more complicated, Lucy had been accepted into the University of Northampton, our local, coming in around the 100 mark in the university hit-parade, to study Travel and Tourism. She was set to begin that coming September and my paranoid foresight had been burning all vacation like some lust-addled Cassandra: one coloring-in exercise per semester supplemented by extracurricular binge drinking and blowjobs. My home-mates weren't much help, what with their reports of campus lust-plots and student-union sexcapades.

"I shit you not, mate," said Rob as he arched his body over the pool table and lined up the shot (staring down the cue, one eye closed, forehead tensed), "I fingered this girl up the bum-hole at the Christmas party in the student union." I sipped my beer in awe as he banged the red in off the cushion, retrieved his pint from atop the fag machine at the side, and took a contemplative chug. "Simple really. Started on the dance floor with a few drinks in us—quite romantic—and then moved away to a dark corner for some privacy. Bing bang bong."

"You're pure filth," said Anne (an ex-girlfriend from when I was twelve, now studying Socio-Bio-Dance Studies with History at some uni up north), twirling her vodka and Coke. I was with her on this one, though slightly impressed. Rob shrugged and eyed up his next shot.

"That's not what your mum said," he muttered as he smashed the cue ball. "You're just jealous."

"Not really. I had my fair share of pulls this past year thank you very much," boasted Anne before breaking out in a blush.

"Did you get fingered up the shitter though?" asked John (a blond pretty boy, studying Applied Agriculture with Media Studies at some university down south).

"No, I did not! You lot are disgusting. I just had a lot of pulls is all."

"Well done," I said sarcastically.

"You can shut up, posh boy," replied Anne. "Just because everyone's asexual at Oxford . . . too busy being butt-ugly and nerds." The rest of the group chuckled. I never have a comeback for this kind of dig. I tend to keep quiet, knowing that a response of any form would be deemed snobbish or elitist.

"Eliot's pussy-whipped by Lucy," suggested Natalie (huge girl, studying Golf Course Management and Experimental PE at some university out east). Ouch: that one was pretty harsh.

"Anyway," I said in a dragged-out voice. "You need to be careful, Rob, you'll be riddled with STIs before you know it."

"Uh-uh, no problems there, bro. I had one of those tests, didn't I." We were all slightly taken aback; I mean that's pretty organized and responsible for Rob. Maybe university was changing him . . . maybe he was growing up. "I shit you not. They shove like a fob mathingy up your jap's eye." Anne, who is half Japanese, doesn't even flinch at this. "It's like an ice-cream stick. And I'm not talking Mini Milk . . . I'm talking Magnum." Everyone gasped with wonderment, the boys squirming in addition.

I wanted to say something about Rochester's "common fucking posts" and "tingling cunts," or Thomas Nashe's "one eye wherein the rheum so fervently doth rain" . . . and what about Herzog going to the doctor thinking he's got clap: *"What have you been up to? Are you married?"* Instead I tried to be funny and said, "Those tests should be like an MOT: annual, and with a little record book for all future purchasers."

"Do you reckon I could take out insurance on my knob?" asked Rob with touching seriousness.

"You definitely wouldn't maintain your no-claims bonus," said Anne.

"Well, I gave someone a rim-job in a club at uni," announced Holly out of nowhere (tiny girl, studying Fuck Knows at some university near Wales). A rapid-fire of chokes and splutters exploded down the line, splashing into an assortment of drinks. That's a bit much, even for us. I found myself transfixed by her teeth and upper lip . . .

"Serious?"

"Of course not! You're such a bunch of douches."

We sipped our drinks, mildly disappointed.

"I knew she was joking," said Rob (I've no idea what Rob studies: perhaps a BA in Throwing Up, or a short course on The Reception of STIs in the Period 2006–9. I'm sure he's told me at some point, but I can't have been listening). He missed his next shot.

"You're shit," said John, his opponent.

I had switched off, thinking about Lucy and how we'd done well to keep things aloft all through that first year; wondering how it would go once she started uni and I got further into my studies. I didn't have anything to say to anyone around me, and longed for my Oxford acquaintances who understood me better; which is exactly how I had felt in Oxford all through my first year, longing to return to my home-mates who, I had convinced myself, understood me better.

"Your mum's shit."


"Cock." That was Jack. He's just seen Terrence walk into the King's Arms. Terrence and Co. He's wearing his blue crushed-velvet jacket (collar up), a paisley scarf intricately folded and tucked, some red corduroys, and a pair of blue and white boaters (no socks). Massive hair, baby face, gerbil nose. Before I got to Oxford, a dandy, to me, was just a comic book; but now I've learned that it's an actual kind of person, though the reality of such a type is something I still have problems grasping. Over the years I have applied qualifications: for instance, I don't see anything wrong with the theorized, aesthetic variation (Oscar Wilde, big fan). But then there's this subset of dandy with no substance; a kind of upper-class grotesque, more toff than artiste. These chaps move in exclusive clusters throughout Oxford, flawlessly reflecting each other.

Am I a hypocrite?

Terrence sees us and smirks, before carrying on to the bar, where he'll probably purchase a quart of port and crack out his snuff tin.

Terrence Terrence: first name Terrence, second name Terrence. He's a ditto; a fellow of incestuous title, one begetting the other, same rubbing against same; a pleonastic preponderance; a tautological tit. He studies English at Hollywell College, unfortunately, like me. He's one of those kids who have two thousand "friends" on mugshot.com. It's ludicrous. Just think about it: if he were to bestow each of his "friends" with the most bog standard of birthday gift—I'm talking a fiver in a card—it would cost him ten grand a year . . . which he could probably afford, but still . . . He says things like mama and mummy instead of mum, and calls champagne (which he has for breakfast) "pooh." You know the type: goes for weekends in Rome, Milan, and Paris, just to snort cocaine off a prostitute's left nipple.

Well, actually, I emphatically did not know the type before I got to Oxford. They don't call it a great seat of

learning for nothing. It was at my entrance interview that
Terrence made his first cameo (what he'd call his début, or,
having been on an extensive gap year, his ɗëɓûʈ) in my
life—


Marching in streets of Oxford, I came to court the fruitful
plot of scholarism. Dad dropped me off on Broad Street.

"Just do your best," he said, gripping my shoulder and
ruffling my stupendous barnet. "There's nothing more
you can do. Good luck, son." What else could he say? The
situation and setting were even more alien to him than
they were to me.

I didn't have a clue where I was and found myself stumbling onto Radcliffe Square, hemmed in by the Bodleian
and All Souls, the spire of St. Mary's Church rising in the
background. The Radcliffe Camera, in all its enlightened
splendor and sanctity, pounced monstrously into view.
The colossal building receded and protruded, dilating and
contracting before my dimming eyes. I stood minuscule at
its base, paralyzed by the dimensions and their impossible
drift into infinity. I clutched my rucksack, my scarf streaming over my shoulder in the wind like a flapping tongue of
dogged bewilderment. The whole building could not be
taken in at once, evading my grasp at its very edges; its
incomprehensible limits. Gazing upward, the golden structure seemed as if it had been placed against a green-screen
sky, leering over me with CGI prodigiousness. But it was
all real. I sensed the floor swaying and my body moving
away from me as the tip of the dome kissed sulky clouds in
strenuous proximity. Then felt I like some watcher of the
sky, when his ken is royally fucked: squashed and stretched;
handed new coordinates; recalibrated. I eventually man-

aged to drag my sorry self away and went in search of Hollywell College.

Having blubbered my way through the porter's lodge (the head porter glaring at me like he wanted me dead, some latent class antagonism animating his inanimate stare—"But I'm with you," I wanted to plead. "I'm with you"), I was shown to the common room by a group of surprisingly good-looking students with names like Rupert and Cecilia stuck to their breasts (*"here to help"*). Fuck me, I could smell the stench of fear and ambition before I even entered. Girls with grandma pashminas and electric-socket beehive hairdos (the kind of mop private schoolgirls spend hours crafting for optimum "just got out of bed" effect) flitted about the room, and boys in brand-new suits stood stiff. Fewer people looked like horses than I had anticipated, but there were one or two for sure: facial features wrenched upward by some counter-gravitational force that only breeding can buy. I was casual in jacket and shirt, unbuttoned, and jet-black jeans. My bouncy, sun-kissed hair gave me an appearance of . . . well, how the hell should I know? I haven't a clue what impression I give.

This was where we were to wait till picked off, one by one, by a cocky undergraduate who would lead us to the firing squad. Pool table, Sega Rally, buzzing Coke machine, and shelled-out newspapers were to keep us preoccupied in the meantime. I couldn't be arsed to make conversation with the competition: too frazzled and hung-up about what they might actually have to say. Instead I stared blindly at a copy of *The Times*, cultivating my best don't-talk-to-me pose. A right bell-end to my left had already formed a harem, preaching some shit about how poetry was the essence of truth and existentialism the curse of the novel. What a wanker, I thought. I mean, what a *wanker*. That was

Terrence Terrence. He was like an exotic bird, and I couldn't tell whether he was dangerous or tame. He said sentences that ended in "like" (which sounded more like lake), "actually" (hactually), and "so," applying major tremolo to the vowels so that they had a trombonic quaver of social pretension. In fact I noticed that a lot of people did this, always in a nonchalantly posh manner. Out of boredom and nervousness I silently completed many of his sentences for him: "I've done quite a lot of practice interviews at school, soooooo . . ." *you might as well give up now, scum*; "I should have lots to talk about, you know . . . I mean I read *Ulysses* this morning liiiiiike . . ." *a complete twat.*

Deep breaths. Deep breaths.

I checked the timetable on the notice board and saw that I had a couple of hours to kill. I was getting mobbed left, right, and center by pompous conversations about favorite authors and books, and people spitting the heinous falsities of their personal statements—how many schools they planned to build in Rwanda on their gap year and how their favorite hobby was volunteering at their local soup kitchen, which, remarkably, they managed to balance with all their sporting commitments as captain of six different school teams (rowing, lacrosse, shooting, water polo, equestrian dressage, interbreeding).

I'm in over my head, I'm in over my head. Shit shit shit shit shit.

Then Terrence began showing off his insider knowledge of Hollywell College, most likely gleaned from the untappable private-school network of gossip and know-how, spurting rumors that Dr. Fletcher (the English Literature Fellow) was notorious for favoring pretty girls. Apparently there had even been an inquiry into this by the college dean, but few complaints about Dr. Fletcher ever resulted in serious action, what with him being the superstar of the Senior Common Room.

I went to the toilet like a sprinkler set at five-minute intervals and gorged chunks of skin from my already battered fingertips. *Settle thy studies*, soliloquized a voice inside my head. *Settle thy studies, Eliot.* I shut myself in a cubicle with a car-crash edition of *Doctor Faustus* and lapped up cringing A-level annotations, priming myself for interview regurgitation.

Back in the common room, some time later, I heard my name being called like never before; as if it were being sucked through a vacuum cleaner:

"Eel-iot Larmb."

And again: "Eel-iot Larmb."

"Here."

"Thart's gurrreat. Fellow may." I understood that he meant for me to follow him, and rose with a sudden flurry of panic and trepidation.

This lad (a volunteering third-year) had stocky inclinations—could be hard if he wanted—and a face like the back of a shovel. He carried a piece of paper that bent and crumpled in the wind. (I was to sit in a secret room for half an hour and analyze the contents of this sheet, preparing clever-clogs things to say about it in my interview.)

"Ah," he said, peering at the paper. We were walking along the grassy edges of the main quad, boxed in by neat angular buildings straight out of the movies. "We read this poem for a tute last week."

"Oh yeah?" I was anxious but alert, trying to keep up.

"Yah. It's about the pleasure of the chase. Bloody good poem."

"I see." *Pleasure of the chase, pleasure of the chase.* I fumbled after the words, desperate to possess them.

"Here w'are," he said, showing me into a tiny birdcage of a room, all the space hogged by a creaky oak table. "Good luck, Eel-iot." He slapped the wind-beaten poem down and shut me in. There was a girl opposite, already under way, reading a passage for a Law interview. Her sheet was carefully colonized by different-colored highlighter pens and fastidious notes. She had tears sliding down her puffy cheeks. Fucking depressing.

It took about fifteen minutes before the words of the poem began to register. I repeatedly passed my eyes over it but nothing went in . . . no discernible subject or images stuck. I wasn't reading so much as looking. It might as well have been written in a different language.

Whoso list to hunt, I know where is an hind,

Pleasure of the chase . . . Come on, Eliot . . . it's all about the pleasure of the chase . . . *What* chase? The chase of *what*? Christ.

Whoso list to hunt, I know where is an hind,

It's a sonnet . . . I think . . . one two three four five six seven eight nine ten eleven twelve thirteen fourteen. Jackpot! Sonnet. Great. Love poem then, right? So why is he talking about deer and hunting and shit? Kinky?

Whoso list to hunt, I know where is an hind,

Oh yeah? Even if you do say so yourself . . .

But as for me, helas, I may no more.

Unlucky.

> The vain travail hath wearied me so sore,
> I am of them that farthest cometh behind.

Midlife crisis? Maybe you should think about getting a nifty little sports car or a nice young bird on the side . . .

> Yet may I by no means my wearied mind
> Draw from the deer, but as she fleeth afore
> Fainting I follow.

Crikey, I know that feeling, mate. Brandy Knox, Year 12. Jesus, she was fit. She had legs like a giraffe and wore tight black trousers (great bum) with that scandalous thong-a-thong-thong-thong peering cheekily over the top. She oozed sex, but I couldn't get near her. Only interested in older boys with shite cars and six-quid-an-hour jobs. I really feel this guy's pain.

> Who list her hunt, I put him out of doubt,
> As well as I may spend his time in vain.

Well, there's no need to be a tosser about it. I'd have your back, be your wingman and that.

> There is written, her fair neck round about:
> "*Noli me tangere*, for Caesar's I am,
> And wild for to hold, though I seem tame."

A little footnote at the bottom told me that the Latin jazz means "do not touch me," which is a bit rude if you ask me.

I do feel bad for him, but I feel worse for the girl/deer/what-ever-the-fuck. Her boyfriend sounds like a right prick: over-bearing, jealous, paranoid. In fact, almost exactly like me. Regrettable really, but okay as long as you don't impinge like this Caesar chap. Come on though, the poet would behave the same way if he had half the chance—he's already said he wants to ruin *my* chances. But is it all worth it? I guess. This girl he's after does seem a bit of a lust-pot—"wild for to hold." Oh yeah? Well, aren't you quite the little—

"Time's up." Spade face stuck his mug round the door and motioned me to follow.

He marched me up a high staircase to a chair outside a door. A chair outside a door on a high staircase.

"Just wait harr until you are called for."

"Okay. Thanks."

I was to be interviewed by the college's two English tutors, Dr. Dylan Fletcher (Senior Fellow) and Dr. Polly Snow (Research Fellow). I had looked them both up on the English faculty and college websites: Dr. Fletcher had writ-ten some groundbreaking study about eighteenth-century poets that I'd never heard of (*The Eighteenth-Century Poets*); a revolutionary monograph on representations of fruit in Milton and Marvell, explored—of course—through the lens of sociocultural Marxism (*The Ambiguous Apple: Towards a Poetics of Fruit in the Writings of Milton and Mar-vell*); a life-changing, radical postmodern account of early modern prose narratives (*The Unfortunate Signifier: Derrida and Elizabethan Fiction*); and *the* definitive account of Wordsworth's something or other (*Wordsworth: Poet*). Dr. Snow was younger and less experienced, having only recently completed her doctorate at Cambridge, and was in her second year of teaching as a Research Fellow at Hol-lywell. I assumed that they were both inside Dr. Fletcher's room, devising death traps and finalizing underhand tactics: carefully positioning my chair so I'd be blinded by the sun; raising their own so that they could look down on me from a height. The pleasure of the chase and Brandy Knox's arse were the recurring themes of my famished brain, every second a minute in the silence of that chill stairwell.

Just as I began to wonder if they had forgotten about me (all day long I had been haunted by a strange feeling that I didn't exist . . . perhaps they had already chosen the students they wanted . . . or maybe they were just watching me fidget and sweat on CCTV), I heard footsteps reverberating from below, winding around corners, growing progressively louder, hunting me down. I sat up rigid. Tense and formal. A girl appeared, decked out in a blue dress that ended just above the knee, a multicolored pastel scarf studded with sequins, and a pair of heels that boldly solidified her calves. Her hair was astonishingly straight (a light brown flirting with blonde) and her face came close to conventionally desirable, though some unidentifiable feature just offset it from being so (was it the nose? the chin? the mouth? . . . impossible to tell). She carried a skinny latte and a black Americano. A reassuring smile peeled from ear to ear.

Phew, just some postgrad, I thought. Ignoring her I slouched back down in the chair, reacquainting my mind with Knox's toosh and giving my nose an experimental poke. I lodged the greased-up digit into my gob for some interview sustenance. The girl had stopped and was watching me.

"Hiya," she beamed. "Sorry—desperate need for a caffeine boost! Just let us settle back down and we'll call you in a minute."

A noise that I can only describe as a thirteen-year-old's voice breaking in slow motion shoulder-barged its way from my throat; a stuck sound clogged with alarm and farce: "O~k~a~y." These two syllables wobbled and clanged like a hand-chime. She disappeared into Dr. Fletcher's room and I could hear much giggling and bustling about.

Fuckety fuckety fuck, I squirmed to myself. What a dick. Supreme start, Eliot, supreme start, mate.

With little time to compose myself, I was asked to enter.

"Sorry about the wait," said Dr. Snow, sincerely but lighthearted, as she tiptoed amongst the piles of books that were flung about the floor like land mines, back toward her armchair. "It's been a long day."

The room was a dream come true, lined wall to wall with ceiling-high bookshelves. Auden, Wilde, Hardy, Eliot, Atwood, Dickens, Austen, Pinter, Yeats, Heaney: the names leapt at me in a flurry of ecstasy, all brandishing intimidating promise. In the center was a low coffee table, surrounded by a sofa on one side and matching armchairs on the other. The table swayed in haphazard splendor with stacks of red-scrawled essays and books, some lying open and bent, others teetering suicidally over the edge. A fridge whinnied in the corner, decorated with postcards and photographs: William Burroughs disdainfully pursing his lips, smart and plain like some demented bank manager; Wilde posing as aesthetic poster-boy on American lecture tour; George Bernard Shaw scowling like a reformist Santa Claus; Salvador Dali balancing a novelty-pencil mustache on his top lip; the startling cheekbones of Virginia Woolf. Modernist prints, all of which I was embarrassingly ignorant of, were dotted about the few patches of available wall space and a perplexing charcoal sketch of a naked female torso and genitalia hung above Dr. Fletcher's chair. It felt like something was being revealed to me . . . something I could never have known. Piercing winter sunlight illuminated the room and set me slightly at ease.

Dr. Fletcher was sprawled on his crimson throne, watching me intently as I maneuvered my way through his scholarly maze. He was a short man on the younger side of middle age and his fashion sense reflected a longing to be hip: his thick black hair was molded into a chunky quiff (possibly a throwback to a Morrissey obsession from his own student days), and he wore a fitted gray blazer over a white V-neck T-shirt (Topman), blue jeans, and some classic Converse sneakers. Despite his attempts at retaining a youthful cool, the flecks of silver peppered through his barnet instantly gave him away. I had convinced myself that I would be slightly starstruck by Dr. Fletcher, though I wasn't quite sure why. He is the type of academic who fancies himself a darling of the media (he calls himself a "public intellectual"): dabbles in radio, obliging the BBC whenever they come looking for an "authority" on any random matter (he was on Radio 4 last month ad-libbing about metaphors of money in a debate about the economy), and has appeared once or twice on *Newsnight Review* as that vaguely good-looking one from academia (though he despises the label "academic," settling instead for "writer" or "creator of ideas"). And, of course, he pens the occasional book review for several literary supplements. He is the Hendrix of the scholarly world and I was desperate to be tutored by him.

"Take a seat."

"Thanks," I said, dropping onto the sofa.

Shitting arseholes: I had forgotten to shake their hands. Oh dear god, no. I might as well get up and leave now. It's all over. (My well-meaning but foolish deputy head teacher, in all her ignorance about Oxbridge applications, had made me practice the art of handshaking in her office the week before: "Now this is vital, Eliot," Miss Hill had said. "Absolutely vital. Look them directly in the eye and say, 'Pleased to meet you' . . . And don't forget to read the newspapers. Current affairs, Eliot. *Current affairs.*")

Dr. Fletcher filled his chair confidently though his frame was negligible, one hand massaging the back of his head, the other his crotch, every now and again venturing upward to wipe across his nose. The eccentric choreography was oddly reassuring.

"Good to see you. Welcome to Oxford University and Hollywell College? I'm Dylan Fletcher and this is Polly," he said in a private-school voice that had been self-consciously toned down, spiced with fashionable glottal stops and rising intonations that he'd picked up from his students.

"Hi, I'm Eliot."

"How's your day been so far? Have they been looking after you?" quizzed Dr. Snow. Great: small talk. This I could handle.

"Yeah, it's been good. Everyone seems really friendly." Who? The pansy existentialist? Spade face? I'm so full of shit.

Dr. Snow rested a pad of lined paper on top of her carefully crossed legs.

"Right then, feel free to dive in and tell us about the poem," said Dr. Fletcher, sipping from his takeaway coffee. I was fixed in his authoritative stare while Dr. Snow sat waiting, ready to scribble notes on me. Silence.

"Urmmm, well, it's a poem, I feel" (oh Christ) "about the pleasure of the chase."

Dr. Fletcher continued to stare unflinchingly, Dr. Snow already penning entire paragraphs and chapters.

"The voice is racked with doubt, almost as if he is like deluding himself, sort of thing. Urrrr, there are moments of kind of clarity where he can like face up to his short-comings, but these are like quickly urr overrun by out-bursts of temptation and stuff."

A stare, a grin, and silence.

"And the form like encapsulates this" (What the fuck is she writing down? "Grade A pillock" or "state school simpleton?" . . . Or maybe she's stealing my ideas . . .) "in the way that like it's like a sonnet."

My sweat expanded and rarefied into the perspiration of terror.

"Coz like it doesn't break down into neat quatrains . . . it's as though the form can't like contain his psychological and urrr" (say it, say it) "sexual turmoil?" (Oh god, I'm blushing. Now they've got me down as a prize pervert.) "You know, it like bleeds over the boundaries and runs back and forth, kind of thing." Woooooooooooooooo, take some air.

"But isn't he just some toff talking about hunting?" asked Dr. Fletcher. Dr. Snow rolled her eyes, somehow managing to keep her smile aloft.

"Errrrrrrrrrrrrrr?"

"I'm just playing devil's advocate," he said with a smirk. "No, I think you're right. Absolutely."

"Of course, the hunt is like a *metaphor* for the pursuit of love," I continued, stressing my flashy use of a poetic device, "and like the deer is a sort of symbol for the evasive, perhaps even teasing female. A bit sexist really" (a supportive nod from Dr. Snow) "but then again the poet is totally alive to male hypocrisy—the other man's ownership of the woman is clearly shown as a negative, I guess, yet at the same time the speaker has like possessive, predatory urges himself."

This seemed to go down well, in that no one was cringing, vomiting, or rolling about on the floor. Dr. Snow continued to jot notes, passing sentence, while Dr. Fletcher placed his coffee cup by the side of his chair.

"So did you like the poem?"

"Am I allowed to?"

"Of course, why not?"

I thought long and hard.

"I think I will do if I get in."

They both chuckled.

"Let's move on. What would you like to talk about?" asked Dr. Fletcher.

Let's see: basketball—English bands beginning with "The"—golden-era hip-hop—Martin Scorsese movies—Brandy Knox's body—my chances of being accepted—you . . .

"Well, I really like the Beat Generation, like Kerouac and Ginsberg—"

"Haven't read them for years," said Dr. Fletcher, possibly lying. Dr. Snow continued to scribble. "Anything else?"

And so we talked about some of my A-level set texts—*Doctor Faustus, Gulliver's Travels, The World's Wife*—Dr. Snow throwing in counter-arguments to test me, and Dr. Fletcher revealing a tendency to disappear into soliloquy: "Gulliver's like a little penis. Being inside the girl's pocket is about wanting to be inside of a young girl, naturally?" I was quite taken with his dark humor and willingness to say anything at all. There was a sense of freedom that was infectious and invigorating:

"Absolutely, Gulliver's resemblance to a cock is tantamount in my opinion. It's a perverted world that Swift creates—everything is magnified or shrunk, and things are mischievously placed in disproportion. But this is the aim of satire, I suppose: to revolutionize the angle of vision and force us into seeing things anew." I didn't know where all this stuff was coming from and was even beginning to impress myself.

"Good," said Dr. Fletcher, finally feeling able to congratulate me. At last I could relax. Palpable relief rushed through my body. "But what do you mean by satire?"

Oh, you bastard.

"Hmm?"

"It's a term bandied about so much that it seems to have lost its sharpness."

"Militant irony?" I speculated, this being a phrase I had heard one of my favorite authors use in interviews on You-Tube. Dr. Fletcher liked my answer and nodded to Dr. Snow, who finally ceased writing. "Right, that's enough I think. We shall be in touch."

Dad picked me up later that evening, rustling a bag of humbugs, the Saints match fizzing away on Radio 5.

"Good day?" (He didn't simply ask me how it went. Usually direct, he felt the need to be diplomatic on this particular occasion.)

"Hmmpph," I said, shrugging my shoulders, watching the formidable colleges disappear through the window.

"Well, did you enjoy yourself?"

I told him I had thoroughly hated the experience.

"Oh, right. All of it?"

"No," I had to admit. "The interview was cool."

"Cool?"

Yeah, it had been. It was like being let in on a big secret. Characteristically, though, I settled for a negative interpretation. "I don't stand a chance, Dad. Look, everyone was so bright and more achieved than me." I slumped a little further into the warm seat. "No, I'm too rough around the edges. Ah well . . . hopefully one of the red bricks will take me."

Slightly disheartened, though more than used to this kind of self-reassuring pessimism, Dad turned the radio up and gave me a report on the first-half action.

I came home from school one day, about two weeks later. There had been a sixth-form party the night before. I was hanging, badly. I lay eagle on my bed—the bed that had suffered the salts of my youth and young manhood—left arm draped upward over left eye in best melodrama swoon. My other arm—my batting arm—was slugging downward, slovenly, grubbing after fly and button with disarming predictability. Maybe a quick limp tug would see me through, or at the very least knock me out. Upper half Lady Audley, lower half plain disorderly, there I lay.

"ELIOT!"

Shit. Dad. Awful image.

I bolted into recovery action, like Frankenstein's monster administered with his first sharp dose of electricity. Trousers up (fly still undone—no time), sat upright, hands conspicuously high in the air: but look how far away they are from *down there*! Of course I haven't been fiddling, it's plain to see! So what if I'm red, it's hot in here . . . and besides, I don't feel so good.

"ELLLIIIIOT."

"WHAT? I'm sleeping!"

"Dr. Snow from Hollywell College is on the phone."

O'er me sweeps, plastic and vast, one intellectual shit-storm. Hast thou rung to holily dispraise these shapings of the unregenerate mind? What sinful and most miserable man am I?

"Huh?" Stalling for time.

"Dr. Snow, from Oxford."

"Okay—I'll be down in a sec."

Charging downstairs, two at a time, I didn't have a chance to consider the possible consequences of the call.

"Hello?" I said, masking my dog-pant breath as best I could.

"Hi, Eliot. It's Polly Snow here."

*S'up. Ringing for a quick natter, are you? I was kinda just getting down to a belter—d'ya mind if I call you back?*

"Oh, hi there, Dr. Snow. It's great to hear from you."

The shock and the dash colluded with my hangover to bring some sick bubbling into my mouth. Oh god, what if she can sense my hangover through the phone?

"I was just ringing to let you know that Dylan and I would very much like to work with you next year."

*Fuck off! You're shitting me, right?*

"Wow, thank you so much . . . that's such great news!"

"We were very impressed with your application and interview, and provided that you get three As this summer, there's a place waiting for you at Hollywell."

*I always knew you'd come round!*

"That's fantastic! I really wasn't expecting this. I'm stunned!"

"We'll be in touch soon with a preparatory reading list. I won't keep you now though, I'm sure you were busy doing something important" (oh Christ—does she know? How could she? She knows . . .) "with A levels getting so close. Once again, we are really excited about working with you. Take care, Eliot."

"Thank you! Good-bye."

"Bye bye."

I put the phone down, off my tits on adrenaline and

endorphins. Mum and Dad, who had been carefully hiding around the corner, eavesdropping, clattered into the living room and gazed at me with unbearable expectancy.

"*Well*, what did she say?"

For a second there, I entertained doing the whole false-disappointment jag ("She thinks I'm not quite up to scratch, but it's okay, guys, don't worry about me . . . I'll be fine").

"I've got an offer from Oxford!"

Dad looked like he was going to cry and did the well-done-son thing with a firm hand on the shoulder, perhaps envisioning a six-figure career in banking and a sports car for Christmas. I performed a victory lap round the living room, eventually collapsing on the sofa.

The next day at school, Miss Hill, forgetting all about her rehearsed handshakes, planted a coffee-creamed slopper on my cheek—"I knew you'd do it!" Then she dragged me into the head teacher's office to show off her wares: "He's in! We got one into Oxford!" I wanted to say, "Hang about, I need to get some As first," but dared not ruin their moment.

Rob ripped me tirelessly at break: "Miss Hill snogged Eliot!" he announced in the canteen.

"No she did not!" I hotly protested.

"Apparently she fellated him." This was Rob's verb of the term: he had only recently discovered it somewhere (probably a porn mag) and was using it at an hourly rate.

"This is bullshit."

"Make the most of it, mate, coz blowjobs are gonna be few and far between at Oxford. I mean well done and everything, but you've really shot yourself in the cock."

"Cheers."

My elderly English teacher, Mrs. Booth, with her jittery blinking act, was the one I really cared about though. I knocked on the English staff room door and she answered, fluttering rapidly.

"Guess what, Miss?"

"What have you done now, Eliot?" she said with mock despair.

"I've got an offer from Oxford!"

She reached up (a tiny lady) in motherly pride, and gave me a hug, almost knocking her glasses off.

"Oh Eliot, well done. I'm so pleased for you."

"Cheers, Miss."

I had just become a big fucking deal. There I was: I knew nothing about nothing, but I was a big fucking deal.

"You're right: he *is* a cock," I say, confirming Jack's nuanced interpretation of our Terrence.

"Oh, he's not that bad," says Ella.

"Well . . . I like him and everything, but he's an absolute cunt," I say, generously allowing Terrence a metamorphosis of genitalia.

Scott brings over a tray of insidious-looking shots—luminous blue—unnatural. These will hurt in the morning. We throw them back and shudder and seethe—sticky hands—bonding. We move to another gunky pub-grub table. A portrait of Prince Charles pulling a pint hovers above us. Heritage.

Megan and Sanjay are conjoined at the end there. He's pining for her. She's got a boyfriend.

"You been up to much?" he asks, confidentially.

"Just a long phone call with Mike."

Sanjay takes a sorrowful, longing pull from his pint. It goes down like shards of glass.

"You?"

"Thought about going gym but realized I couldn't be fucked sort of thing."

I notice that this mention of the gym prompts Jack to look down at his arms and, as subtly as possible, tense them. Nope—the protein shake still isn't doing anything.

Megan nods. She probably hasn't even listened.

"You've gone well red, Eliot," broadcasts Abi.

Great. Thanks for pointing that out to everyone, mouthy bitch.

"Great. Thanks for pointing that out to everyone."

Ella gives a little giggle, knowing how much this annoys me. She's seen me red plenty of times.

The poetry of the pub envelops us. We love it. Just look at our little faces—we bloody *love* it. Take, for instance, the malignant antagonism propping up the bar with his opinion on everything. See how this Voluminous Maximus wrenches his way into any conversation going, jabbering in caps lock:

"YOU FINK THEY CAN WIN A CHAMPIONSHIP WIV A BACK LINE LIKE THAT? YOU'RE 'AVIN A LARFF, ENTCHYA?" he says to his left; "FACKIN STU-DENTS, THEY'RE BLOODY EVERYWHERE, SPENDIN ALL MY TAXIS," he says to his right; "OI OI BILLY, POUR US ANUVVER, MATE—I COULD CANE A BEER, TO BE FAIR," he says to his front; "YOU ORDERIN A DIET COKE? YOU A GIRL OR SUMFINK?" he says down the bar to the right; "DON'T GET ME WRONG, BOSS, I AIN'T NO HOMOPHOBIC OR NUFFINK. I'M A LIB-ERAL KINDA FELLA AT THE END OF THE DAY" (snorts and nods self-approvingly, almost tearful) "BUT I FACKIN 'ATE THE GAYS. THEY CAN DO WHAT THEY WANT S'LONG AS THEY DON'T COME NEAR ME," he says behind him; "TOMATO JUICE? FACKIN TOMATO

JUICE? YOU A GIRL OR SUMFINK? HAHAHA, EH
BILLY, D'YA 'EAR WHAT I JUST SAYS? I SAYS . . ." he
repeats to the left and to the front. It's like cider off an
alky's back to us. He's part of the décor.

We drink with tireless rapidity. It's a functional thing this
early in the night: groundwork. Sipping and gurgling defers
communication and thought, until a few rounds down the
road when, fingers crossed, it'll have the opposite effect.
Oh, how the tables will turn. Despite the intention of
bonding, we are all slightly closed to each other, won't let
each other in, won't give anything away . . . for now.

"Ah mate."

"Yeah, right."

I lave another sip, maybe swill it too.

Ella settles next to me. This makes me feel slightly on
edge, the expectations being so high tonight. It's as though
we are sitting on different benches: I hump and slump,
almost unfolding off the furniture and onto the floor, while
Ella practically levitates, all poise and serenity. Earlier on in
our friendship I would have put this down to our different
backgrounds, but I'm not such a twat anymore. Ella seemed
to arrive at Oxford fully formed—cultured and widely read,
crystallized and polished. Her sophistication and grace were
like foreign goods I couldn't get my hands on. (If I could
just nick some of what she had. The knowledge this girl is
carrying on her . . . her brain is *well* fit.) I spent the first few
weeks of our relationship trying to measure her degree of
poshness: she must have gone to a cushty school, but where
were the buckteeth and frizzy hair? Where the downward
gaze and raised snotter? Was she defying my expectations?
She didn't appear to recoil when I said things like "mate"
or "d'ya know what I mean?," or if I allowed my clunky
Wellingborough accent to ring through. She represented

the world that I wanted to move into: the refined world, the intellectual world, the world of high culture. She was every-thing that home didn't represent: Wellingborough, my schoolmates, and possibly even Lucy.

In fact, she was so different from Lucy . . . *is* so different from Lucy. There's all the common ground with Ella, which seems so uncommon with everybody else: the books we've read, the films and music we like. The daunting intensity that she brings to everything, her vitality, is conta-gious. Plus, there is potential . . . potential for the unknown and for enrichment. With Lucy, though, there is the past, which is hard to shift: the vast photo album of the mind which holds all our memories and first times. And her end-less kindnesses, her undying optimism, her easygoing atti-tude. It's just that we don't have anything in common.

But we have each other in common.

"It's coming to an end, Eliot," Ella says with that melo-dious voice that you'd have to call well-spoken but not plummy. I notice that Jack is keeping a careful eye on us from across the table.

"I know. It sucks. Do you think we'll all keep in touch?" I ask. I hope so, though I know it's going to be tough. After all that's happened, I can't tell if finishing uni is a relief or a tragedy . . . all the drama; all the heartbreak and confu-sion. I think we share too much history to lose one another though; we've held our thorny secret for so long. But try-ing to keep it buried has done us no good. I need to talk to her . . . explain my feelings. I just need to be open.

"Well—"

My phone is vibrating demonically. Lucy again—I'm sure of it. This time it's a long-drawn-out frenzy. Must be a call. I would answer if it wasn't for Ella. I ignore it and look

at her, each burr and buzz a rampant betrayal. It feels like
the bench is moving . . . tremoring under the pressure of
my secrets. She must be able to tell: she's practically rattling along with it. I smile. I can't say what I really feel.

"Probably not *all* of us, eh?" I say, answering my own
question.

★

Lying in the hairdressers. The back of my neck is being
ground into the china rim of a basin, arched and tense.

"Is that temperature okay for you?"

It's unbearably hot. I can feel my scalp blistering and
swelling. Is she emptying a kettle on my head?

"Yeah, that's fine thanks."

It's a semi-chic salon: black tiles and marble surfaces,
extra-large mirrors, bowls of wrapped humbugs, piles of
male grooming mags.

"Is that pressure okay?"

Do it harder. Harder. Go on, *harder*.

"Yeah, that's fine thanks."

I can almost feel the sheen of the trainee's peroxide hair
as she lurches over me, giving my head a rub and a tug.
Flecks of shampoo make darts for my eyes and slipstreams
do mischievous runners down my forehead.

"Got the afternoon off work then?"

"Nah, I'm a student."

"Oh right, cool."

She starts kneading my head like she's fashioning a man
out of plasticine.

"What do you study?"

"English?"

"Oh right, cool."

We are reaching nirvana on the head rub. I close my eyes and strain after relaxation.

"Where do you go to uni?"

"Oxford?" I say, apologetically.

"Oh wow. Are you like well clever then?"

"I don't know about that," I say modestly.

"How did you get into Oxford then?"

"Well, I guess I was clever enough."

"No need to be arrogant about it." She continues to rummage through my mop. I wonder if she can tell from that angle that I'm blushing. "So what do you want to do with that?"

"With what?" I ask.

"An English degree."

"Oh, I see. No idea really."

"Typical."

"*The suburbs are dreaming*," sings the stereo. "Typical," echoes the babe. He's next to me with one of those shower-cap contraptions on his massive head, waiting for some color to set, flicking through a magazine larger than his body. "Hey gal," he says to my head-fiddler, "ask him about his thesis."

"What did you do your thesis on?" she says obediently.

"You wouldn't be interested."

"How do you know that?"

"It's so boring."

"Why did you do it then?"

"Okay. Well, I uh, oh you know, I looked at doubles in Shakespeare through the, uh, lens of dialecticism," I stutter in embarrassment.

"Oh, okay."

"Yeah, see, it's pretty dull stuff . . . I guess."

"So are we talking like the Master/Slave dialectic from *The Phenomenology of Spirit?*" she says as she squeezes some conditioner into her palm and lathers it up.

"Urrr, yeah, kind of," I say, rather stunned. "Exactly, really."

She thinks about this for a second while she begins to rub the conditioner into my hair. "That's a bit anachronistic, isn't it?"

"What is?"

"Applying nineteenth-century philosophy to the early modern period?"

"Told you," says the babe. "I hated that thesis . . . he lost so much sleep over it; it really tired me out. I'm the one who has to bear the brunt of all the stress and hard work, you see. I am anti theses, that's for sure."

I look up and my eyes meet the babe's in the mirror. We share a reflection and I watch in astonishment as large, bulbous bags begin developing beneath his eyes. His hair thins and recedes slightly, like something in a time-lapse movie. I urgently need to go for a slash . . . I feel like I'm gonna split if I don't get out of here soon.

"Here, how does the color look, fella?

I've had bare blonde put in it

innit."

says the babe,

his speech turning colloquial,

the accent all chavved up.

"Gonna look proper phat."

            "Huh?"

           "Gosh, Eliot, don't irk me with your

               ghastly false ignorance, okay?"

he says,
posh as a swan.
"It proper fucks me off. This one
finks everyfink's so

polarized. He can be a
frightful old bore."
"Which plays did you look at?" asks the trainee.
"Sorry?" I mumble, not knowing where to look or what
to think.
"Which plays did you write on . . . for your Shakespeare
thesis?"
"Oh. *Henry IV* mainly."
"One or two?"
"One."
"Hotspur as Hal's double?"
"Yeah."
"Makes sense. Hotspur being the dutiful son that Hal
should be . . . And then I guess you have Falstaff represent-
ing the opposite possibility available to him. Two poles of
being: the ambitious and the waster; the worldly and the
simplistic; the aristocrat and the lowly fool."
"Well yeah."

"Things aren't that transparent though,
are they, Eliot?"
says the babe.
"It
just ain't as fucking easy-peasy-
lemon-squeazy as you're tryina tell
yourself. It ain't so black and
white, boss."

"What are you
talking about?"
I ask.

"Pardon the equivocality
for a second—"
"Stop punning!"
I scream.
"It's
linguistic onanism!"
"—but ain't you being a bit
of a wanker?"

Do you ever feel like your life is in a constant state of rehearsal? Like you're always wondering when the clinch is going to come? I feel like an eternal sub. "Late?" exclaims a customer to my left. "What do you mean, *late?*"

"I'm sorry," says the stylist hovering above him—the stylist who has broken the rules. "We should have washed that off five minutes ago. The timer didn't sound, I'm afraid. I apologize . . . it's entirely my fault."

"I do believe that's your alarum,
Eliot.
Wake the fuck up."

It's a most twenty-first-century scene, here in the King's Arms, here in our twenty-first-century scene.

The start of a century, it's a nothing phase; those first two decades a lacuna in the hundred-year sweep. It's a nominal dilemma born of numerical obstinacy: the '40s are the forties and the '80s the eighties, sure, of course, but this here decade is nothing but the slops of numerous misfits. Some settle for the noughties, smacking as it does of nihilism and reprobates. But that's rather dismissive, is it not? The next decade doesn't get much better: the teens? Sounds like some crappy American high-school flick. And what about 2011 and 2012, those big uncooperators? Shall we reformulate and go for a duodecade and octennial followed by eight decades? Shoot me for being pedantic, but I have had a few pints.

What we are facing here is a problem of—

"*Would*," says Jack, watching a tall brunette walk past with her friends. She notices his attention and looks at the ground, smiling. All the girls spin to grab a peek, but I continue doing what I'm doing, drink in hand, dreaming. My bladder is starting to fidget.

"You'd do anything?" says Abi, always resistant to the notion of another girl being considered attractive.

"Yeah, but he's mad for it," Scott says, harping on Jack's Mancunian roots.

"Lad!" remarks Jack, qualifying himself. Ella doesn't appear to be enjoying the tone of the conversation, picking a crusty old coaster to pieces. Scott, greatly excited, is fiddling about in his trouser pockets. He's playing with his touchy-feelies: softened washing labels cut from jumpers which he rubs in moments of nervous energy—is this kid private school or what?

"You fiddling with your touchy-feelies, Scott?" I ask.

"No," he says, hastily placing both hands on top of the table and blushing profusely.

"Bless him?" says Abi. I flinch as my bladder ups the ante.

As I was saying, what we are facing here is a problem of conceptualization. We just don't know where to place ourselves, and neither will history. The Roaring Twenties and the Swinging Sixties we ain't. Can't be. We resist totalizing models and interpretations; we don't provide the chronological shorthand. We're a loose bunch: a confused series of tenuously associated, random events. How will we be referred to? How will they homogenize us? Or will we be overlooked as an untimely mass of singularities? We have no foreseeable narrative, untaggable as we are. Ours is a lost period, shopping around for identity, spiraling off in referential chaos.

"Back in a sec," I say, rising from the table. Need the toilet—time to break the seal—will be pissing like a racehorse from now on—the three rooms leading there are rammed—playing dodgems on a full bladder—reached capacity—at least five people give me the glare as I buoyantly pass—collisions and spillages—lube me up—fetid smell—slide me through—suspiciously wet door handle: the Gents.

What we do have, down here in the fledgling twenty-first century, is performance. Our entire tangible lives are performance; we are consummate professionals. The performance of self is nothing new of course; but it's never been so rampant, so vital, so fundamental.

"Where's Eliot?" Sanjay will be saying at our table, just returned from the bar.

"Toilet," someone will reply ("Toilet?" if that someone is Abi), and Sanjay will say "typical" because it's typical for me to be in the toilet.

Performance: rampant, vital, fundamental. Our lot follow celebrities, red circles flashing round their defects—their unforgivable cellulite and unthinkable lack of abs—and adjust ourselves accordingly. We turn on MTV, where the M stands for Materialism, and make our demands, warp our expectations, perform performance. Even our language is performed: the twenty-first-century phrasebook all cliché and slang, empty razzmatazz and Neanderthal droning.

Undo fly—keep head up—stare straight ahead—do not look down—do not eye the steaming stainless steel—dripping bubbling reflection—I am not inspecting your tackle—I repeat, I am not inspecting your—I am strictly focused on the job in hand—ten seconds of dry delay—seriously, I am not looking at . . . and we're away.

Performance is foremost a qualitative notion, here in the twenty-first century. It has a competitive edge. For instance, one of the girls I knocked into on the way to the toilet was a strong 7 and her friend a close 6 (10 being absolutely hypothetical, of course); the cocky barman, with his irresistibly punchable five-year-old face, is a Grade A bell-end. Moreover, the condom machine in the toilet boasts that it can make me "last longer" and "raise my sexual game," just as the junk mail on my BlackBerry promises "prosperous lovemaking" and offers to "boost" my "manhood" for only a few dollars a month. He that farthest cometh behind, fainting follows, in this, our most twenty-first of centuries.

Shiver and repackage—quick check of the mirror—rower type next to me delicately tweaking each strand of hair—someone vomming in the cubicle—another, the next along, having his beeriod—rower type now surreptitiously testing his guns—anonymous character still chucking up. Ready to reload, I set off for the bar.

A blip in time then, this, the awkward, tentative first decade. Sure, we remember the '90s well enough to associate with the twentieth century still, but why would we want to do that? Let's run away from that. We're the veterans of the twentieth and the rookies of the twenty-first; old and young, corrupt and innocent, all at once. Innocence didn't last long, mind. It only took a year, one worldwide NY day, for the last century's hangover to rekindle into more drunken abuse. Hair of the dog: reckless advice. And so now we'll spend the entirety of this century—our one stab at a clean slate—running away, Atlassing burden on our backs. But as we well know, there's no such thing as a clean slate: dates and numbers don't change a thing, don't help us forget or remedy. They couldn't even bring the Internet crashing to its knees like they threatened to.

7—2—1—8. I enter my PIN at the bar. A line of Jägerbombs for all: my treat. The shots plunge into the long trail of energy drinks—those festering pits of liquid marzipan—a chain of splashing dominoes. We're going nuclear.

Another toilet. Not a toilet in a pub. A toilet in a club.

A toilet in a club, three years ago, on my very first night at Oxford.

"Freshen up."

It was Freshers Week, and I was in a club called Filth. I was a fresher in a toilet in a club called Filth. Not a toilet in a pub, but a toilet in a club, a club called Filth . . . and I was a fresher.

"You gots to freshen up. Freshen up for the pussy."

These words were being said—shouted, chanted, sung, rapped—by a Nigerian toilet attendant (he attends a toilet in a club called Filth, not a toilet in a pub or anywhere else, but a toilet in a club, and that club is called Filth). They are standardized lines, to be heard verbatim in every two-bit nightclub across the country (which begs the question: is there a training manual for this gig? In fact, these crude one-liners make me nostalgic, reminding me of those formative, underage nights out in Wellingborough, sneaking past unwitting bouncers with our elaborate facial-hair ruses and comically deepened voices. "Nostalgia," from the Greek *nostos*, meaning a return home, like the return of Odysseus and the other Greek heroes of the Trojan War . . . and like me tomorrow when my parents collect me and take me back . . . ), but on this particular occasion they were being said—shouted, chanted, sung, rapped—in a very particular club, and that club was called Filth.

"No spray, no lay."

He loitered at the sinks with his array of cheap designer scents, rolls of tissue, a bowl of chewing gum and lollipops, and a saucer for tips.

"No splash, no gash."

(If only I was making this stuff up! But this is no jock hysteria, no vulgar lashings of lad loquacity. This is about as George-Eliot-George-Gissing-naturalistic, Capote-Wolfe-Hunter-new-journalistic as it gets up in here . . . up here in my fuddled muddled head, where it's nothing but a huddle of puddles of beer and shot memory.)

He wanted to wash our hands for us. I and my fellow cock artists stood staring ahead at the wall while he shouted his idle threats. It's a piss-take of a sales pitch.

"No splash, no gash, my friend."

The words were so unfortunate, so tragic, poking their elbows and digging their fists as they struggled from his barely anglicized throat.

"No tissue, no issue."

He was suggesting that if I didn't use his tissues to dry my hands (at a price, of course) I would be free from sexual escapade; sexually unfortuitous; coitally inauspicious. We could go one step further, noting the polysemy of "issue," and argue that he was threatening me with infertility . . . which is a bit harsh, mate . . . I just wanted to take a leak. But he didn't mean this. He meant no splash, no gash.

The music boomed from outside. It was brutal. It was violent. It was hard to concentrate.

"You touch it, you wash it."

This one is trickier than his other riffs—more experimental in technique, the meaning more opaque. It doesn't have the easy rhyme or associative imagery of "no splash, no gash," or the transparent cause and effect of "no tissue, no issue." For a start, the logic is problematic. Presumably the object of his expression (the "it") changes—we are being asked to make a referential leap: he isn't promoting genital cleansing (you touch your cock, you wash your cock). No, just clean hands (you touch your cock, you wash your hands). Yes, he wants us to wash our hands. Then there's the awkward aural correspondence: the interplay between "touch" and "wash." The half-rhyme jars, what with its

vowel shift and exchange of the hard "ch" for the whole-
some "sh." It lacks the deliberate barbed-wire knottiness of,
say, a Wilfred Owen half-rhyme:

> Sit on the bed. I'm blind, and three parts shell.
> Be careful; can't shake hands now; never shall.
> Both arms have mutinied against me – brutes.
> My fingers fidget like ten idle brats.

By this stage he'd got me thinking so hard (what with my
first ever tutorial just five days away) that his slogans were
useless.

"No moo-arny, no poo-narny."

Essentially no money, no vagina. It folds under analysis.

I avoided washing my hands, and slugged back out into
the club.

I entered a sea of hot-pants and high heels, miniskirts
and makeup. Unstylish lads, double fisting (a bottle in each
hand), cut horrific shapes on the dance floor and around
the bars—dancing without due consideration for rhythm,
time, or aesthetics. There was zero individualistic self-
expression on display. Just confused particles banging
about in a cell . . . a scrambling sickbowl of shifting shapes.

I couldn't stop thinking about Lucy. She flittered in and
out of my head, snagging on my mood and nicking that
mysterious void behind the chest. We had cried when we
said good-bye that morning, back home. I was heading off
into the unknown, and I guess it was doubly unknown for
her. "I'll miss you," she'd said as Mum and Dad sat waiting
in the car (Mum clutching some anticipatory Kleenex),
allowing us space to perform our couple's duties; the
momentous send-off like black-and-white lovers during
wartime. "I don't want to leave. This summer, with you,

has been so—" I paused as dewy tears fattened and rolled down her cheeks, clogging my throat. Her shoulders began to dance. "Hey, hey," I'd said, pulling her in, in an attempt to suffocate the abandon that was threatening to undo us. "I love you, you know that?" "I love you . . . too." I kept kissing her head, just above the temple where her fringe lay matted against salty skin. "I'll see you next week, won't I?" "Yes," she said in a whisper that she'd never intended to sound so broken and hush. I think we were both surprised at just how much we cared. Love isn't realized in its telling though, in its endless repetitions of three words, but in moments of doing, of happening. She was delicate in my arms, and I felt all the weight of an unexpected wish, sudden and instinctive, to gently break her into little bits and pack her up; take her away with me forever.

Trying to block all this out, I joined my new acquaintances at a booth. Most of us had been introduced in college at the welcome cocktails in Lecture Room V earlier that evening. There I had carefully begun to select my team, picking out potential mates, trying them on and designating their roles: Jack (the joker), Ella (the fit one), Abi (the dark horse), Megan (the quiet one), Scott (the butt of the joke), Sanjay (the even keel). Sorted. So many faces, so many hairdos, so many outfits, so many accents, so many stories. My stomach had been empty and my voice wobbly, my head working overtime with each person I met: *Are we going to kiss? Philia or eros?*

This was nothing compared to the type of experience Rob claimed to have had during his Freshers Week just a couple of weeks prior to mine:

M8! Gash everywhere!
Drownin in minge! I
FUCKING LUV UNI!!

The music blared with deafening drumbeat and skin-stripping bass, the unfavorable conditions we favor for social engagement. I was trying to talk to Ella. She struck me as intimidatingly luscious (philia or eros?)—

"SO, WHEREABOUTS ARE YOU FROM?" she shouted.

"THE TOILET . . .YOU?"

"NAH, DON'T NEED IT."

"WHAT'S YOUR SUBJECT?"

"YEAH."

We took glugs from our special-offer mixers.

"DO YOU ALREADY KNOW ANYONE HERE, LIKE FROM SCHOOL?"

"NO—IS HE COOL?"

"ME NEITHER."

My phone rumbled in my pocket. It was Lucy:

> Hey baby. Met
> ne1 nice? Up
> 2 much? Tb x x

Sticking to my script, Jack was establishing himself as the joker of the group, miming lap dance in Megan's face (eros or philia?) as he fidgeted his way into the booth.

"THE BLOKE IN THE TOILET," he shouted through jester's grin, " 'NO SOAP, NO GROPE,' HE SAYS . . . SO I GIVE HIM 20P, GOT ALL LATHERED UP AND THAT, AND THEN HE WOULDN'T DROP HIS TROU-SERS! . . . WHAT A RIP!" Frowns and polite giggles. "CAN I GET A GROPE OF YOU INSTEAD, ABI? MY HANDS ARE CLEAN AFTER ALL!"

"YOU'LL HAVE TO GET ME ON THE DANCE FLOOR FIRST . . . SHOW ME YOUR MOVES."

"AFFIRMATIVE."

We battled our way into the depths of the heaving mass. By default, everyone in this region was steaming drunk, including us. There was no other way we could bring ourselves to do it. The girls dropped their bags in a pile and we instinctively circled around, as though we had rehearsed the occasion over and again. The formation soon unraveled as we pranced about, sandwiching each other and pairing off. I was lodged tight between Ella and Megan while Jack skipped around us maniacally. Scott was waving a bottle in the air, pointing at imaginary targets; I clicked my fingers every now and then; Jack fondled whoever was nearest. None of us knew what to do with our hands.

Did I think how coarse my hands were, and consider them a very indifferent pair? I had certainly thought of being ashamed of them before (reading led me to it), and it had crossed my mind earlier that day, when my parents took me out for lunch at a café round the corner from college. We had just finished unloading my belongings into my first home away from home (that room so cold and unloving when I opened it, Mum instantly running around with a J-cloth and dustpan, yellow rubber-gloved hands scrubbing last year's occupant clean from the sink). Dad treated me to a panini, a wedge of chocolate fudge cake and a pint of Coke, struggling to hide his own nerves more than I. As my greasy hands fed the panini into my mouth, I noticed that no other first-day students seemed to be dining with their parents. Perhaps they were all at real restaurants on the High, or maybe they had already left their folks, under way with forming friendship groups and establishing parts.

"The conversations that people must have in here, eh?" said Dad, looking around with reverence. He liked to believe that everyone in the city was associated with the university in some way—the girl behind the counter a prizewinning poet, the *Big Issue* seller outside a respected philosopher. "And now it'll be you having those conversations, son."

Mum dabbed her eyes with a napkin. I was speechless.

Walking back to the car, Mum slipped me a tenner, as she always does, our little secret. We smiled mischievously and I mouthed thanks, Mum winking, code for *don't tell your dad*. Desperation took hold when it came to the final good-byes, the car doors now open, ready to take my parents back home where I had been comfortable and content. Dad slipped me a twenty after our last embrace and told me not to tell Mum.

"Thanks, Dad." I was beginning to sob.

And they would cry to me from the car, waving their hands:

—Good-bye, Eliot, good-bye!

—Good-bye, Eliot, good-bye!

But I hadn't read that yet.

After a few tunes had dropped, our theatricality intensified, rising in confidence as the alcohol climbed to our heads and shook about, mixing my thirty-quid cranium cocktail. We oozed nightclub sewage, dripping with sweat, more and more items coming undone. I was doing the flatulent robot and Jack was performing the paraplegic pogo. It's easier for girls, just wiggling and grinding, while we have to toil through our best health and safety hazards.

Jack hooked an arm round my neck and patted my chest. "Legend," he shouted.

"Thanks a lot." He wrapped me in a front-on hold and lifted me from the ground, the people around cautiously moving aside. I guessed that we were now best friends.

Lucy was still trying to reach me from her distant night:

Oi, y rnt u
txtin me bk?
X

(The capital X is significant. Firstly, it's singular. The standard x x says everything is dandy; all's peace, love, and harmony. The shift to the single x is momentous: a signal of no small dissatisfaction. Secondly, it came in the capital form. This is really disconcerting. It's like an aggressive (but wholly unerotic) kiss, or a rough, thin-lipped, push-away kiss.)

Ella backed into me and I found my right hand stealing furtively round her waist. She pressed her bum in and I pulled her tighter. She crushed my phone against my leg, smothering Lucy's calls. We swayed and writhed, a split second off the beat. Jack grinned away as he swung and swiveled from Abi. The music steam-engined ahead.

"You know," Ella shouted as I leaned my head in, "this song samples The Clash."

"Sorry?"

"The Clash!"

"Yeah, I love them."

Ella smiled over her shoulder, our bodies packed together. "The original is far superior."

"Totally."

"They're such a seminal band, don't you think?"

I was doing an esoteric form of the headless chicken behind her. "Oh yeah. Seminal. Course."

"I always think—"

"Huh?"

She reached her hand over her shoulder, grasping me round the back of my head so that our faces were almost touching. "I was saying that Strummer's voice is too unique to remove it for the sake of a sample. It's like absenting the soul from the music."

My moves were now fusing into the constipated otter.

"Absolutely."

With her warm lips practically attached to my ear she added: "And don't you reckon they're so much better than the Pistols?"

"Yeah. It's like a category error to even compare the two."

She smiled appreciatively and refocused on her minimal dance routine.

Should I be doing this? Guilt squirms inside my arms, its back against me, slipping and sliding, bumping and grinding, and on and on, pulling along and along, splayed and sweating, heaving and purring, and on and on, our para-tactical prance. And then more fluid with sultry swirl of linked hands at hips and goose-bumped ear to lips of cheek neck shoulder as I arc down to hold her: we enjamb.

Jack had pulled Abi. There he was, clinching her arse, her arms draped round his neck. Sloshing about they inspected each other's gums and fixed one another's root canals.

> K, I guess ur
> out and about.
> It is ur 1st nite
> @ uni I suppose!
> Im goin 2 bed
> now. School
> 2moro. Nite nite
> x x

Ella turned to face me—we were dancing cheek by jowl. Oh shit, is she lining me up? Lining me up for a tonguing?

I waved my head in the air Stevie Wonder–style, endeavoring to keep my lips away from her whirlpool mouth: that vortex of wet chamois and nibblers, of soft smells and lubrication. Her low-cut top framed a most grave discussion between my eyes and her breasts. There was a subtle streak of moisture tickling the purgatorial gap at their center—that no-man's-land of taut skin and bone. Flashbacks of the summer with Lucy strobed through my head: picnics in the sun, hanging at the shopping center, evening trips to the cinema, bedroom snuggles with the door closed, our hotel rendezvous . . . She had told me to have fun, not to worry about her because she'd be round before I knew it anyway, and that she'd miss me muchly. Enjoy yourself and get settled in, she'd said.

We're coming closer, the parameters more enabling, more forgiving. You're drunk . . . maybe it *is* okay . . .

The music stopped.

The lights crashed on.

Our eyes dilated, flooded by harsh reality. Game over. We found ourselves in a pit of spilled toxins and enervated hormones, bottles and glasses strewn across its sticky base. Like wood lice exposed by an upturned slab, everyone scuttled away to the cloakroom or the exit. Ella and I pulled apart unawares, standing ruefully askance, peering at each other with dead-end curiosity. Soon we were stepping outside, our sweat clinging tight in sudden surprised coldness as it met the nighttime air.

As a group we had fallen together pretty sharpish, and once these things set they don't change much. Ella and

Jack were the key players for me, and I identified them as such from the off. During Freshers Week I went for a couple of coffees with Ella and she scared me shitless with her boundless chat about books and my suspicion that she had made her way through Dr. Dylan Fletcher's reading list at least twice over. She had already met Dylan for a drink and an informal chat about the forthcoming term. We exchanged films and albums, Ella lending me some Miles Davis records and a Fellini collection, politely accepting the first two seasons of *The Sopranos* in return. For some reason, I never told Lucy about any of the time I spent with Ella. As for Jack, well, he had already vomited in my bedroom sink by the end of the first week. We were that tight. I remember hanging with the lads one night and Jack gallantly suggesting that Ella might be the prettiest girl in our circle: "Ella's blatantly the fittest bird." Everyone concurred (although it was clear that Sanjay had a hankering for Megan, despite Mike, her boyfriend from Warwick Uni, hanging around all the time), yet I felt too guilty to say anything . . . as though an admission on my part would be a direct betrayal of Lucy (whom I had been texting nonstop) and would somehow reach her.

The hangover from Freshers Week had just about dissipated when Ella approached me by the memorial bench and the large terra-cotta plant pots at the tip of the quadrangle's untouchable grass, so that we could walk to our first tutorial together. There was an inquiring slant to her head as she held a clutch of books and a refill pad against her chest. The warm light of tutors' rooms and first-year dorms glowed all around us. It was late afternoon, already dark, smoky and crisp.

"I'm oddly excited," she announced through a creamy giggle, stepping into the golden fringe of the lamp outside Staircase XII.

"That's one way of looking at it. Personally I'm bricking it."

Certainty of academic shame pressed down on my diluted brain. Michaelmas term meant the Victorian paper, and Dylan had let us choose our first-week authors: Ella and I had both opted for Thomas Hardy (I'd read at least one of his novels, which made him an instant front-runner).

"I didn't email my essay off till five in the bloody morning," I said, yawning performatively. As I recall, it was a clunky, rookie rant, about omniscient narration and the relationship between narrator and character. That old chestnut. I hoped Ella had written something better so that she could lead the discussion while I recovered in silence from my sleepless night.

"I handed mine in yesterday afternoon," she said with a hint of bookish pride. "Thought it best to give Dylan as much time as poss to go over it, you know?"

There was something about the excitement of the unknown that enhanced Ella's allure. The color in her cheeks—a color about to grow bolder in heated literary discussion—signaled her passion and vitality. Her pondering lips, holding question and support on their soft, vanishing brinks, fixed me.

Up in Dylan's room another first-time tute was winding down. We knocked and entered. Pausing mid-sentence, Dylan looked up, greeted us with a smile, and continued on.

"Do you think that the hysterical energy of Dickens's worlds, as you've put it, ever threatens to negate depth of character?" posed Dylan. A fidgety wave of silence engulfed the room. "Indeed, what *is* character in the case of Dickens?"

Fuck me, thought I. I'm glad I'm not on the end of that. I began to tremor in anticipation of what he might have in store for me. Ella and I gladly sat to the side while Terrence and Megan (the other two Eng Lit freshers in the college) drowned on the sofa like startled infants, grappling with uncooperative thoughts and tongues.

"Ermmm, well, kind of, I guess, he . . ." Terrence disappeared into the all-consuming black hole of his head.

"Well, he's like more interested in surfaces, right? Like, caricature and absurdities?" suggested Megan. "Humor and sentimentality stifle the possibility of depth and roundedness, don't they? So . . ."

*It's all about the primacy of style* . . . I tested the opinion in my head, wondering how it would sound if released through my state-school gob. I felt drastically uncomfortable with such thoughts and doubted if I'd ever be able to play the academic.

Dylan interceded by answering his own question. His room had barely changed since my interview, bar a few new front covers gracing the floor. It was as though his entire world had been crystallized upon discovering me . . . as though he had reached the peak of his career and was holding on for dear life . . . or something like that.

"Okay, better stop there. We've run over." Relief poured from Megan and Terrence, who were stuffing their papers and books away. Was that a first edition of *Great Expectations* in Terrence's hand? The snot-nosed fucker . . . (I soon learned that he would always bring first editions to tutes. There we were with our spine-crippled Penguin Classics, and there was Terrence with leather-bound firsts and calf-skin presentation copies.)

"Who do you want to write on for next week?"

"George Eliot?"

"Great. Make sure you look at some of her essays as well as the novels. *Scenes of Clerical Life*, of course. And check the poetry too. No one writes on it. How about you, Terrence?"

"Brontë?"

"Which one?"

"Oh, urrr, Charlotte, actually . . ."

"Okay. Compare her sisters too. Right, get your essays to me by Wednesday evening at the latest. Okay?"

"Cool. Thanks, Dylan."

"Yeah, thanks."

As Megan and Terrence shuffled their war-hardened arses from the room, Ella and I moved over to the main sofa. We kicked off with some chitchat about our essay styles and some banter (an appalling word with much currency in Oxford) about writing no-no's and can-do's. Handing mine back to me, Dylan said, "I can tell you've worked hard this week, Eliot, but you need to be more concise and find a cutting edge. It'll come though." This advice was so abstract to me that he might as well have told me to find a formula for the meaning of life or simply to give up. Handing Ella hers, he said, "There's some great stuff in here, Ella. I'm excited about what you might have in store for me over the next three years. You're very stimulating. Well done." Ella blushed and thanked him.

The first panic rumbled into action after a mere two minutes, when Dylan and Ella were discussing a character I couldn't even remember: bollocks, which one was Arabella again? I congratulated myself on an unsurpassable ability to retain fuck all. Look, mate, I've got a twenty-first-century hard-drive head . . . files get deleted, okay? All I needed was a quick rummage through my recycle bin and it would come trickling back. What I did have, however, was a vivid recollection of lounging about at home over the summer, reading *Jude the Obscure*, listening to *Kid A*, and contemplating how harmoniously the two came together . . .

Ella and Dylan seemed to be getting along tremendously, nattering away with no regard for oxygen and consistently making each other laugh, while I tried to remain inconspicuous. Maybe they would forget I was there. Hey, I'm a good listener.

"What do you think to that, Eliot? I recall you saying something contradictory to Ella in your essay . . ." said Dylan, catching me off guard.

Huh? Hadn't I written two thousand and five hundred words of absolutely nothing? And what was Ella just saying, because I caught none of it?

My cheeks flamed up like hot air balloons.

You're on your own here.

"Ermmm, well, I'm not quite sure what Ella means. Could you clarify briefly?"

Phew, that's a wily response, Eliot, I thought to myself. You've done well there, mate: bargained for time *and* alleviated the pressure—admittedly by placing it all back on Ella, but it's dog eat dog up in here. Rather tactical this tutorial malarkey, but I'll soon—

". . . does that make more sense?"

Missed it again. No idea what we're talking about.

Dylan grinned an anticipatory "well done" my way, inviting and permissive.

"Errrrr, yeah, I guess that makes sense. Well, like, I kinda guess that, uh . . . well, you know . . . despite what I said in my essay . . . I think that I, ermm, sort of agree with Ella really." Full stop. Discussion closed.

Dylan freestyled for a bit, improvising ideas and spitting mad lyrics in an experienced rescue bid. I wrote it all down verbatim (these pearls would be useful come exam time). Eventually his flow began to lose its momentum and I sensed a question forming. Oh god, please don't . . . (The trick here is to keep your head down—make eye contact and you're absolutely fucked—and pretend you're writing something erudite and pressing . . . essentially, run your pen back over the words you've already written, fattening them out and digging them deeper into the page. So long as you appear to be busy you're alright. No questions asked. The relative merit or efficacy of what you're doing is irrelevant . . . just so long as you're doing *something*. It's sound English logic and you can't mess with that.)

Sure enough a question arose like a threat I had hoped would never come to fruition, and was greeted by silence (except for the feigning scribbles of my purposeless pen). Implicitly, the question (which I can't even repeat) was meant for me: I had been the silent party for far too long and Ella had already earned her keep. I was quite affronted, to be honest. I mean, here I am, politely minding my own business, and all I get for thanks is this.

After gazing at me for ten seconds, hopefully, then hopelessly, Ella swooped in with a sophisticated answer—something about the fracturing of the absolute and how poeticity performs this by, you know, doing all that . . . Oh, I don't remember! I was certainly impressed, though I felt pathetic, dumb, grateful. I owe her for many such courtesies.

Throughout the tute I was recollecting the previous night's colorful phone call from Rob, who had rung to inform me that his first few weeks at uni (somewhere up north) were incomparably better than mine. Here I was, already getting down to an essay, listening to how he'd *already* got his "dick wet." I didn't need that. I really didn't. "Ah man, she was frothing at the gash!" What a twat.

"Oh really?"

"Yeah. To be honest I've been poking bare clunge since I got here."

"Yeah?"

"Hell yeah. Proper prodding it."

I can't handle this. Read a book, you fucking imbecile. "All I've got time for is working. Sucks cock."

"No way, man. Not ragged any hotties?"

"I've got a girlfriend, haven't I? Lucy?"

"Oh yeah, fair play . . . But so what?"

"Gotta go, mate, essay to write."

"A what?"

"Essay."

"Shit. No sight of one of those for me. What is it?"

"Oh nothing. You know, Thomas Hardy."

"Who?"

"Books and shit."

"Fag."

"See you."

"Yeah, bye."

After forty minutes of noncommittal responses (all boiling down to bugger all) I plucked up the courage to offer a comment (having soundchecked it in my head for the past five minutes, one-twoing it while Ella banged on about Hardy's "poetics of ambiguity"). "It seems to me," I nervously began, "that Hardy wants to whip the reader into a miserable pulp . . . kind of thing" (I mean just look at me: I'm living proof). "Just as you think things can't possibly get any worse, he like buffets you on the head again, but a little bit harder. He pushes it to extremes. Like that bit when Old Father Time kills his brother and sister and leaves the suicide note" (Is this a memory I need right now?) "it's well crushing. How is the reader meant to like recover from that?" (I have got the right novel, haven't I, because they're both looking at me like I'm chatting breeze.) "It's so like fragile and brutal all at the same time. So moving . . . in a way. The terseness of the suicide note, contrasted by the like complexity of Jude's reactions, is true to life sort of thing—things happen fast and are over quickly" (unlike this tute) "yet we continue to assimilate and suffer long after, if you know what I mean?" (Get on with it . . . I need to get on with it.)

"Oh please! *'Done because we are too menny,'*" blurted Dylan, who had been patiently allowing me to dig my own grave. "It's so facile and contrived . . . surely it inspires nothing but laughter!" (Well, if you put it like that . . .) "It makes me think of Wilde's remark" (excuse me?) "that 'one must have a heart of stone to read the death of Little Nell without laughing,' which could have been better applied to the death of Jude's children. It's straight out of Victorian melodrama."

(I'm looking at Ella. What could I have done?)

"Ermm . . . well, you know . . . it's like . . . kind of . . . well . . . absolutely . . . I mean it's ludicrous! That's what I was trying to say. So unrealistic . . . removed from reality. I agree . . . totally."

Like I said, I'd soon get the hang of this tutorial jazz.

Dylan smiled, Ella frowned, I blushed. And then I wondered what Lucy was up to back home.

A waiting room. I'm on a hard chair that affords no comfort. I can hear sounds of terror and confusion. I'm trapped and burdened by impending bad news. Silence. Is it safe? Is it safe? It's dark and I shiver . . . a nightmare of being back in the womb . . . a dispossessed return . . . depersonalized . . . Something bad is coming—

Sudden noise. Back in the King's Arms.

There's a bunch of Americans to my right, yawping and like oh-my-godding. They're everywhere in Oxford, drawn by its filmic sweeps and dreaming pointy bits. They ramble on about *Harry Potter* and *Brideshead*, experiencing the city through a screen.

"I need a Guinness and a Gem," says their spokesperson.

No you don't. You would *like* a Guinness and a Gem. You don't *need* them. You're not going to keel over if you don't have them . . . if anything you'll be less likely to.

Their sense of entitlement trumps ours. We're just a fascinating subspecies . . . quaint and formal . . . less assured and too self-mocking.

"And I guess I'll have a Stella."

You guess or you know? Shall we wait a bit until you find out for sure? And, by the way, these statements need a softener—a "please" or a "may I"—to take the edge off. I purposely raise my game in compensation:

"Alright buddy. Could I have eight pints of Fosters please? Nice one." (Well, I *could*, but am I going to? Shut up!)

Two round-trips see my purchases over to the gang.

"Cheers, bruv."

"Nice one, boss."

Looking around the table I see a gallery of wear and tear: the body bags saddled beneath the eyes; the corduroy frown lines ironed into the foreheads; the resident sweat patches. We're all frayed and scuffed, barely held together by gel, wax, and creams. Sanj is blinking again, bless him.

Maybe it's all the emotion; the sense of occasion dragging his lids and weighing his brow. I refrain from pointing this out. It would appear that his lucky Fred Perry is starting to have its effect though: Megan is sitting up close to him, nibbling her nails. She is an example to us all, maintaining her relationship with Mike without any incident for three years, despite living miles apart. Maybe this is what Sanj is thinking, ruing the fact and identifying tonight as a last chance. Well, if his shirt has its say in the matter . . .

"At the end of the day, I can't think of anything better than a bevy of pints with you lot at the end of the day," says Jack, trying to reboost the momentum. He's recognized the undesirable lull.

Thing is, we're hitting the quarter-life crisis. I know, it's tragic. You may think I'm being OTT (*hello?*), but why should the only generic crisis be of the midlife variety? For a start, the midlife crisis is a touch presumptive, is it not? I mean, what makes you think you're going to live that long *all over again*? Of course the quarter-life crisis could prove not to be a quarter-life crisis at all: it could be the middle, the two-thirds, the five-eighths, and so on, depending on how far your individual time-travel goes . . . You just can't tell. These things can't be calculated till after the fact. Who knows how long you've got? Whatever it is we're going through, it's a bloody crisis. No, hang on, I've got the magnitude all wrong here: it's a *fucking* crisis. Life has been sped up super-broadband style, so we can't afford to wait till we're forty to have a crisis. And that's another thing about us: we want everything *now*. There's no time to wait, no time to explain. I've got to stop letting it get to me so much though . . . I'm too old for this shit.

But what have we got to complain about? What on earth could constitute crises for us, so young and brimming with potential? Well, I can't account for everyone, but maybe Sanj is burned from the intensity of Law Finals and having doubts about his future at a Magic Circle firm where the pressures will only rise exponentially, a slave to corporate boredom; maybe Abi is heartaching over the lack of love in her life, all her promiscuity and pulling initiatives no substitute for genuine bonds; perhaps Megan is realizing that if she's still with Mike now, after all this, she's gonna have to start getting used to the idea of being with him forever . . . (*Should I get married? Should I be good? Astound the girl next door with my velvet suit and Faustus hood?*); Scott is almost certainly despairing over his future: the expensive education—illustrious prep schools, Eton, Oxford—and now not a clue; as for Jack, Ella, and me, that's going to take much longer to convey. That's what tonight is for.

A load of first-years from our college enter the pub. We all look up, slightly put out. They're so fresh, virtually ejaculating with hope and ambition.

"To be young, eh?" I say.

"To youth!" exclaims Jack, raising his pint aloft.

"Hear, hear," we cry.

"Bitches," mutters Abi. It's tough for the older lady in student society.

The last three years have retarded us all. Apparently you're meant to "find yourself" at uni, but all we managed to do was get even more lost. It's like a game of hide-and-seek where the seeker can't be bothered to finish the job . . . can't be arsed to look in the drawers or under the bed. I came of age and age came of me. It was all rather becoming. At least I think it was. Maybe it passed me by. We're twenty-one, which is to say we are slightly more specialized eighteen-year-olds. Twenty-one used to be the age when you got the keys to the home, but we can't open anything except our gullets.

We chug.

"You should be paying for tonight, *solicitor* Sanjay," jokes Abi with a sarky sound effect on her voice. "You're the one with the hench salary coming your way—lucky shit." Sanjay looks consummately depressed, burdened by the toxic City connotations of his future: perceived enemy of art, literature, and soul.

"Second that. Me and Scott are just poor gap-year vagabonds now," says Jack, reminding me of their plans to travel the world for several months. Scott seems embarrassed by their anti-prospects, all too willing to trade the idealism of his wind-in-the-hair route for some of the soulless City bread—all those loaves and fancy rolls—that Sanjay's going to be getting his hands on.

"If anyone should be minesweeping for free drinks it's Eliot—he's the one who hasn't got a clue what he's doing next!" quips Megan. I don't think it was meant to sound so cruel, but she's right: I really haven't got a clue.

What's it going to be then, eh?

I look around the table: some of the slightly-above-average minds of my generation destroyed by madness, starving hysterical naked, dragging themselves through the—

"Hi, I'm so sorry. I haven't had a chance—"

"Eliot! I've been trying to get hold of you all—" The signal in the King's Arms is terrible. I jump from the table and head to a corner, left index finger plugged into left ear, pressing the phone harder against the right like it might absorb her voice better.

"Sorry, I didn't hear that. It's my last night, you know, I can't spend it checking my phone all the time . . ." Slightly quieter, I say, "This might be the last time I see some of them."

"There's something I need to talk to you about." She pauses. "Why haven't you been answering your phone?"

"Sorry. What's wrong?"

"I need to tell you something . . . but I'm not sure how . . ." Her voice trails off into silence. "Where are you?"

"The King's Arms. I told you that, hun. What's going on?"

"I don't know if that's a good place to hear something like this."

Cautious eyes glance over from the table, trying to gauge the seriousness of my call: Ella, Jack. They talk amongst themselves, hypothesizing and screenplay plotting. I turn my back.

"What's going on, Lucy?"

"Eliot, I—"

The phone is beeping, like it's censoring a long illustrious obscenity. I look at the screen and see the usual mountain of signal incrementally dropping to a mere doorstop. She's gone. Was she crying at the end or was that the dwindling connection? I try calling back, but there's still no signal. I try again. *Sorry, it has not been possible to—* "Fuck," I mutter under my breath.

I head back over to the table. The others can tell from my vacant look that something is up.

"Everything okay, mate?" asks Jack.

"Yeah, fine." It wouldn't have taken them long to deduce that Lucy was on the other end. That might explain their timorousness: Lucy always did fit uncomfortably with Oxford. And somehow hearing her on the phone just now reminds me of that . . . a disembodied Lucy . . . not fully present . . .

"She's quite shy," I warned Ella and Jack, down the college bar the night before Lucy's first visit to Oxford. It had been nearly two weeks since we had said good-bye and I'd left for university, but it felt like we'd been apart forever.

"I'm sure she's lovely, Eliot. We're all looking forward to meeting her," Ella had said with a tender maturity that made me want to fall for her that little bit more—

Why am I torturing myself with memories? How am I ever going to be in any kind of moment if I can't just let things go? But past incidents are what I'm full of and I must continue to play catch-up. It's not a question of an A side and a B side, of present and past, for it all feels contemporary to me; it all goes into the making of tonight. It's the only way I am going to make sense—

Okay. Lucy's first visit. My nerves were threatening to get the better of me, grabbing me by the balls and letting me know who was boss as I waited for her at the bus stop outside Sainsbury's. The heavy air and sodden gritty pavements compounded my fears, the rain teasing out all those grimy smells peculiar to wet weather: dank hair, moldy cardboard, dog tongue, oil-swirl puddle. Different worlds—home and uni, love and friendship—were coming together and the atmosphere was thick with portent.

As I've said before, Lucy wasn't—isn't—the academic type. This made me anxious about bringing her to Oxford, where I had expected everyone to be so otherworldly and lofty. But maybe I wasn't giving her enough credit. It's hard to be rational though, or to feel secure, when the thing that really sets you apart from other lads is your brain and excellent literary knowledge. Most girls simply aren't interested in brains and excellent literary knowledge. They are worthless commodities . . . valueless on the modern-day meat market. If a girl, however, was to say to me, "Hi, my name is Nicole and I am a huge fan of *fin de siècle* novels that explore the theme of degeneration," I would bet my entire student loan that I'd have her in the sack before you could say Bram Stoker's *Dracula*. Obviously none of this mattered to Lucy. She must've liked me for other reasons that I couldn't make out.

Part of me felt a growing preference for separate spheres: keep Lucy to myself, tucked away in our private enclave, far from the baying and spitting of the public forum. I could smuggle her into my room and lock the door . . . disconnect the Internet cable . . . divert all calls. I could even—

"Hey!"

Lucy's bus had been and gone.

"Huh? Oh . . . Sorry! I was a million miles away."

"Hehe." She didn't say this as such, but it comes close. It's her code for gentle humor or self-deprecation in texts and emails (as in "bless me" or "how silly is that?").

"It's great to see you," I said, accompanied by a kiss and a hug. And it *was* great to see her. She looked vitalized, aglow with uncertain excitement, wrapped in her shimmering gold scarf, shaped enticingly by white skinny jeans. Still approaching eighteen, this must've seemed quite an adventure: away from home in an unknown city, with a boy (yours truly), and the promise of sex and alcohol (in no particular order). Most importantly, though, free from the obtrusive presence of "come and sit with us" parents.

"Have you missed me?"

"Of course I have. Terribly!"

"Good," she said, untroubled by the irony of greeting my intimation of suffering as a positive thing, as only a lover can.

"You?"

"Of course."

We strolled arm in arm to my quaint and pretty college. When we passed through the forbidding archways, into the main quadrangle, Lucy unlinked from me, donning an impenetrable armory of puzzlement and suspicion. She attempted to take it all in: the perfection of the grid-imprinted grass; the palpable sense of history emblazoned in stained glass and weathered stone; the Gothic points and angles, aslant from our accustomed reality; the threat of an alternative life. Already she seemed to be turning away. I boasted futile gems of college history as we made for my staircase: how many prime ministers went here, which movies and TV shows were filmed on site, the roll call of alumni novelists and athletes. I was pompous and proud, but mainly awkward.

She spent, it seemed to me, an unusually long time in front of the mirror in my room, preparing herself for the bar: lip gloss, mascara, bracelets, perfumes, straighteners, heels, hair spray, bronzer. Who did she want to impress? I wallowed in sudden paranoia: she didn't go to all this effort for me . . . she *must* be looking to impress my mates . . . Oxford lads . . . *has* to be . . . maybe she's seen my new photos from Freshers Week on Mugshot and taken a fancy to one of the guys . . . maybe she's got a crush on Scott . . . she *must* have a crush on Scott . . . she wants all the guys to be attracted to her . . . she's after their hard-ons and chat-up lines. The gungy cogs of my jealous mind went into overdrive. (In a cooler, more collected moment, I realized that she was doing it for herself. It was her shield. She was responding to her difference in age and a presumed deficit in sophistication. She wanted to fit in. And she was doing it for me. She wanted me to feel glad that she was around.)

"So what are your friends like?" she asked, rooting for some preparatory information as we bustled out of my pigsty.

"Oh, they're all lovely. You'll get along fine."

"That's cool."

I thought I picked up a quiver of anxiety in her voice.

"Don't feel any pressure though. Just be yourself. I've told them you're quite shy anyway . . . so it's not like they're expecting much."

"Well, thanks a lot, Eliot."

"What?"

"I'm not even shy," she added, coldly.

As we descended toward the Hollywell College bar, a dungeon buried beneath the quad, sharp voices and bellows ricocheted against the walls of the stairwell, echoing like a frenzied swimming pool. I felt tense as I imagined the nerves that must have being consuming Lucy. When the door swung open we were drowned by an instantly doubled hoorah. My crew was sitting over by the jukebox playing a game of 21s or Bunnies or whatever. The laughs and cheers were caricature, the shouts superficially aggressive: "Get it down, you Zulu warrior . . . Get it down, you Zulu CHIEF CHIEF CHIEF CHIEF."

"Everyone, this is Lucy . . . Lucy, this is everyone," I said, interrupting their drinking game.

They all seemed taken aback . . . was Jack checking her out? Motherfu—

"Hey, Lucy. Here, take a seat." Ella pulled up a stool. "I'm Ella."

"Hi," said Lucy, shaking Ella's hand and smiling her razzle-dazzle smile. Her summer countenance, with its sultry contours and soft textures, couldn't have been more incongruous with the humdrum *mise en scène*: the drab chipped furniture, the low arching ceiling, the lumpy underground brickwork, the weak septic lighting. She's an effervescent Eloi kidnapped by Morlocks in an alcoholic subterrain, dramatized my essay-fagged brain. They belonged to different genres: Lucy all dream vision; the scene a lowly Anglo-Saxon dirge. I had breached some code of formal decorum by bringing her there.

Lucy sat smiling.

She won't start any conversation . . . I know she won't . . . she'll just sit there, smiling.

"So what do you do?" ventured Sanjay.

What do you mean, what does she *do*? Well, she sleeps and eats, shits and pisses, takes regular doses of oxygen, and stretches her limbs when she needs to get from A to B . . .

Me. She does *me*! Alright?

"I'm in my last year at school." (They already knew this, of course.)

"Ah, cool."

"Hehe." (She didn't actually say this.)

"Have you started applying to any universities yet?" offered Megan.

Yeah, probably none of the ones you did. Jesus! *She's not the academic type*, okay? Leave the poor girl alone.

"I'm not quite sure if I'm going to go yet," she said, coloring up slightly. She peered at me, as though she was bothered about how I'd respond. I had the feeling she was only considering uni because of me . . . like it was what I would've wanted . . . or expected. "The uni at Northampton has a pretty good Travel and Tourism course, so I might look at that . . . I'd have to get the grades first though!" I hung my head, waiting for the inexorable judgments of my brainy mates. I wanted to apologize to everyone. I relinquished Lucy's hand under the table and fiddled in my pocket for my wallet.

"Oh cool," said Jack. "My big sis works in events management . . . same kind of thing, right?" Lucy nodded readily. "Yeah, she loves it. Gets loads of free tickets for things." I glanced up, surprised not to find everyone staring at me in disbelief or giving Lucy condescending looks. No, they were all listening intently, and drinking their drinks as per normal. I took Lucy's hand back in mine.

"I think Eliot secretly wants me to apply to Oxford Brooks," she said, giving me a cheeky sidelong look.

"Hah, keep you nearby, eh?" said Jack.

"Exactly . . . that's the one thing that puts me off though!"

Very funny now . . . quite the sense of humor on you there. You've got all my friends laughing . . . well done . . . oh, funny girl. This is depressing.

"Hehe, only joking, Eliot!"

Get off my hand.

"Hey, you should get a drink and join in our game," said Ella overenthusiastically.

"What are you playing?" I asked.

"Categories. Do you know how to play, Lucy?"

Lucy shook her head.

"It's dumb," I said.

"No, I want to play," said Lucy.

"It's easy," continued Ella. "We pick a category and then go around the table taking it in turns to think of an example. If you can't come up with one or if you repeat one that's already been said, you have to down your drink. And, of course, you have to drink while you think!"

"Okay!" said Lucy.

"What category are you on?" I asked.

"We just did Oxford colleges," said Jack. I could sense Lucy's enthusiasm dying a very sudden death. "How about poets? Or famous scientists?" Oh fuck . . .

"Ermmm, I think we'll just go to the bar and get a drink. You guys play on though. What do you want to drink?" I asked Lucy. I was terrified she would say something like Smirnoff Ice or WKD . . . hell, why not a bottle of White Lightning in a brown paper bag like we used to drink down the rec. Lucy carefully surveyed the bevies on the table. The boys were on pints, Abi and Megan were sharing a bottle of rosé, and Ella was sipping a glass of white.

"Mmm, I'll have a glass of white wine please."

"Sure."

We got up and headed to the bar, the sticky floor threatening to tear our shoes from beneath us. "Eliot," came Lucy's shadowy whisper over my shoulder. "Whereabouts is the loo?" Her scent made me crumple.

"It's through the corridor over there. Are you okay? Happy and that?"

"Yeah . . . I'm fine."

"Okay."

I couldn't tell what I was so nervous about. I rested my arms on the sloppy bar. "Alright buddy. I guess I'll have a San Miguel and a white wine please."

(My phone has just vibrated against my thigh again. It's not a call this time—just the two sharp buzzes of a text message. Lucy, can't you see I'm trying to explain you here?)

I watched the narrative unfolding in the long mirror behind the bar. There were a couple of lads rattling away on the foosball table, a misfit assembly poking and jabbing at the quiz machine, and random groups of library refugees spattered about, small-eyed and finger-biting. My lot were chatting excitedly.

Are they discussing Lucy? Evaluating her? Passing judgment and sentence? Compliments or criticism? Or are they just kicking off their drinking game . . . ?

An interminable two minutes swelled around me as I watched for Lucy to return from the loo and waited for my round. And there she was, walking over to the gang and sitting—

Why the fuck has she gone and sat next to Jack? What's she trying to do? Betrayal! My insides punched me heavyweight slogger style as I brought the drinks over.

Here's your bloody wine. I'll just sit on the other side from you then, shall I? Fine.

"Thanks," she said, taking a swig.

"S'okay."

So I was next to Ella and Sanj, and Lucy was next to Jack and Scott. Jack, then Lucy, then Scott; or Scott, then Lucy, then Jack, depending on which way you look at it. Abi and Megan appeared somewhere in between. But Lucy was next to Jack and Scott, and Scott and Jack were next to Lucy, and they're both lads . . .

Her chest heaved slow and full as she sat up, absolutely straight. I didn't quite catch what Jack said to her but she chuckled lavishly, baring her shiny white Kodak smile. Lucy's laugh is a force of nature: rich and voluminous, it borders on the dirty. It's a sexy laugh, for sure. A laugh you want to be responsible for . . . a laugh you want to provoke and roll around in, lapped by its gurgles and rumbles, tongued by its air and chimes. You want to ride the wave of her guttural joy. But you want it to yourself . . . you strive for exclusivity. Okay, I want it to myself . . . I strive for exclusivity. A laugh is for the other as much as for the self, nearly always a collaborative project, and I want Lucy's to myself.

She was laughing again, this time more vigorously, and Jack was starting to look a tad overencouraged. Even Scott was smirking. They both watched her as she bubbled and wriggled, gazing wide-eyed at the drink in her hand, down there on the table. I took rapid pulls from my pint and showed a little seethe. Lucy was an exotic to Hollywell College, being actually fit and not conforming to the private-schoolgirl fashion model so dominant around here. They're carbon copies of each other, the Hollywell anti-babes: big fuzzy hair, draping scarves like wizard's sleeves, gilet, jogging bottoms (Jack Wills, not Sports World), and ugly Ugg boots. Lucy was demonstrably not one of them, with her straightened hair and high heels.

"Is this your first time in Oxford?" inquired Ella across the table.

Who gives a flying fuck?

"Yeah. I don't know why that is really."

"Well, you're in for a treat," said Jack. "We'll show you some of the hot-spots tonight . . . have a little boogie and that."

"Hehe," etc. etc.

Oh fuck this.

Recognizing an unrecognizable girl, Terrence Terrence, who had just dropped into the bar to purchase a tipple, came over to our table and pulled up a stool.

"Terrence?"

"I don't believe we have met," he said, extending a hand to Lucy.

"Hi," she said, smiling. "I'm Lucy."

"Terrence. Pleased." Terrence kissed Lucy on the top of her hand, which made her giggle. "Is this your paramour, John?" he asked me. Throughout that first term he had called me John. I have no idea why.

"Eliot. Yes, Lucy is my girlfriend . . . from home." I don't know why I felt the need to add this last bit—like it would grant her some leeway or something.

"Oh, I see. How very . . . parochial." He crossed his legs effeminately. "So which college are you at?"

Lucy chuckled some more, this time at the assumption that she might be an Oxford student. "I'm still at school," she answered, taking great pleasure in sipping her wine. I dropped my head once again. Terrence sat up . . . perked, even.

"A babe in the woods! How positively charming."

"I like your outfit," said Lucy. Terrence, fancying himself a thespian, was wearing yellow tights, mascara, and eye shadow.

"I've just been at rehearsals, *so* . . ."

"What are you rehearsing for?" asked Lucy, eager to show interest.

"A student production," I dived in, before Terrence could baffle her with some play she'd never heard of.

"Ah, that's cool."

"Yah, I really want to go into theater after uni, actually. I love to tread the boards, liiiiike . . ." a dickhead.

"Oh, awesome. Like panto?"

That's not *theater*, I snapped derisively in my head. He means *serious* stuff . . .

The whole gang erupted with laughter and Terrence darkened with embarrassment. They thought she was joking . . . they thought she was breaking his balls! Lucy had just become a heroine.

"Well, errrr, no, *actually*. Shakespearean, *so* . . ." He uncrossed his legs in the hope that it might alleviate some of the ridicule.

"Oh right, that sounds lovely," Lucy said in recompense. I think she was upset to have made him so uncomfortable. Jack and Ella were visibly delighted with Lucy's presence. (You're welcome.)

"Do you like Shakespeare?" asked Terrence.

"Can't say that I know any. Did he write *Romeo and Juliet?*"

"Are you okay for drink?" I asked Lucy, in a desperate shift of—

(There goes my phone, *again*. Lucy, give me a chance to explain you! I'm going to need some space to get this done! But I suppose I am alone in my quest to level things tonight.

I notice that Jack and Ella are standing over by the quiz machine, holding their drinks against their chests and funneling chat into each other's ears. Jack slaps his empty pint glass on top of the machine and appears to split for the john. Ella, left on her own, clocks me and smiles. She's coming over—)

After a bit of reshuffling and a few more drinks, Lucy found her way back next to me. We were on to our fifth or sixth.

"Hello, stranger," she said.

"Hey. Where've you been all my life?"

"About two meters away."

"Hehe" (I didn't actually say this). "Sorry if I've been a bit tetchy. And I know you're not shy . . . I shouldn't have said anything."

"It's okay, Eliot," she said, snuggling against me. I kissed her. "I wish you would just relax."

"I've missed you really bad this week and I want you to like it here is all."

"It's okay, don't worry."

I bit her on the nose, gave it a little lick, and she screwed her face up, playfully . . . adorably.

"You're so cute," I whispered.

"And you're silly," she whispered back, smiling.

"Are you having a nice time anyway?"

"Yeah, it's cool." I was pleased to hear it. "Scott and Jack seem really sweet. Jack's great. He's *so* funny."

Oh fuck off! Why don't you just marry him if he's so perfect?

"How about that for a first tute last week," I said to Ella, turning my back on Lucy and cultivating a conversation I knew she'd feel alienated by.

"I know," said Ella, surprised by the seeming spontaneity of the question. "I'm so relieved to get it out of the way. I didn't know what to expect."

"I wasn't banking on Dylan knowing so much about Hardy. He must've read everything . . . I don't get how he remembers it all."

"Totally. I felt so dumb."

"Yeah, right! You said so many interesting things . . . like all that stuff about the poeticity of Hardy's prose . . . and, errrr, the influence of like evolutionary thought, you know?" Ella modestly shrugged this off and turned to Lucy.

"Have you read any Hardy?" she asked, wanting to include her in the conversation.

"No. Can't say that I have."

"What kind of stuff do you read?" asked Ella.

"She's not interested in reading," I answered for her. I could feel her hand relinquishing mine under the table.

"No . . . I guess I'm not."

She was unhappy now, I could tell. She looked demoralized; disheartened and challenged. I had done it. But why was I trying to show her up? I was purposely making things difficult and I didn't even know why. I simmered in guilt.

"I don't blame you," said Ella. "You'd just wind up making boring conversation like us." She gave Lucy a supportive smile. All the encoded comments and body language weighed down on me like a universal betrayal.

"Right, let's head off. I can't be fucked to go out any more," I announced, getting to my feet. "I've been partying too hard this week . . . I need a quiet one for once." (Did you get that, Lucy? I've been having fun *without* you.) "Come on, we're going."

"Fair enough," muttered Lucy, rising to the racket of screeching stools.

I wondered if she was actually relieved to bring the evening—her trial—to a premature close. She said it was a shame, that she had been having a good time. But I felt otherwise.

Later that night, back in my room, we got undressed and made up. There in the depths of our inexperienced bed we learned about greed and jealousy, about give and take. I held her in my arms to let her know I was a fool. I kissed the back of her neck to show her I had been unfair and tickled the inside of her legs to undo my wrongs. She had made all that effort for the both of us, and we had gone to bed early. Awake, I spooned her through the night while she slept peacefully, to show her how much I needed her. I spooned her throughout the night to show myself—

Ella has taken the empty seat on my left. Swollen tears form around the outside of her wineglass and drip down the stem to its cloudy base. She fiddles with it absentmindedly, turning and tilting its curvaceous body, drawing attention to its transparency.

"Let's make this a bloody good one, yeah?" says Jack as he ferries another round to the table. There's nostalgia in the timbre of his voice: this one's for all the other great nights, yeah?; out of respect for everything gone by, yeah?; let's just have one last fucking good night—*yeah*? "This night is real," he adds, nodding in approval at his new pint.

The windows in the King's Arms have steamed up, the nighttime streets looking like they've been soaped over, obscured by the forces and emissions of the pub. Pockets of energy throb throughout the place.

"So, have you got much planned at home for the next few weeks?" asks Ella.

This is my chance. We've got some privacy and she seems to be really focusing on me. I should just tell her how I feel and deal with the fallout afterward.

"Yeah, I've got quite a lot of, uh, you know, stuff on, I guess," I struggle to say, bottling it, thinking about Jack and Lucy and a whole range of other potential obstacles. I'm a humdrum conundrum, my mind and mouth no longer bedfellows, no longer on speaking terms.

"Oh, okay."

The night is young. Plenty more opportunities will present themselves, I'm sure. No need to start panicking just yet.

So here we are, gaping zeros of insufficiency, trying to mouth genuine feeling but coming up short. The feeling's there alright; the momentousness isn't lost on us. It's hard. That's all.

"Let's just have one final fucking good night, yeah?"

"Time to move on?" asks Sanjay, testing the mood.

"Defo. A round of tequila for the road?" suggests Scott.

"Doubles, pussies!" challenges Abi.

Everyone laughs and chatters, shifting around in ready assent.

Without arrangement or silent signal, Ella and I hang back.

"You seem sad," she says.

"Err . . . it's just the weight of the occasion," I say, somewhat misleadingly.

"Yeah. For three years, a night out like this seemed so trivial . . . so habitual, right? But now all of a sudden it's . . ."

"Meaningful."

"Yeah."

I finish the watery dregs of my pint and look up at her. I look up at her because I don't know what else to do. I go to say something but change my mind.

"Ready?" she says, probably to avoid whatever I might've been boiling up.

"Yeah."

It's time to check my phone. I can't ignore it any longer. The others are slightly ahead, having downed the tequilas, weaving their way through the door and onto the pavement. I pull it from my pocket, shuffling around to ease the tightness of the jeans.

Got it. Unlock . . .

There are three missed calls, and my inbox contains a couple of text alerts from my voice mail, and then there's . . . aha, here's the one we need . . .

Open it, open it.

# Bar

I've turned my phone off.

I wasn't expecting that. I just don't know what to say . . . what to think . . . what to *do*. I mean, how the hell has this happened? I'm going to need time . . . time to figure all this out.

We've left the King's Arms. We shoved those tequilas where the sun don't shine and split. Time for progress; momentum; the logical next step.

So we've moved on to a bar. Not a pub or a club, but a bar. A bar: it comes somewhere between a pub and a club. But it isn't a pub or a club, coz it's a bar. It's basically a step up from the pub on the going-out scale: the drinks are unjustifiably more expensive, the lighting is darker (with bursts of neon), and there is a mini dance floor of sorts toward the back there. The girls in these joints make considerably more effort: shorter skirts, tighter shorts, higher heels (I clock Scott rubbing his touchy-feelies as he checks out our new environment). And it's more metropolitan than a pub, which is quaint: all moldering "ye olde" pretension and fix. On the other hand, it's less ferocious than a club (where we leave all dignity in the car park, outside Argos, sodden in the rainy queue). But like I said, it's halfway between the two. See: our world does have form and order, an internal logic . . . kind of thing.

There's a hierarchy of conversational possibility in the pub-bar-club equation (although the twat chugging a yard of ale over by the fag machine might not agree). The *pub* is the most sociable: there we kotch about, rhapsodizing on our specialist subjects of not-a-lot. We can actually be heard. In a *bar* the music has to dominate—there's a dance floor to be taken care of. Bar noises have a greater tenacity. Conversation fragments and simplifies, tending toward gossip and vulgarity. A vast improvement, one might think. As for the *club* . . . well . . . that's where language utterly degenerates into blubbering white noise: monosyllabic phrases, polysyllabic belches, aggressive consonants. It's unadulterated shit-chat: "Drink?," "Piss?," "Dance?," "Number?," "Shag?" But we'll get *there* in good time.

The tequilas have really done the trick. Jack's transforming into hyper mode: Turbo-Jack. He's skipping around to the music, sidling up to random girls, doing the epileptic string-puppet. He's been saying "fucking A" ever since the bouncers granted us entry. He is starting to unwind.

"You need to watch your mate," warns a stern dude, arms folded, face like a Meat Supreme (Stuffed Crust), as he polices his harem of grinders, Jack rubbing against its fringes.

"Whatever, mate."

Jack is oblivious. I have always admired, maybe even envied, his insouciance. How he can turn his surroundings into a Jackocentric universe without being egotistical or selfish; the gravitational force around which we orbit, drawn and maintained. Like all of my university friendships, we only exist to each other within Oxford, never crossing boundaries of home and origin, but I think I've got a pretty good sense of him. Within Oxford we are an effective fit, sharing perceptions about the state-school/private-school distinction, and cultivating them to our own comedy ends. But the chip on his shoulder is smaller; there's no inverted snobbery or lurking resentment. He has gone at things more vigorously than I, game to mix and establish himself. Less fettered in many ways.

I'm going to have to level with him at some point tonight, though I can't see how it can possibly go well.

We are making our way toward the flash bar (the bar inside the Bar), flanked by rude-boys and stumbling-somethings.

"Whose round is it?" I shout, broadcasting that it sure as fuck ain't mine.

"I'm on it," replies Sanjay, withdrawing a fat wallet and positioning himself so as best to attack.

It's heaving in here. A real cock fest. I'm surrounded by blokes in tight shirts. They ripple and bulge like steroid blancmanges, their clothes bought at least one size too small to give the lie of muscularity. Most are simply plump. All the men around me are obsessed with size: puffing their chests and holding their bevies in ways that deliberately accentuate their guns. They call the bar-ladies "darlin" and "sweet'art" and frown at fitties like me. Performative cunts the lot of 'em. Girls wriggle about in the byways and swellings while these men stand sturdy, inspecting, like farmers at a cattle market. They watch stiffly, effortlessly emitting their rigor-mortis charisma, occasionally saying *"would"* when a particularly fine specimen flits past (because they would, of course). They are meant to appear intimidating (obviously the best way to attract the opposite sex is to look like you're going to punch them); but actually, it seems to me, they're just bricking it. They're uncertain about what to do with their oafish bodies and bubble-wrap heads. Mark their sweaty brows and disconcerting sways. Shit, these guys are nervous wrecks, even if they could kick my head in.

"Wahey, check it out," says Sanjay, gesturing toward our right. We all follow his motion. Jack and I don't look best pleased. A random is trying to get in there with Ella. Fuck me he's good-looking. Don't you just hate that? When you know someone is a better deal than you? When your ego has no choice but to admit tail-between-legs defeat? This guy is tall and tanned, with long golden locks scraped back off his face. His white shirt is stylishly cut—fitted is the term, I believe—and his sleek black jeans encase legs longer and rounder than my own. Ella is politely smiling and nodding. If I was a girl I *would*. Jack makes an unannounced dash for the bathroom.

Watching the blunt servitude of barroom show-and-display, with its speculative pulling bids and trade deadlines, makes me think of Lucy's message more and more. I thought tonight was all about Ella, but now I'm not so sure. I'm all over the place.

I start reaching for my phone but put the urge in check.


Oxford is filled with memories of Lucy. She's everywhere—every restaurant the scene of a date, every path the route of a stroll, every establishment with an alcohol license the setting of a ridiculous lovers' tiff. It's the dates that really stick, what with all visits being a date of sorts . . . containing a date . . . an occasion. I languished in perpetual heat and stickiness during that early period, all underlined by a dull ache in the balls, getting hard-ons walking down the street, buying some groceries, returning library books. She always left her mark: the fervid smell of her perfume in my room, puffing from the sheets and pillow at the slightest tap; last night's wineglasses on the desk with tiny puddles of white left at the bottom; the room a bomb site of sexual warfare and going-out costume changes— the strewn clothes, the balled-up Kleenex, the rash-inducing massage oil capsized at the foot of the bed.

I tried so hard. Punting across the gnat-gauzed river, I would misquote Tennyson and exhaustively point out anything of remote historical insignificance—"That's where [insert poet] studied," and "That's where C. S. Lewis got his inspiration for x, y and z"—until Lucy pulled out a pair of sunnies and a creased issue of *Heat*. Or the picnic in University Parks when I sat on duck shit and got stung by a bee. And how about the time she returned the copy of *Lucky Jim* I had lent her in an attempt to make her a bit more literary.

"What did you think?"

"He irritated me so much!"

"Who? Kingsley Amis or Jim?"

"Yeah. Why can't he ever say what he thinks? He has all these humps about everything but never actually comes out with them. Just seemed so weaselly and weak."

I was incredibly surprised by the concision and perspicacity of her critique. I really hadn't expected it. And it was a strong argument: one I didn't like, feeling as it did like a covert attack on me.

"Errr, okay," I said condescendingly. "I think you've missed the point a bit. Maybe I should've given you something easier to start with."

And who could forget the Valentine's Day when I booked a bicycle-rickshaw to transport us to our restaurant on the corner of Little Clarendon Street? I sat fuming while she enjoyed the cyclist's gratuitously bulbous buttocks and chunky calves as he rode standing up, a mechanical specimen of some masculine ideal. The meal was equally unforgettable. When the waiter asked if I would like to try the wine, Lucy watched expectantly, like she thought I'd be good in such situations. I choked violently and tapped some instant access sweat from my forehead; "Yes, that's fine thank you," I concluded. And then, as if things couldn't get any worse, Lucy's chicken turned out to be undercooked: "Does this look pink to you?"

"I don't know . . . is it meant to be like that?"

"I don't think so."

"But you've already eaten half of it."

"Do you reckon I could get salmonella?"

"Are you sure chicken isn't always like that?"

"I don't know . . . can't be."

"Should I complain?"

"I don't know. What do you reckon?"

"Do you want me to?"

"I guess."

"Excuse me . . . waiter . . . oh hi, thanks. This, err, chicken appears to be, err . . . is this chicken, like, raw . . . do you possibly think?"

"I'm sorry, sir. I could check with the chef . . . but she has eaten over half of it."

"I know, but she only just realized you see." (Lucy waiting.) "Can we have this deducted from the bill possibly, at all?"

"But, as I say, sir, she has eaten over half of it." (Lucy thinking about how the rickshaw-cyclist would deal with the situation.)

"I won't pay for it."

"Yes you will, sir." (Lucy measuring my worth.)

"Okay . . . I guess that's fine," I said to the waiter. "I mean, you have eaten over half of it, honey. Can we just get the bill then, please?"

But her visits were the absolute highlights of my time at Oxford, especially early on. They were all I wanted and looked forward to. *She* was all I wanted. What I'd give to return to the innocence of those days, rather than the nightmare pageantry of now . . .

What am I talking about? How could I overlook the college summer ball at the end of first year? I remember Lucy in my room, making diligent use of the mirror, again. Her syrupy smells and preternatural sheen; those lithe bends and generous smiles. I lay on the bed, hands behind head, legs outstretched.

"Shouldn't you be getting ready too?" she said, turning away from the mirror for a rare second (I was going to say a *fleeting* second, but I'm not sure that they occur in real life, do they?). She had been in preparation for half an hour already, but I knew that her handicap was at least forty-five minutes (allowing up to one hour for special occasions, which I suppose this was).

"Yeah yeah, I'm on it."

I had never worn white tie before and was delaying the ordeal of attiring myself. Before Lucy arrived I had trawled the Internet for instructions on how to put the outfit together, a sobbing mess of inadequacy and defeat: they're not buttons, they're cuff links; that's not a scarf, knobhead, it's a waistcoat. For all that I could tell, the sole purpose of this preposterous costume was to crush my lower-middle-class spirit, as well as making me look like an impractical tit. So I ended up ringing Scott for some private-schoolboy advice, this shit being like pajamas to him.

I spotted my opportunity when Lucy momentarily turned her back to search through some bags, and leapt into manic action: firstly trip-wiring and sack-racing with the trousers, I then locked the waistcoat in a sleeper hold, body-slammed the shirt to the ground, and administered a clothesline/elbow-drop combo to the bow tie. I was roughly dressed in fifteen seconds flat. In sharp contrast (having taken care of the surfaces and the icing: immaculate makeup, complex hair), Lucy slipped into her dark green silk dress with supreme ease. Her supple figure undulated in—those soft curves and pliant grooves making their bends adornings—to find its most perfect rhyme in the elegant lines of the garment. She'd pitched the makeup just right—ceramic lids, fruit crush lips, gentle shimmer—avoiding some of the arts-and-crafts horror shows that would be on display at the ball (clown colors, pizza faces, embalmed corpse lacquer, freshly squeezed tans). Makeup terrifies boys: young girls wear it to look older, old ladies wear it to look younger . . . either way we're just confused. But Swift had got it wrong in Celia's scummy dressing room: Lucy was beautiful beneath it all, and upon her transformation I was speechless—partly because I was out of breath from sumo-wrestling my outfit onto my body, and partly because the bow tie was slicing my throat, but also (to fulfill the queasy line) because she was stunning. I already knew this, of course, but the eventful glamour of the evening and the lack of oxygen going to my head emphasized the fact.

I stole a nervy arm around her waist as we left my room and strolled toward the main quad. The college's metamorphosis into a summer ball was odd: a troubling mixture of grand, historical architecture and rusty fairground poverty; seaside Meccano and carnivalesque carnage smuggled in through the back door (dodgems, Ferris wheel, merry-go-round, hog roast, shot bar, candy floss, casino, photographers, chocolate fountain). Kids in tracksuits and hoodies would've been just as congruent as us pricks in our penguin garb.

I fell painfully self-conscious over my walk, as though I had forgotten how to put one foot in front of the other in any convincing or sensible manner. I knew that Jack was accompanying Ella and kept an anxious eye out for them, fearful of bringing Ella and Lucy together on such a unique occasion, like heavenly bodies capable of an apocalyptic collision. At this point in my Oxford life, I was already well under way with the process of forcing Lucy into the "Home" box—that tempestuous compartment of my brain where it is forever windy and bleak, also known as "The Past," "Limited Horizons," and "Failure"—and to let her out would create all sorts of problems. Meanwhile, I had managed to boss Ella into a grand treasure chest which bore plaques like "The World," "Upper Class," "Culture," and "Success," scribed in some kind of exotic calligraphy that I liked the look of. I wondered where I belonged in the apartment blocks of Lucy's imagination, or whether the terrain of her psychogeography was entirely different to mine—a rambling countryside of happy interminglings perhaps, or carefree vistas of disorganization and liberality.

We bumped into Jack and Ella over at the vodka-jelly shot bar. "It's been so long!" exclaimed Ella, who'd seen Lucy just two weeks ago, grabbing her and kissing every cheek going. What's the protocol in these situations, because I'm never sure? One kiss; one on each cheek; a cheeky third—what the hell, have four! Me and Jack stood there trading silent complicity.

"You look lovely!"

"Thank you! (hehe) So do you!"

"That's such a gorgeous dress!"

"Hundred pounds from Mango," revealed Lucy, briefly jutting a hip and dropping a shoulder in catwalk pose. "I really like your shoes!"

"Eighty quid, House of Fraz!"

"They're so pretty!"

"Oh" (giving Lucy another kiss; Lucy beaming) "it really is nice to see you again!"

Me and Jack continued to look at each other like mildly aware cows.

"Alright mate."

"Alright bro."

"You look hot."

"Cheers. Fifty quid. Hire . . . innit."

"Nice."

"You look ravishing."

"Cheers. Hire. Fifty quid."

"Sexy."

"Stop it, you're making me blush."

We moved farther into the ball. I always felt a surprised sensation to be out and about with Lucy, even though she visited at least every other week. I would spend the days and nights between doing the old imaginative substitution on any girl–guy combo I saw. But now she was really here: not the idea of her, or a representation of her, but the girl-in-herself. It's a shame that I could never seem to relax and make the most of it.

Inside a flashing, booming marquee (its wooden boards and canvassing having ingested the entire quad) we began our habitual quest for a lower plane of consciousness and ordered a hefty round at the bar. Nerves needed quelling, doubts burying. Lucy had just finished her A levels and uni

was now settled upon as a definite plan, so a sense of cel-
ebration animated the night for her, though I didn't particularly share in this.

We were sat around a table covered in confetti and
sequins, some helium balloons in the center anchored by
champagne bottles, when Terrence Terrence made a raucous entry with the Decadents (a members-only drinking
society), of which he was president at the time. There they
were in their thousand-pound uniforms (ludicrous maroon
tails), with their floppy hair and ra quiffs, their wet secret
handshakes and double-barreled names. There are only
eight Decadents at any one time, eligibility depending on
family wealth and notoriety and therefore being highly
exclusive. Ella and I had always mocked these Archibalds
and Maximillians as they swanned about in the quad for
pre-dinner drinks at any one of their fortnightly affairs,
and we would persistently rekindle our debate over which
spot in the higher reaches of the college would best serve
a sniper. Admittedly, they invited Ella to all of their events
(being widely regarded as the second-hottest girl in college) but she scornfully rejected them each time, too aware
that invitations were reserved solely for arm candy.

"Fuck," I muttered to myself as Terrence clocked us. His
pencil-thin lips twisted into a cunning, deprecating smile.

"What's that?" asked Lucy.

"Terrence," I replied.

"So?"

"Darling," he said, now reeling in front of us. "I must
ask, have you brushed up on your Shakespeare yet?"

"Oh god, no. What would I go and do a thing like that
for?" said Lucy, couching her response in a laugh. As with
most things in life, Terrence had no answer. "I always seem
to catch you in fancy dress," she added with charming

innocence. We both passed our eyes over his elaborate tails. "Another play?"

Touchéd by Lucy's line of inquiry, Terrence opted for a different approach: "We've snuck a couple bottles of absinthe in—plus some other more delightful substances— if you care to join us for a tipple in the Ashberry Suite? It's hired out especially for the Decadents, actually. We go a long way back, sooooo . . . I bet you would like to see how the real movers and shakers of Oxford indulge themselves for once, wouldn't you . . ." He paused, inviting Lucy to remind him of her name.

"We'll be fine," I said.

Terrence lodged his tongue between gums and top lip, scrunching and rubbing his nose, arrogantly advertising the mound of cocaine he'd been snorting in the toilets.

"Okay then, Eliot."

"I can't stand that dick," I said bitterly once he had managed to stagger a few meters away. I could see Jack frowning and Ella nodding, halted on their return journey from the bar, as he regaled them with acidic pleasantries. "I mean, he's such a *dick*. I can't think of anything worse than sharing a drink with that gang of douches."

"You're silly," said Lucy, the glow of the red wine beginning to spread across her cheeks. "You shouldn't let things get to you so much."

"Do you guys want to come over to the Ashberry Suite?" asked Ella, Jack following behind. "Apparently there's loads of free booze up there, and to be honest I quite like the idea of scrounging stuff off Terrence!"

"Sure," I replied. "Sounds good."

"Are you serious?" said Lucy.

"Yeah, why not? Come on, it'll be a laugh." Lucy's surprise was remote and understated, but the trace of disbelief in her voice turned me defensive. "Lighten up. It's a summer ball!"

Up in the Ashberry Suite, surrounded by private-school troubleshooters and eager female supplements, I proceeded to get fucked to such a degree that I was incontrovertibly fucked with Lucy and utterly bereft of any chance of getting fucked that night. The more I drank (torrents of emerald green flaming their way down my raspy throat) the soberer Lucy seemed to become.

"Why are you talking like that?" she asked, after I had been showing off to one of the junior lords, trying to act like I belonged in their company, while Lucy looked on, bemused and unsettled.

"Like what?"

"I dunno . . . like posh I guess. That wasn't your normal voice just then."

"Stop being so small-minded," I spluttered, reaching for a glass of port from a side table. Ella and Jack looked on, like accidental intruders. "You just don't get me." Before Lucy could respond (signals of affront winding tight about her lips and cheekbones), Terrence pushed his way between us, wielding a pewter tray laced with lines of powder.

"Check out Guy Fawkes over here," I said through a mouth that was no longer my own. It felt like there was an alien inside my body, using my eyes and my tongue, steering my limbs irresponsibly.

"Well, do you want in on the plot, liiiiike?" he said, offering Lucy first.

She didn't even bother to muster a word. The sharp look of disgust was enough.

"Good sir?" he said, turning to me.

"Oh. Are you sure, mate?"

Terrence nodded, holding the tray out on one hand, the

other tucked behind his back like a butler, a demented smile transfixed on his face.

"Wow, thanks. That's really kind of you." I wasn't exactly interested, but I was intensely flattered, the idea of coke being so bound in my head with the socialite scene I knew I'd never be a part of. I pressed one nostril in, like I'd seen in the movies, closed my eyes, and cleaned a line from bottom to top like a sinister Henry Hoover whose smile grows wider as he goes. Straightening up, I vigorously shook my head, desperate to reorganize my collapsing face. "You're a legend, Terrence. Thanks."

"Don't mention it," he said, that shit-eating grin truly stuck. "We should all do our bit for charity when we can."

"What?" Before I knew what had happened I was slumping into Jack and Ella, all the absinthe inside of me unleashing a sudden bout of voodoo. The scene had turned dunce and inane; double, double, toil and trouble. My face went like fag ash, my eyes popping Cheshire Cat balls. I lolled in Jack's arms, head slopping on his shoulder, a veritable kicking k, as he dragged me like a first-aid practice dummy to the toilets. In the Gents he punted the cubicle door cop-raid drugs-bust style, lifted the seat (all amber bejeweled in splodgy cock nectar) with the end of his foot, and lowered his casualty onto the floor. He was in a war movie, dragging his bloodied best friend back into the trenches and begging him to hang on.

With a china wallop my gut unfolded and I heartily hurled, like there'd been a dead badger decomposing in my stomach all evening. Go on, let it all out. There, there, that's it. (Infant memories of *keep it in the bowl, Eliot, keep it in the bowl* . . .) That's it, let it all—I want to die—let it all out. There's a good—

After many jolts and experimental maneuvers Jack got

me back into the ball. Things were dying down though—a few kids lying in the bushes and flower beds, pairs heading off hand in hand, the more hardcore still dancing—and I couldn't find Lucy anywhere. I fell all the way up the stairs to my room and clumsily fed the keys into the lock, but it was already open. Inside I collapsed into a heap trying to remove my clothes, winding up on top of the bed with a shirt halfway over my head and trousers at my knees. A familiar form, neatly tucked in, stirred quietly beside me.

"Lucy?"

She didn't reply, turning over so that her back was against me. I placed an arm around her, attempting to spoon but ending up more like knife and fork as she nudged me away. "Just go to sleep, Eliot."

"Wanna get it on?"

"Sleep!"

I tried to protest, arguing that I wasn't ready for bed yet, but I must've passed out mid-sentence.


We get ripped for cocktails and beers.

"She's doing well for herself . . . as usual," says Megan, looking over at Ella and her chat-up assailant.

Sanjay and Scott are laughing away with each other about something.

"Beer garden?" suggests Abi.

"Definitely," says Jack, returned from the toilet and eager to get away from the spectacle of some chump hitting on Ella.

I wish I could turn to Jack, like I used to. It's just not possible anymore. But when I broke up with Lucy, he was the first to know. I can still remember putting the phone down. We were no more. That's what Lucy had become to me by the time I started my second year: the voice at the end of the phone. Or, to be more accurate, the silence at the end of the phone. Either way I had terminated her with my delayed fingering of the red button. I had terminated us.

The summer itself had been okay, the regrets of the ball at its start so easily absorbed, young lovers trading daggers for roses in days, hours, minutes. It was all classic, in fact, until the very end of the vacation when Lucy was poised to start at the local uni. She assured me of the relative insignificance of this, citing how she was only going to be studying down the road and living at home anyway, yet I still found myself slumped on my bedroom floor with a notepad on my lap and an edition of Shakespeare's son-nets spread across my knee, like it was about to take off, drafting an unnecessarily momentous letter. I had even borrowed a copy of *The Oxford Book of Love Poems* from the college library at the end of term in morbid anticipation of this difficult transition. It wasn't a bill of separation or any-thing. Quite the opposite: I wanted to tell her how much I loved her and how I would do anything to keep us together now we'd both be at university (maybe some potent words of affection would divert her attentions from any prospect-ing lads during Freshers Week). But I couldn't find a con-vincing manner for sublimating all this poetical material into a natural voice. If my degree was meant to provide me with any kind of transferable skills, applicable to every-day life, then surely it was for moments like this. The scrunched-up balls of paper accumulating around me like miniature, undeveloped brains suggested otherwise. Shakespeare just wouldn't bend to my needs and I couldn't integrate the anthology's sentiments with my own feel-ings. In what was meant to be a spontaneous outpour of lover's resolve and romantic declaration, I found myself resenting Lucy more and more, as though my struggles with the pen were directly related to her unliterary mind. How was I ever meant to express my inner thoughts if she couldn't even understand me? The blank page stared back. With twelve months of lofty knowledge and reading swirling about in my head, I couldn't find a voice. I was silenced by quotations and styles not my own. Maybe it really was Lucy's fault. I eventually discovered the answers, however, in the liner notes to a Luther Vandross record. Lucy said I was sweet when I earnestly handed her the letter (with my chick-flick face of bravery and heartache), but that I needn't have bothered: we would see each other soon and she wasn't at all worried.

And then this. What wonderful shapes we tug ourselves into when crying, wrested and wrenched from our sane center of gravity. I squirmed and flailed like an emo gymnast after that three-hour phone conversation where we confirmed our incompatibility. I couldn't even do a traditional fetal position, clawing and grasping after nothing at all: a preposterous proposition; all arse over tit. And then I blew my nose, triggering and firing with full circus frivolity. How unfortunate it is, that moment which makes you want to laugh when all you want to do is cry. But comedy is never too far from tragedy, its awkward accomplice: yellow-stockinged Malvolio, distraught and abused.

I scraped myself up off the desk, surprised not to find a chalk outline of my mangled body, and began the short trip across the quad to Jack's staircase. A gang of testosterone-troubled rowers was emerging from the college bar, decked in garish boatclub blazers and epilepsy-inducing ties. Insensitive to my private pain, they stumbled about the quad in drunken embraces.

"I fuckin love you, man."

"You're the greatest, bro."

Dodging their assault course, head down, I reached Jack's stairwell and traipsed the three floors up to his room. "Errrr, alright mate?" he said, reluctantly opening the door. His cheeks were flushed and he was buttoning his trousers. He peered cautiously over at the bed, as if to ascertain that the coast was clear.

"Ah mate," I said, stepping within.

His room was a mirror-image duplication of mine. There was the duvet crumpled into a mound on the bed, the dirty dishes and tea-stained mugs rocking about on the floor, and jumble-sale litterings of clothes, as though their irresponsible mannequins had all done runners.

"Ah mate."

"I know."

"What happened?"

"Ah mate."

Jack sat on a swivel chair, his back toward the desk where a laptop blinkered and fanned. He looked faintly nervous, realizing that we were about to tread uncharted territories of friendship and disclosure. It was the look of someone battling to keep a straight face . . . like he knew a smirk or giggle would be the most inappropriate response and had therefore become a distinct possibility.

"It's over. Fuck me. It's over, mate."

"Ah shit."

Shouts and song filtered in through the window: "WE LOVE YOU, HOLLYWELL, OH HOLLYWELL, WE DO; WE LOVE YOU, HOLLYWELL, OH HOLLYWELL, JUST YOU . . ."

"Bell-ends," remarked Jack to make me feel better.

"Yeah. Right."

"So what happened?"

"Ah mate."

"Ah mate?"

"Yeah."

These words might seem inadequate, but we'd grown so tight over the first year of uni that all it took was a certain intonation, maybe a facial expression or two, and we understood each other clearly.

"Mate, I'm sorry."

My face was a back catalogue of tears: the swellings and the puffs; the glints and the gleams; the snail trails and the mires. This made Jack fidget a little more.

"Why's the tissue box in the bed, you big wanker?" I asked, momentarily discovering a distraction in humor. But it was forced.

"Let's keep this about you, yeah?"

"You're right . . . you're right. Ah mate."

Jack turned his music down (some morose indie song) as I sank into a chair (rolled-up socks, boxer shorts, and a baseball, all riding up into my crack and lower back).

"Is it for good, do you think?"

"Yeah, this is it. It's over, mate. Definitely. I think."

"I'm sorry, man."

"Thanks."

"Do you wanna like talk about it . . . and shit?"

I nodded slowly. Lucy had become somewhat of a regular fixture in Oxford during our freshers year, so Jack and the crew had observed us plenty of times. And it had worked quite well, the whole distance-relationship thing, though there were odd moments of confusion and miscommunication. Of course it was difficult, her being at school and me trying to settle in, obliged to go out on the lash all the time. But that's unavoidable; necessary as such. Jack had shared it all, what with the frequent "ah mate" chats in the early hours when we were meant to be banging out essays or fixing seminar presentations. By this point we were veterans when it came to the sophisticated, heartfelt convo:

"It was kind of mutual, I guess," I said at a struggle. "Ever since she's started uni, four weeks ago, there's been like a distance between us, mate." Jack nodded to demonstrate his sensitive understanding on the matter. "She's been cold kinda thing, if that makes sense. I don't know. Ah . . . it's just . . . you know." These were complete lies, even though I had convinced myself of their truth. *I* was the real reason for our breakup. And yet it wasn't even me who had brought matters to a head, opting instead to let things splutter along as they were. No, Lucy knew better than I did and she had the courage to broach it. She said that I was pushing her further away, or pulling myself further away, depending on which way you look at it. Apparently I wanted things that she could never be a part of.

"It's alright, bro. Let it all out and that."

The other issue, which Lucy hadn't perceived, and which I wasn't going to verbalize for Jack or anyone else, not even myself, was my feelings for Ella. Nothing was clear on this front, but she was making me uncomfortable with myself, as well as making it increasingly hard for me to be around Lucy, or even talk to her. I was far too confused to see it, though.

"My jealousy's gone into overdrive. Ever since her fucking Freshers Week. It's bullshit. It's been eating me up, and—" I noticed that Jack was switching off. He had stopped nodding and murmuring and was staring off into empty space. "Everything okay, mate?"

"Oh, yeah. I feel bad for you, man," he said, not so convincingly.

"Something on your mind?"

"Nah, it's stupid."

The more I had got to know Jack, the more I sensed a dark void rumbling away somewhere beneath the good-time exterior, adding pitch and ore. He was unequivocally the funnyman of the group, and the whole college seemed to love him for his easy laughs and clownery. But I had glimpsed more substance than this. Not that we ever talked about it.

"Mate, tell me."

"Nah, just girls innit." Now this really caught my attention. Jack had had a few fresher pulls, you know, the standard dance-floor/house-party affair—a passionate kiss here, a greasy handjob there—but he'd never revealed anything more settled or profound. I was ready for extra dimension . . .

"Oh yeah? Got your eye on someone, have you?"

"Hah, well, I guess, kind of. It's a bit awkward though, mate . . ."

"Do I know her?"

"Well, uh, that's kind of the—"

"Evening!" said Ella, entering the room without knocking. "Ah, Eliot, glad you're here. I've got your DVD," she said, waving the copy of *Harold and Maude* that I'd lent her. Then she clocked the situation, looking around and lurching backward. "Who died?" she asked sarcastically. "Why are your tissues in the bed, Jack? You filthy sod!"

"Eliot and Lucy broke up," he said at speed to change her focus, and possibly to change mine. I was momentarily contorted between diverging lines of thought.

"Oh."

I wish I had paid close attention to Ella's reaction. But I didn't. I had returned to self-absorbed thoughts of Lucy: thoughts of Lucy bawling in a heap on her bed, without me there to comfort her and tell her it was all going to be okay; of Lucy bawling to her brand-new uni girlfriends who wouldn't understand, just wouldn't understand, being ignorant of our history and ignorant of *me*; of Lucy getting balled by some horny chump now they'd finally managed to get me out of the way. And so I didn't pay close attention to Ella's reaction. But I'm almost certain it would've gone something like this: her face slackened, unscrewing and falling into the involuntary mask of disconnect (the flat mouth and relaxed cheeks, the unwrinkled brow and sunken eyes) as she looked from Jack, to me, and then down to the floor. Then she dropped absentmindedly onto the empty sofa. Having come from the college library you can bet she had books on her lap, neatly stacked and obedient to her pose, the film resting on top. Then she would have thrown her long thick hair up and over, continuing to stare into space as her fringe fell back down and across, once again, into its original place.

"I'm really sorry, Eliot. You must be—"

"Don't worry about it. It's just a shit situation is all."

Jack slumped in his chair, swiveling in guilt for exploiting my bad news (my terrible, terrible news) to avert attention away from his rogue tissue box.

"Give it time and things will become clearer," she said with tender levelheadedness.

"I guess. Maybe."

A silence of inexperience, but not immaturity, subsumed us all. We each picked our points of invisible interest (at our feet, on the ceiling, out the window) and gazed accordingly.

"I'm so pissed!" said Scott as he barged his way through Jack's door, unwittingly joining the commiseration exhibition. "Filth, anyone?" He'd come straight from the college bar, wielding the dregs of a pint in a plastic cup. "You been cracking one off over there, you demon wanker you?" he teased, motioning toward the incriminating tissues.

"For fuck's sake, Eliot and Lucy have just broken up, alright?" snapped Jack, shaking his head and straightening up. "Show some fucking sensitivity or something, yeah?"

"Shit the bed," said Scott in disbelief as he fell onto the sofa, next to Ella. "Is it true?"

"Yeah mate. Don't worry about it."

Scott did the malfunctioning robot, searching for an appropriate response, his drunken glaze twinkling uncertainly at the unwanted delicacies of male friendship.

"So what does that mean, for you guys?" he asked obscurely, looking from me and Jack to Ella.

"Scott, for fuck's sake!" exclaimed Jack.

How hard it is to share another's grief. Am I being deliberately melodramatic in deploying such a weighty word? Should that which tugs at my heartstrings tug at anyone else's? Are these stirrings contagious, passing freely from breast to breast? Wishing to assuage my gloom, my tense commiserators showered me with presence and considered silence. I wanted to know what Ella was thinking, I remember that much, but her countenance was as inscrutable as the conundrum apparently troubling Scott's dulled head. He wore a pained expression of concentration, but the thoughtful solution came quick enough:

"Abdul's?" (by which he meant our local kebab van).

"No no no no no," intervened Jack, snapping out of whatever funk he'd been in the whole time. "You were right first time around. Filth."

As we are walking away toward the beer garden, I feel a hand tugging me back and around. The others keep walking. It's Ella, escaped from her man.

"Kiss me."

"Huh?"

She places her warm breath inside mine.

We pull away from each other, the kiss having played out its moment, this rupture in the general movement of things. We didn't hold one another, Ella going for the sudden lunge as I turned around, and neither of us pulling the other in during those surprised split seconds. Panic-stricken, I dart my eyes around the bar, terrified at the thought that Jack might've seen. Ella's eyes are still slightly closed, her beautiful face tilted downward, her bottom lip hanging moist and culpable. She slowly raises her head, taking it all in. She needed a diversion, but even so I don't think she really knows why she did it. For a second she possesses a moony translucence—the outlines mutable and dissolving—but then she sharpens and merges into something more emphatic, like I'm adjusting the color and contrast on a television set. Before me is the delicate nose and distinguished, arcing mouth. But beneath all this there is damage, and I must tell her that I accept my share of responsibility. She looks at me speculatively and turns her head.

Should I tell her that she's the one for me, that deep down I've always felt we belong together? I've been thinking about it all night and here's as good a chance as any to come through. "I . . . I'm going to go to the toilet," I say.

I leave her and don't look back.

The toilets are hidden underground so I make my way down a congested set of stairs, like the simultaneous inlet and outlet of a football stadium, the flow stilted and rowdy. I find a vacant cubicle and shut myself in, the lock broken but the door staying approximately closed. The floor is wet. Soggy clumps of tissue—whole reams and streamers of the stuff—decorate my hovel. I drop the lid (the underside not worthy of consideration) and plonk myself down, resting my left arm on the toilet-paper dispenser to my side. I'm clouded with guilt and confusion, a screen of obfuscation.

I think about Jack, and what he would have to say about what's just happened.

I think about Lucy. I thought I was ready to move on for good . . . to go for her opposite; but I should have always known that Ella and Lucy aren't opposites at all. Hanging on to Lucy felt like a backward step . . . an admission that I wouldn't ever leave my past behind. And now that's not even an option. I've left it too late.

I think about Ella . . . how she views the last couple of years . . . her hopes for the future. Nothing becomes clearer; I can't begin to see through her eyes. I try to imagine myself in her place, but the history is too complicated and tragic, thwarting any powers of empathy or imagination that I might possess.

I think I want her. But is it Ella that I'm after, or the idea of Ella . . . everything that I've allowed her to represent? I just can't tell anymore.

I think about her standing upstairs, alone on the barroom floor, trying to shake it all off before making her way outside to the others.

I think about the time I met her father . . . He came up to Oxford, a high-powered City lawyer, to see his darling girl and take some of her friends out for dinner. I was running late, meeting the gang and Mr. Franklin at a swanky restaurant—a conservatory-type gig with atmospheric

candlelight and origami napkins—situated at the foot of
the Banbury Road. I dashed into the place, sweat on my
brow, decked out in T-shirt and jeans but thankfully not
trainers. I was expecting a casual affair, knowing that if my
folks were to stage such a date it would all be very low-key
and informal. There everyone was, around the center
table, already chewing oil-glazed breads and ripe olives,
tall velvet menus held out in front like hymn sheets. The
glass bottles of still and sparkling, red, white, and the one
empty seat next to Mr. F were the first things I noticed,
before registering the unfamiliar appearance of my familiar friends: Jack, Scott, and Sanjay in jacket and tie; Abi,
Megan, and Ella in cocktail dresses. I briefly flirted with
turning and leaving, going home and changing, or just
plain hiding, until Jack, facing my direction, raised his eyebrows and announced, "Here's Eliot" to the table. Mr. F
and his wondrous daughter, sitting on his right, turned to
smile and beckon me over.

"Hi everyone, I'm really sorry I'm late—" I said at speed.
I began to murmur an excuse but my throat got stuck on
itself and emitted nothing more than a pathetic gulping
sound. "Nice to meet you, Mr. Franklin," I said as he deci-
mated my lower-middle-class mitt in his deal-breaking
claw.

"Please, call me Jeff. Great to see you, Eliot." He
motioned with his spare hand to the vacant seat on his left.

I timorously settled in, wafting a napkin so large over
my regrettably denimed lap that it created a veritable
breeze. I passed my eyes over the company one by one.
Cheers fellas, real classy of you, in your smart attire, all
savvy and alive to decorum. I felt betrayed. At least I could
be thankful for being placed outside of Mr. F's constant

line of vision . . . but he had noticed . . . it had been duly noted.

The only other memories I have of that evening are my shyness and Ella's voice. The first is self-explanatory (inferiority complex, chip on shoulder, sulking inadequacy, general feeling of self-loathing). The second came as more of a surprise: Ella is, well, *posh*. As though especially for the evening, her voice had acquired the assured drawl and occasional squeaks (unexpected and startling) of upper-class speech. Her large bear of a father reeked of corporate green, with his formidable tan and crisp suit, the sparkling Rolex and general mastery of events. I felt abashed . . . how had I ever deigned to come so close to such a princess? I almost wanted to apologize and give my word that I would never bother his daughter again.

Most of all, I couldn't believe Jack with his black jacket and navy tie, hair neatly combed, and his pre-watershed topics of conversation. His sophistication was off the scale and I felt myself slumping lower and lower to the floor.

On the way back to college, where Mr. F would treat us all to pints at the bar to show his matey, down-to-earth side, Ella leaned into me—right in front of her father—as if inviting me to put an arm around her waist. I dithered, hesitant to find myself embroiled in a lawsuit, until she nearly ran me onto the road with her lowered shoulder. Placing my arm about her, she pressed in even tighter and squeezed my hand as it rested on her hip—

I rise from the toilet and head back up the stairs, out to the beer garden. In some ways Lucy's revelation should make my decision easier (and where the fuck did *that* come from?), but it hasn't, and the switched-off mobile in my pocket is burning a hole through my leg, demanding action, begging engagement. So I am not best pleased to see everyone else playing with their phones when I find them in the beer garden, participating in a brief textual interlude . . .

They r sittin round some outdoor heaters & theyve all got their phones out. Y, u might ask, given th@ its r last night all 2gether? I agree, its anti-social 4 sure, lol. But it's xepted: every1 needs a break from small talk & hard drinking @ least 1ce in a yle.

& so they take a min 2 communic8 with the absent. Or perhaps it would be more xpressive 2 say the "absent-presences"; the absent-presences of their *inboxes* & *sent msgs*. They text 4iously with speedy C21 thumbs & techno +vanced h&s (it's evolution baby).

"I number-eight this song," snarls Jack, without looking up from his phone.

"Lower-case-y?" I ask.

"It's number-two repetitive."

"What lower-case r lower-case u talking about?" interjects Abi. "It's an absolute tune!"

Jack: "confused face symbol."

I'm with Jack on this 1.

"Letter-n letter-e number-one lower-case-c Ella letter-x me?" I feel like asking, but clearly don't. It's 2 complic8ed. They wouldn't understand. Lol. (I don't mean "lol" @ all. It's just a textual ✓. There's nothing "lol" about me & Ella . . . it's a v complic8ed m@er.)

Evry1 frigs their phones with reck< abandon, ratter-tat-tapping & waving them in the air to catch some signal.

It's weird how these days u can b in the public & keep up the priv@ @ the same time. R mobs r r little boxes of privacy, like a physicalized subconscious. E.g. Scott is texting his l8est luv (some girl in the year <) 2 c if she's out 2nite; Sanjay is razzin through his sent msgs 2 make sure he hasn't done anything stupid (drunk txts r dangerous); Jax just playing mob games (sad really); & Megan & Abi r sharing texts & lol about them. I'm complic8ing over Lucy, contempl8ing my options.

I feel like txtin this 2 every1 dear:

> Depth was lost a long time ago. You can mark its vanishing point somewhere around the middle of the last century. Fullness of character is but a myth we hear about in documentaries and textbooks, all reedy-voiced and alien. For a while there, just before us millennial babes were plucked prematurely from our historical orbit, everything was surface; all must-haves and money-back guarantees; three-for-twos and buy-one-get-one-frees. But we don't even have that any more. Just lovers in the night, reaching and recoiling.

But like that's ever going to happen.

The beer garden is rammed.

"This is where it's at-sign number-two-night!" declares Jack.

Ella is the only other 1 not fiddling with a phone.

"Number-four real," I say distractedly.

We r all lost 2 each other, putting up walls and shutting ↓. Lol.

R m8.

These musing memories of the past do not simply—oh, how does it go? What comes next?—traverse my indolent brain (yes, that's it) like flitting phantasies . . . though often they do. I am a creature of both sensations and reflections and must make the record as I see fit.

You see, I *am* in control.

This is nothing new—my inability to block things out and move on—and I have not been passive in my missing of Lucy. She's imprinted all over my body . . . lodged in the nooks and crannies . . . and I did indeed make one notable rescue bid not long after the breakup. It began with me standing huddled in—

"Do you want a drink, mate?" Jack.

"If you're offering?"

"Course . . . Everything alright?"

"Sweet as a nut."

I was standing huddled in my black duffel jacket and paisley scarf at the Oxford bus station on Gloucester Green, round the back from the George Street Odeon. Lucy was settling into her new university life and I was consistently fucking up the process of moving on. I dug my hands deep into my pockets and hid half of my face in the scarf.

We're trained to stand stationary, there on the purgatorial platform, observing the delays and dues on the most depressing TV screen you'll ever see. The episode is bollocks—all numbers and middle-of-nowhere place-names; no pictures, no music, no action. Everyone watches with slight grimaces of perplexity, newspaper rapiers tucked under armpits; briefcases, suitcases, rucksacks piled about feet. The thistles and nettles prising their scraped heads and necks through the concrete tiles spark unspoken questions about hope and fear, security and abandon.

I caught the 16.15 to Wellingborough.

> Hey. I'll b there in
> two hours. That ok?
> x x

The question on the end was entirely unnecessary. We had already arranged to meet up earlier that morning, so I knew it was "ok"—or at least green-lighted. All I was doing with that question was wishfully stretching my tentacles out for further connection, straining and longing for

> K x

I retreated with severed limb . . . a throbbing stump of sadness. That solitary kiss; the response reduced to one harsh letter, one destructive plosive; that cutting K.

> Cool. Lookin 4ward
> 2 it x x

I wasn't sure what I was traveling toward or even what I wanted. I just had to go. It was me who had unconsciously engineered our breakup for so long, yet there I was, yearning for return, dragged under by nostalgia's fierce undertow. I watched the countryside straddling the dual carriageway's yawning asphalt as it rushed through the window frames of the coach. I gripped my phone in case of reply.

My destination was a coffee shop round the corner from the bus station in town. Destination, of course, shares its etymological root with destiny. But something told me that destiny had bugger all to do with this. Destiny could get up out of it. Destiny could fuck right off.

I arrived before Lucy, opening the door with its nosy-parker bell on top. It was a standard café of the type you find in every town or city. There were the aggressive thwacks of coffee strainers on the counter and the fizzing of rampant milk-steamers; the busy chatterings of hob-nobbers and casual meeter-uppers. I expected a few student characters, each to their own, buried in textbooks and night-out reverie, but of course there were none: it was Wellingborough. I took my place.

Might she know everyone in the café? Had she become acquainted with every punter in our hometown . . . now more her hometown than mine? Of course not. But in my head . . . in my head . . . All these new people she had let into her life, traveling up her motorway in bumper-to-bumper traffic, the other side of the road from me. *Me*, in the outbound lane. *Me*, alone. Everyone in there was rooting for her, as far as I was concerned. A tricky away game when even my home form was far from stellar.

"Hey," I said, scrambling from the table when she glided in.

"Hi." Her tone was obscure. We did that nervous dance of greeting, unsure whether to peck, kiss, hug—a pat on the back?—or just smile, until we practically head-butted each other instead. She seemed fuller, galvanized, adjusted by new experiences and knowledge. Not cerebral knowledge, mind. Carnal. But that was probably the brushwork of my imagination; my restless distorting eye.

"It's good to see you" (that's me).

We sat down opposite each other in interview formation. There hung an invisible barrier between us, blocking my soft signals, fortifying her guardedness.

"How's things?" I asked.

"Fine. I'm hungover."

"Oh right. Heavy night?"

"Yeah. I drank far too much."

"Was it a late one?"

"Yeah."

"Who were you out with?"

"Friends."

"Do they have names?"

"Yeah, but you wouldn't know them."

"So? Why won't you tell me who you were out with?"

"Eliot, stop it."

"Whatever."

With each jealous thud of my jackhammer heart Lucy recoiled a little further into herself. She chewed the inside of her bottom lip, not sultrily like she used to, but anxiously.

"What do you want to drink?"

"Just an orange juice."

"Don't you want a hot drink?"

"No. You know I hate caffeine."

"Fair enough."

She stopped me as I got up. "Eliot . . ."

"Yeah?" I said, spinning round like tortured lover in romantic movie . . . heavy . . . giddy . . . longing for revelation . . . say it, please, just say it . . . give me anything and I'll take it.

"Can you get me a chocolate twist as well?"

"Sure."

After surviving a barrage of options from the bloke behind the counter, I returned to Lucy and settled down for the long haul. "Oh, I have a gift for you," I said, pulling a paperback from my jacket pocket. "See what you think." I placed it on the corner of the table: Iris Murdoch's *Under the Net*. I'm not entirely sure why I did this—to impress her? To continue molding her into my idea of the perfect girl? To remind her of our differences?

"What do you want, Eliot?"

"I don't know," I stuttered, surprised by her directness. "I just wanted to see you."

"But why?"

"Because I miss you, and—"

"You can't do this," she said. I sat back, stunned: *but thy more serious eye a mild reproof darts, O beloved woman!* "You can't push me away and then try and pull me back in. You know?" (Yeah, but I thought—) "You can't put me down whenever you feel like it and just expect to pick me back up again," she said, talking about me like I was a demented forklift truck. "I've been settling into my new life," she continued. "You knew I was going to need some space for a while. But that's all." (But *I* didn't need you to need space, did I? I mean just think about—) "You're the one who goes quiet and distant, for no reason, until jealousy or curiosity brings you back round. I love you, but you can't keep doing this to me."

"Sorry. I didn't realize I—"

"You made it seem like you'd lost interest. You were lovely all summer and then you changed again as soon as we went back to uni." (*Dramatic pause.*) "You went quiet."

"You're the one who changed though," I countered, unadvisedly, knowing that she was spot-on. "You're too obsessed with your new life . . . your new friends."

"No! That's what you *wanted* to happen," she said, growing more animated. "That's how you'd pre-planned it in your head. You chase tension, Eliot." (Well, I hadn't bargained for this.) "It's like you expect bad things to happen—you don't trust anyone, and I don't understand why. No one's ever even done anything horrible to you! Your life is constant plain sailing."

"That's not true!" I retorted, stung by the venomous truth of her dart.

"Look, I can't do this," she said, welling up. "I'm not right for you—you know it and I know it . . . and it makes me so unhappy . . . makes me feel awful. All I've ever wanted is for you to want me as much as I want you and just accept me as I am . . . like I do you. But I don't think you can. You used to, but that's all changed now you're comfortable at Oxford."

"Please Lucy, just let me—"

"Eliot, stop it. You don't even know what you really want, and it's messing with my head. It's not fair."

"Sorry."

She shriveled when I reached out to touch her—a reaction so alien that reality seemed to be betraying me.

"I'm gonna go," she said. "I promised I'd meet some friends."

"Oh."

"We can't keep doing this."

"So why do you stay in touch with me?" I said in last-ditch desperation. "Why do you reply to my texts and agree to meet up?"

"Because. I can't help it. I can't imagine cutting you off. But this isn't good."

We sat for a while, saturated in silence.

"I have to go. Text me later or something . . . when I'm less tired."

"Okay then."

She rose and disappeared into her new landscape (that once familiar landscape), absorbed by its canvas and colors, all hostile to me, the non-integrated object. She didn't say bye and neither of us drank our drinks.

The bus jibed and cajoled me all the way back to Oxford, mercilessly grinding away at my fresh wounds. Stopping at every place conceivable, and many inconceivable, it took my misery on tour: Northampton, Towcester, Silverstone, Brackley, Bicester . . . The show garnered an underwhelming reception, what with virtually no tickets sold. At each stop we rolled up to, no one got on, no one got off. I was alone in my unhappiness, performing to an empty house. Even the stocky bus driver seemed to resent having to chauffeur such a sorry excuse for a man.

My second year was off to a disastrous start. Not only was there the loss of Lucy, but I also found out that I had fucked up my first-year exams, or "underachieved" as the two-sentence report that landed in my pigeonhole put it. Dr. Dylan Fletcher, who was fast establishing himself as an absolute legend, took me under his wing (a blokey pint at the Turf), and convinced me not to feel disheartened by my results. He said that I showed a lot of promise and that some people just develop more slowly than others. Apparently he had absolute faith that I was going to have a breakthrough at some point in the next two years and I took his word for it. Why not? I liked his approach. He'd even hosted a debauched house-party for his students at the start of the term, welcoming us all into the new academic year. I tried to enjoy myself as best I could but it was fucking hard, what with Lucy cramping my emotional and psychological style. Most of the others crashed at Dylan's after, drinking and dancing into the early hours, but I snuck off at the height of the shindig to wallow pitifully in front of Lucy's Mugshot page.

And that is precisely what I did when I made it back from Wellingborough to my room, which had donned a decidedly bleak aura in my absence. I fired up the slumbering laptop to renew contact with the world and recharge myself at the mains. Then I did the habitual rounds: uni email, personal email, some sport sites and, yes, mugshot. com. Like everyone else I slaughter whole swaths of time on the latter. Pathetic. My Mugshot inbox blinked two new messages and an update notified me that I had been "prodded" by two "friends." How thoughtful. Jack had scribbled all over my "face": "Mmmmmmmmate! When are you back from home? Large one down Scrot Lounge tonight . . . keen? Peas x." Then, as I do every single day, still, I clicked on Lucy's "face" to torture myself with the latest. Always at this moment my stomach plummets and my ticker accelerates in dreaded anticipation; the anticipation of something that'll make me curious . . . paranoid . . . jealous . . . livid . . . sad. Signs of a life in which I don't exist. Never gets easier. It throws me.

"Lucy has been 'caught' in 7 photos," advertised her status update.

Fucking great, I thought, prepping myself for the stalker's gloom of compulsive investigation. These would be shots from her night out with her new friends: the root of her hangover. What am I expecting to find when I search through her photos, and her friends' photos, and her friends' friends' photos, getting lost down inadvisable back roads of dubious connection?

Exhibit 1: This one was fine. This one I could handle. It was pretty much inoffensive. Just Lucy in group pose, in some club, yes, with three gf's. I noted that one of them looked like a tangerine . . . sure to be a bad influence.

Exhibit 2: Lucy and man. Probably a rocket scientist or future Nobel Laureate from her Travel and Tourism course. My palms clammed up like soggy bread, but it was okay . . . they were just standing next to each other. Fine. Besides, although I couldn't make out his face, which was distorted by the snapper's clumsy thumb covering half the lens, he looked like a chav.

Exhibit 3: What? *Hugging?* I leaned closer into the screen and administered deep breaths.

Exhibit 4: This was more like it. Strength in numbers. A motley assortment of boob tubes and quiffs. People that I just don't know. A harmless gang of drunken counterfeits, their faces melting into horror-show shapes. Grim as, but better than that last one.

Exhibit 5: Now we had a problem. Now we had a big fucking problem. She was on a sparse dance floor, grinding on that bell from Exhibits 2 and 3. She was facing me, obliviously taunting me, excluding me. He was behind her, leering over her, mortar-and-pestling her, his face blocked by Lucy's. His hand-that-was-not-my-hand gripped her hip and her arse was slipping and sliding all over his parasitic cock.

Exhibit 6: This was the stomach-churning masterpiece. A Caravaggian scene of epic betrayal. That "lad" was eating her face. Or was she eating his? It's hard to find precision in these matters. But they were kissing. They were kissing, okay? There was something recognizable about the guy's pose . . . maybe it was just because I had been in his position so many times myself. It was obvious that neither was aware of being caught by their "friend's" scandal-cam, which somehow made it worse: I was seeing something that I was never meant to see.

I didn't dare confront the finale . . . the money shot. The dry metallic taste in my mouth and the trembling of my body let me know it was time to turn away. No Exhibit 7 for me.

I know that I am probably misrepresenting Lucy and I regret it immensely. I wish I could truly convey her . . . the poetics of her geometry: the longing arcs of her shoulders; those slender, inquiring fingers and pouty knuckles; her smooth, tight neck; those infant ears like time signatures on a piece of music . . . but it's never enough. And then there's Ella, who hangs over these memories like a gauze, forcing me to squint as I struggle to make sense of everything. In old age such recollections might seem like a gift, purified of any poison . . . pleasant reminders of flesh, limbs, and sexual possibility . . . harmless messages from the subjective historian cloistered in the head. But for now they are raw. They disorientate, carrying so much consequence and import.

I feel as though I am forever haunted by thoughts of Lucy. I'm haunted by—

A murky vagina, ghoulish in its sinister ferocity, loomed down on me, stared across the room at me, winked its rheumy eye at me, as Ella pressed tight against my thigh. (I'm sorry . . . the memories are starting to come thick and

fast, and I must allow them . . . it's the only way . . . I am
straining for intelligibility.) We were intimately packed on
the sofa in Dr. Fletcher's room. Dylan stood by the window fondling his crotch.

"Anyone want a cuppa tea?"

"Ooooh, yes please. Three sugars," piped Megan, who
was perching on the edge of a sofa perpendicular to ours.

"How very artisan," said Terrence, sunk back next to her,
one leg crossed over the other in the feminine form, twirling
a pen and balancing a leather-bound notebook on his lap.

I hadn't slept much the night before, what with seeing
Lucy's "moving-on" pics on Mugshot and having my insides
hung up to dry. The whole scene took on a giddy, almost
hallucinatory quality.

"I bet you've had cunt on your mind all week," the vagina
seemed to be saying to me. It was Dylan, in the corner, to
the left of the meticulously placed sketch of a naked female
torso and crotch (directly above his teaching chair, directly
in front of my sofa, directly yet silently testing me), as he
fiddled with kettle and teabags on a rickety side table.

Megan immediately took the bait (Dylan's chief aim
and pleasure being to get a rise from his female students).
"To be honest, I don't see why he has to be so profane. He
uses the *c*-word so much and I can't see any artistic or philosophical justification for it."

Handing a steaming cup to Megan before lurching into
his throne with a cup for himself (this roughly signaling
the beginning of the tutorial proper), Dylan smiled a smug
note of satisfaction.

"Need there be a justification for it? What's wrong with
some gratuitous cuntery?"

The tute was on John Wilmot, the Earl of Rochester;
that libertine poet, all sex, guts, and booze. I had borrowed

an Oxford University Press edition of the complete works from the Hollywell library, an orange train ticket poking out from the top. I always use train or bus tickets for bookmarks (unlike Terrence, with his gold clip or peacock feather). I like the sense of a journey, as if the book is going to take me somewhere. As for Dylan's language, he had worked hard (in a manner that suggested not working hard) to reach a stage where he could be as open and irreverent with us as he liked; to be a mate; a *young one*. We were so impressed to hear a tutor swear and act like one of us that we didn't think to ever take issue or question the content. He enjoyed playing the windup merchant and therefore it was difficult to be offended. Megan felt differently about old Rochester though, who, unlike Dylan, hadn't earned our respect by throwing parties and organizing trips to the pub:

"Well, quite frankly, the endless, ahem, c-words seem a bit misogynistic to me," replied Megan, heating up, her voice wobbling with all the righteousness that was simmering inside.

Was I a mug? Had Lucy been playing me for a fool? I knew we weren't together anymore, but wasn't it a bit soon to be doing all that? And god knows how many others there had been. I could hardly call her a slut, or a slag, or a whore. But I wanted to. *Fucking slut.* No, too strong. I looked to the charcoal vagina for answers, but none were forthcoming.

"'And may no woman better thrive, that dares prophane the cunt I swive!'" performed Terrence with extra thespian attack on the obscenity. "It's fabulous, Megan, what are you talking about? It's so full of bite and wit, actually . . ." All dandies fancy themselves libertines, so of course Terrence would embrace the aristocratic hedonism.

"Alright, Terrence," said Dylan dismissively, displeased by the prospect of anyone else relishing the word, but mostly not wanting Terrence on his side. (I think he dislikes him as much as the rest of us.)

It's not like I hadn't ever thought about it myself. Of course I had wondered what other girls would be like— those rogue phantasms that pop into the head when they shouldn't; my dream team raring for the call-up from my wanking bench. Put me in, coach, put me in! But I'd never made it reality . . . I mean, Jesus Christ, I didn't actually want to move on, did I? And I certainly didn't want Lucy to.

"Come off it, Terrence," said Megan. (Dylan smiled: an interstudent face-off really gets the juices flowing.) "That bit when the poet follows the lady around the park, spying on her sexual escapades . . . it's nothing more than pure woman-bashing. Listen to this . . ." She picked up a threadbare edition of Rochester's poems which had apparently been hurled across a room and smashed against a wall or two, the victim of some heinous domestic violence. The page was most carefully marked though by a bright pink tab, her disgust lovingly organized and considerate. Megan rolled her eyes at Terrence and glanced across to Dylan for a permissive signal. Dylan was spread-eagled, caressing the back of his head. She coughed and swallowed.

> " 'So a proud bitch does lead about
> Of humble curs the amorous rout,
> Who most obsequiously do hunt
> The savory scent of salt-swoln cunt.'

Yeah, Terrence, great fun!"

Terrence tossed a nod of superiority Dylan's way, hoping for a laddy laugh or some sign of mutual appreciation.

Dylan was having none of it, lifting his tea to snarling lips. Ella was unusually quiet, sensing my exhausted condition perhaps: my shifts and my fidgets; my yawns gaping after sunset. Ordinarily you could expect Ella to jump in at this point and teasingly chastise Dylan for his flippant misogyny before explaining to us all exactly why Rochester was so filthy, and whether we were meant to find it profound or simply vacant. On this particular occasion she wasn't giving any tips, however, keeping her head down and picking at her pen.

"Forget the morality, or amorality, of it all for a moment," suggested Dylan, cocking his right leg over the arm of the chair. Hand on forehead he gazed into the upper reaches of the bookshelf behind Terrence and Megan, searching for ideas as though they might be stored beneath the Longman *Milton*, behind Coleridge's *Table Talk*, grinding on Montaigne's *Essays*, snogging Spenser's *Fairie Qveene*. "What are the *words* doing? Where is the poet in all this? Whereabouts is he in relation to his style?"

Ella had stolen my tactic and was pretending to write, industriously running her pen over the only two words on the page: "Rochester tute." What's with her?

Terrence did some improv—a bloated answer that ended up getting lost down a dead end of empty terms and crude generalizations, salted-and-peppered with "like"s, "actually"s, and "so"s.

"But why be so explicit?" asked Dylan, completely ignoring all of Terrence's points. "What are these 'spermatic sluices' and 'cunts filled with unwholesome juices' *doing*?"

I had a gnawing desire to text Lucy and interrogate her. But how could I? Did I have any right? Well yeah, actually; I did. Her dirt was all over the Web; it was in the public domain . . . so now she had to face the shit-storm. You heard: now you have to face the shit-storm. That comes with the territory. And besides, I wanted her to know how badly she had fucked me up.

Dylan geared himself up for soliloquy, the mechanisms of his brain creaking into action. Megan cowed her head. The vagina maintained a poker face.

"For all of its seeming explicitness, isn't experience just being held at bay?" Why, of course; quite. "Cunt stands for everything and anything here. It becomes the transcendental signifier." You took the words right out of my mouth. "So does it mean anything at all? Is it actually graphic or is it simply a way of deferring meaning and evading experience?" We twitch with faux-scholarly reflexes: mmm, well yes, one might . . . one could . . . most curious . . . "And is the self taking refuge in this empty space or is the self being placed under constant erasure?"

Maybe it would've been better to have never seen the evidence. Sure, that would've been the healthier option. At least that way I could have had a decent night's sleep and my road-kill ego would still be intact. But I *had* seen it. And I had wanted to see it. I had sought it out. Let's face it, every time I click on her Mugshot "face" I am slightly disappointed not to find something scandalous or upsetting. I long to be fucked up. How dare you not fuck me up sooner. *Fucking slag.*

No, still too much.

"He's outside of experience," I said, breaking my conspicuous silence for the first time. Ella looked up at me, surprised. I was surprised myself, slipping into autopilot: "Libertinism is ostensibly about the direct gratification of the senses and lust, right? Yet language only forms a barrier for Rochester. It doesn't bring him any closer to his subject. It merely distances and self-mortifies, like he's on the outside looking in." I shifted in my seat, getting more upright. Terrence nearly dropped his notebook. "His vicious tirade on the promiscuous lover is ultimately futile: it may be brutal and damning, but it's only words. He is helpless to affect what he sees. He's merely left with his own fear and loathing, hidden behind a stylistic screen and mask."

"Absolutely," said Dylan, smiling and putting his book down. I noticed that the others were all scribbling away, and found a garbled version of my thoughts flicking and curling across Ella's stunned page.

At the end of the tute Dylan asked Ella to stay behind for a quick chat. I think he had noticed her unusual lack of gusto, and apparently her essay that week had bombed. I was too busy angsting over Lucy to really care. I wondered what she was doing and weighed up the chances of seeing her soon.

Jack's determined to enjoy this final night. Aren't we all? Yes. We're all agreed on this one.

"Let's just have a good night, yeah?" he says again, with hammed-up seriousness, shrugging his shoulders in fake appeal like it's a decision that needs to be made.

"Let's just have a good night, yeah?" I say, the agreed response to the call.

"Let's just have a good night," chips in Scott.

"Lads on tour, lads on tour, lads on tour," sings Jack to the tune of a footy chant, wielding a beer in each hand, as we settle into a booth inside the bar.

"Fuck me, this is going to cane in the morning," says Sanjay. The warning isn't necessary.

Jack and I pair off in the conversational arena. "Is it time to have a man chat yet?"

"You mean like a final 'I love you, bro'?"

"Yeah. It won't be the final one though. You ain't ever gettin' rid of me, baby."

"As I feared."

"Oh, how we laugh!" exclaims Jack in his best private-school imitation. He's had long enough to perfect it these past three years.

"Oi, me old mucka, leave it out," jeers Scott in horrifically rendered cockney. Ever an old Etonian, despite his best efforts to cut those ties, he sets off a round of giggles.

"Haha! Do you remember the first time we met Scott?" begins Jack.

"Oh come on, guys," pleads Scott, instantly ruing his pained attempt at joviality. "We've heard it a million times before."

Jack doubles over, choking on mute laughs, eyes scrunched shut, all teeth and gum.

"Please?" tries Scott, a last-ditch plea, delving into his pockets for the touchy-feelies.

"Oh god!" I'm fighting back the hysterics. This is more like it. "It was in your room as well, Jack, in Freshers Week."

"Oh haha how we haha laugh hahaha!" He's red, shaking and bubbling, a volcano of mirth.

Scott is now gulping his beer in individual stabs, blushing horrendously—like he always does—bracing himself for the story he knows will come.

"Fuck me, I can't breathe," pants Jack.

"Unfortunately not true," mutters Scott, momentarily lifting his lips away from his security pint.

". . . when Abi necked that whole bottle of Lambrini," continues Jack, "and then Scott . . ." he breaks off, tugged under by our wave of roars ". . . he says . . . he says . . ."

"Hahahahahaha," we cry in unison.

". . . he says, 'Gosh! I've read about girls like you in the tabloids . . . but, well, you know, gosh . . . I never knew you actually existed!' " Jack tilts back on his chair, throwing his face up to the skies, convulsing rapidly, tears streaming down his tensed, muscular cheeks. Scott buries his face in his hands, shaking his head, surreptitiously enjoying his claim to posterity.

"Bless him," comes Sanjay, "he'd never seen an actual living girl before!" (the routine conclusion to the skit).

The girls arrive at the booth, ogled by a troop of lads just over from us.

"What's so funny?" inquires Megan, her tipsy voice slipping off her tongue.

"The Lambrini story," explains Scott with dejected airs. Ella rolls her eyes and Abi shows subtle signs of pride.

"Ah, I'm gonna miss the posh sod," I say to Jack, returning to our private dialogue.

"Me too . . . . What am I talking about? I'm going halfway round the world with the tosser!"

"Hah, yeah. Good luck."

"Fuck. Nah, it'll be hot. He can pull them in with the Hugh Grant and then I'll give 'em the bit of rough they're really after."

"Teamwork."

"Exactly," says Jack before darting at his glass for another swig. "It's a shame you're not coming with us."

I would've been up for it as well, but things weren't too easy between me and Jack when they organized their gap year a few months ago . . .

Ella cautiously watches us from across the table, full of care, chewing on her straw and pretending to listen to Abi's conversation.

A roving bar-lady infiltrates our booth, showing off her utility belt loaded with strawberry-and-cream vodka shots. Her looping earrings glitter under the neon lights and her waddling bum shakes from side to side like drink in an unsteady glass.

"Anyone for shots? Only two quid each," she says.

"Are they as sexy as you?" asks Jack, always quick to stir cheeky vibes.

"Of course. They're scrummy."

"Scrummy you say? Will you do one with me?" She is remotely fit, I suppose, but this is irrelevant.

"Shots all around and one for yourself," I interrupt to end the cringe. The waitress smiles and begins administering our tooth rot.

"Trust you to jump in there before me," mutters Jack.

I shoot a quick look at Ella, whose face, though motionless, seems to be telling me something. My heart whimpers. What does he mean? Nothing, nothing. Stop being so sensitive. He doesn't know, does he? How could he . . . I've kept it from him all this time. My stomach flutters and my skin prickles with heat. I'm being overly paranoid . . . reading too much into things. He could've meant anything . . .

I'm remembering a certain night (of course I am, what other night could it be?). It begins at an English Literature drinks party halfway through a royally shit Michaelmas term. English Drinks: the once-termly gathering of Hollywell's literary students and tutors (about twenty in all) for minor nibbles and major inebriation. There we stood in a snugly fitted room, named after one of the college's illustrious benefactors, guzzling wine gratis. (Some tables and chairs pushed to the mahogany sides. Shimmering book cabinets with leather-bound guts. Rippled carpet hugging old cambering floorboards. Lighting sleepy, temperature soft and warm. Window seats with deep, crimson cushions looking out and down onto pitch-black quadrangle scene. Armchairs and sofas, portraits and chandelier. The door rattles shut with each coming and going: private.)

I pause to note that Rob had been in touch earlier that

evening to let me know that he was there for me after the
breakup with Lucy:

"Rooted anyone yet?"

"Huh?"

"You know, *porked* anyone? Have you moved on?"

"Too soon, mate. I'm not even thinking about that."
That was a lie—the possibility of being sexually promiscuous all of a sudden was scaring the shit out of me.

"Okay. Well, if you ever need to talk . . . Why not come
and visit me in . . ." I had switched off. I knew he was only
going to suggest I went up to his uni, wherever it was, and
laid some of his mates or a selection of the eager freshers
he had primed.

"Yeah mate, maybe. Busy term . . . so I doubt it."

"Whatever."

"I've gotta go."

"Working again?"

"I'm going to a drinks party actually."

This combination of words was a self-evident redun-
dancy to Rob; a silly tautology: one drinks at all parties,
right? Otherwise what's the point?

"That's what I'm talking about! Big club night?"

"Actually, no. It's a little get-together put on by my tutors
for—"

"Your what?"

"My tutors."

"Why would they do that?"

"Well, it's for—"

"You're such a fag, mate. I worry about you sometimes.
Nah, what you need is a couple of pints of snakebite, a
sweaty club, and lots of hot girls to rub yourself on."

"Bye then."

"Peace."

And so I went to the party. We began in circles. Nervous clusters crystallized around their respective oracles: a pair of postgrads, bedraggled by advanced knowledge of Joyce and Woolf, bookending Dr. Polly Snow; a brace of first-year girls plus awkward lad, tirelessly topped up by Dylan's trigger-happy claret and Sauvignon Blanc; Cassandra, the young new medieval tutor, blending with third-year finalists and their thoughts of apocalypse; and me, Megan, and Ella, scavenging the egg and cress, the tuna and cucumber, the cheese and tomato, staining our teeth against the bitter grape of the red, a nervous cluster in want of its oracle. (Terrence was absent, thankfully, being too exclusive for such an event.) The air was charged with excited expectancy: the prospect of hobnob-bing with our tutors and absorbing grand, vaulting thought.

"I'm gonna get absolutely fucked tonight," I said on the down-low to our orphan group. "I think I'm halfway there already."

"Lightweight," ribbed Ella.

"As if," I remonstrated. "I've only had a sandwich all day" (the standard line).

"We need to corner one of the tutors," said Megan ambitiously, staring in the direction of Polly. "Bloody post-grads kissing her arse and getting in the way . . . Let's head over and make ourselves apparent," she suggested, unable to relax.

"I guess," said Ella as she refilled her lipstick-signatured glass.

Setting off on our seven-meter expedition over to Polly, a bumbling old man blocked us in our tracks.

"Mmmmmmmmm hullo th-th-there."

Simultaneously alarmed and amused we took stock of this most unexpected creature. He had old Fellow bespat-tered all over him: the tweed jacket and velvety cords; the

tufty nostrils and mischievous twinkle; the incoherent babble of drink and arcane knowledge. The port glass in his
right hand suggested a lifetime devotion to the hard stuff.

"Hello?" said Megan, jaggedly.

"Hello," said Ella with more humor.

"W-w-w-well, aren't you a p-p-pretty wibble thing," he
said to Ella, swaying and nodding somnolently. This guy
must've been fucked off his tits for the last fifty years.
That's what hanging out in libraries does for you.

"Excuse me?" she said abruptly. I was surprised: I had
expected her to forgive his sleazy aspect for the quirky,
grandfatherly character he clearly played.

"Are you Polly and Dylan's b-b-b-b-bright wobble young
things, hmmmm?" he asked, leaning so far forward on his
toes that I was primed for a catch.

"Yes," jabbed Megan with a hint of finality in her tone,
desperate to dispense with this inconvenience in order to
get to Polly.

"We're second-years," added Ella as an apologetic modification. Megan glared at her.

"Ahhhhhhhhhhh," sang the old man, wavering between
wonderment and death throe. "T-t-t-ttto b'young," he
dreamed out loud, his bulbous eyes momentarily hidden
by wrinkled accordion lids, as though rolling the idea back
and around in his once lucid head.

"I w-w-w-w-w-w-was Fellow here, a long wobbly t-t-t-
ttime ago. Wrote on James and Hardy, hmmmmm?"

Groping after a bottle from the side he topped the girls'
glasses liberally, holding the vessel limply round its head and
leaning into them, splashing puddles of red all over his shoes
and the light-gold carpet. Bored by his gendered focus and
my own empty glass, I slipped away to the drinks table.
Glugging from the wings I watched Ella throwing back her

hair and laughing generously. I marked her sophisticated squints of consideration and her full-bodied enthusiasms: those tilts and flutters and sways. I could smell her careful fruitiness from across the room, coming in traces and then waves. A stylish, miniature blazer pinched her about the sides, contrastingly fanning her chest and hips into distract- ing outlines above and below. In the course of making these observations we slozzled another glass each. It looked like Ella was going to drink me under the table.

Then a familiar rumble in my trouser leg. First Jack:

> S'up bruv. U
> English fags
> comin out after
> drinks? Reckon
> I cud smuggle
> in 4 free booze? X

Then Rob:

> U got ur dick wet
> yet? Yeh boi!

"Alright?" came Dylan's voice as I tucked my phone back into my pocket. He was scouting through the mass of opened bottles on the table, testing them for dregs.

"Oh, hi Dylan."

"Enjoying the evening?"

"Yeah I am, thanks," I said, hurriedly swallowing back a stodgy sandwich of mysterious content.

"I need heavy booze, and quick," he confided, nodding toward a group of master's students who had fallen to bick- ering amongst themselves about some inane literary point.

"All they want to do is talk about bloody English. Factory-line academic sycophants! It's such a bore. Why talk shop?" he asked rhetorically, filling his glass to the brim. "Can't they talk about music, or the last film they saw, or who they're shagging?" He took an eager gulp. "Tossers."

"Completely," I said, squirming at the thought of all those pre-planned questions I had lined up about his latest research, his book on Wordsworth, and the English course. I couldn't take my eyes off Ella.

"How do you think she's doing this term?" he asked.

"Huh?" I said, embarrassedly.

"Ella. She doesn't seem her usual self."

"Oh, she's fine. I guess things are more serious now we're studying toward Finals. You know how she is—she's incredibly driven. She wants that First so desperately."

"Of course, and so should you. You're both more than capable."

We sipped our drinks. I felt tense.

"But she hasn't said anything to you?" he added.

"Not at all."

"I'm sure it'll sort itself out, whatever it is." We refocused on our glasses of wine, having run out of conversation, but were soon joined by Polly and Ella, plus an ebullient Megan, visibly thrilled by the tutorly company she had managed to gather at last.

"Drink up, drink up," goaded Dylan, resuming the role of ringleader, replenishing drinks and holding court. Megan chuckled boozily at his every word while Polly poked fun at his outlandish statements. Bobbling back and forth and side to side, Megan binged her way by the gallon. Even Ella was starting to lose her balance, the drink circulating through all our bodies with destabilizing intent. I leaned into Ella to offer support, grateful for the contact.

Quickened by the greased frivolity of his primmest student, Dylan was prodding away with bawdy conversation.

"This one gets so wide-eyed on the drink. You're a little minx, aren't you?"

"I knnnnnow you're after a rise, Dddddylan," said Megan, gluing her words with sloppy slurs.

"I've already got one, thanks."

Usually antagonistic to Dylan's ribaldry and bite, Megan spewed a grotesquely fulsome laugh. The social parameters had expanded with alcohol-bloated flaccidity to incorporate all possibilities.

Amidst apologetic good-byes and excuses (long cycle ride home, essays to mark), Polly made her exit, leaving Dylan singularly in charge. The telltale rouge in Megan's cheeks deepened as she polished off another glass.

"Here, knock this back," coaxed Dylan, minesweeping the empties for abandoned remains. He wiggled a half-filled glass in front of Megan's nose.

"I know what you're doing, Dylan. I'm onto you, don't you know. You're tryin'a get me pissed," she said, rising to a comic squeak on the last note.

"I'm your tutor. I only have your best interests at heart."

Megan giggled a little more. Ella leaned against me with weightier dependence and I stole an arm around her waist. She didn't seem to be enjoying Dylan's performance and hardly offered a word.

"I think I've had enough," voiced Megan's rolling head, slipping free at the hinges. Lurching backward and then forward like a suddenly released spring, Megan let loose her evening's wares all over the floor. The crimson pool of vomit mutated into an increasingly larger organism as it soaked into the carpet. Those once innocuous-looking sandwiches were now sinister and monstrous, bedeviled in their lumpy rot. Dylan brought the evening to a sobering close, locking the door behind us and leaving the pool of sick to fester overnight for the cleaning scouts to discover the next day.

Out in the quad, once Dylan had hastily fled home with bicycle and reflector jacket, Ella and I piled Megan's carcass onto one of the caretaker's trolleys and dragged her to her staircase.

"Bring out your dead! Bring out your dead!" chanted a group of freshers sitting on one of the benches, blowing smoky swirls into the cold night air.

We lugged Megan up to her room and dug out her keys from a tan handbag. Her room was neat and orderly, with pot plants on the windowsill and picture frames carefully positioned all about. We laid her onto her purple sheets and I filled a glass of water at the beautician-like sink. She sprawled out on her back, her chest slowly rising and falling, a slight linger before each exhale. Her bare toes scrunched and wiggled, her hair scattered carelessly across face and pillow. Ella and I watched her melt into otherworldly terrain.

Once we had buried Megan we sloped off to the wine merchants on the High. Absurdly jealous of Megan's comatose state, we needed another bottle or two to help us on our way. Returning with a plastic carrier bag now chiming against my leg, we turned into the stillness of Radcliffe Square. That late at night, the library magically appears, sudden and sheer: *I've been here all along*, it says. *Where have you been?* It rises and grows out of the black, gaining in stature as you walk around; adding extensions, levels, windows, pillars, alcoves, like some untrodden region of the mind. We were heading back to Ella's room to continue the drinking, just the two of us, though I can't remember at whose suggestion. It was probably unspoken; simply intuited by the imperceptible palpitations in our pants. *Is this what you came here for?* taunted the Radcliffe Camera, snap-shotting me in its bookish glare. *Get all the way to this hallowed bed—hallowed* seat *of loving—of* learning—*just to get laid?* Who said anything about getting laid? Leave me alone. *And what about Lucy?* Oh, get out of it . . . keep your nose in your own books. *Ella is well fit though, mate, to be fair . . . she spends a lot of time in here with me, actually . . .* We turned out of the square and onto Catte Street.

"Would you rather have a nipple on your chin or a chin on your nipple?" asked Ella as we finally made it to her room. I pondered this while she clattered about, flicking on a couple of lamps and revealing her treasure chest of trinkets and charms. Loose clothes modeled themselves over an armchair, stacks of CDs crept up the side of a desk, a small unit of shelves went wobbly at the knees with books (all containing first-class scribbles), and a chest of drawers stood stocky, topped with necklaces, rings, brace-lets, bangles, lipsticks, eye shadows, mascaras, and a privi-leged mirror.

"That's a no-brainer," I said, dropping into the armchair, the two bottles in my lap. "Nipple on chin. If I had a chin for a nipple it would poke out from my clothes like a little boob. And besides, I could just grow a beard."

Ella placed her keys on the desk and awoke the laptop from its hibernation. She bent over the screen and key-board so that her body almost mirrored its right angle, her dress lifting slightly, teasingly, so that I was forced to look in a different direction. She began scrolling through her music library.

"It's got gender significance though, that one," I contin-ued, trying to disguise my awkwardness. "I mean, if you were a girl you'd have to go the other way." I fidgeted with unready thoughts while Ella double-clicked her selection and turned the dial up on the supplementary speakers. "The goatee get-out clause just wouldn't apply. You'd look like a tit." Lucy frowned over her shoulder to acknowledge the atrocious pun. "And on the upside, a chin for a nipple would give you a slightly bigger . . . well, you know."

"Boob?" she said, walking toward me.

"Hah, well . . ."

"Tit?" now standing directly in front of me, the music firing up behind her with cinematic timing.

"Your words, not mine. It would be kind of lopsided, but still . . ."

Ella smiled, her lips dancing disarming potential. She lifted the carrier bag from my lap and took it over to the desk where a bottle opener awaited. The song was "Boy Child" by Scott Walker, with its ripe plucks of the guitar and atmospheric strings . . . music from another planet. As Scott's mellifluous voice poured from the speakers, I went to the laptop.

"Tune."

"Of course." Ella planted a glass of white on the desk. "There you are." She sat on the desk chair, her own glass in hand, watching me nose through her music files, down on my knees, there by her side. Her library was impeccable; almost a carbon copy of my own. Our music snobbery gave us reference points (along with our nerdy love of literature and film) and we had indulgently used them all for the past year, cross-referencing and consulting our expanding network of allusions, our growing common sense. Basically all the stuff that I had never shared with Lucy.

I continued to scroll. There was Joni. (We both favor her experimental jazz period over the earlier folk warblings— *Mingus*, *The Hissing of Summer Lawns*, and *Hejira*, with black-

and-white Joni, bereted and cloaked, coming out from the cover like an apparition of painful wisdom and dare-do.) There was Scott. (I'm all for the eponymous LPs, 1 through to 4, though Ella feels that he really hits his stride on *Nite Flights* and its increasingly obscure successors.) We agree on Motown, pedantically differentiating between performers and artists—The Supremes, The Temptations, and The Four Tops on the one hand; Marvin and Stevie on the other. As she said of the latter, they're uniques, stepping outside of the Holland-Dozier-Holland hit-making machine. I concur. She understands the crucial differences between Prince and Michael Jackson, and why the US's rejection of The Kinks was a good thing, forcing the band inward to make provincial classics like *Village Green Preservation Society*.

I switched to "The Electrician" from *Nite Flights*. "You don't mind, do you?"

"Of course not."

We stayed in position—me on the floor, Ella on her chair—and sipped our wine as the song's eerie intro coaxed us into silence. (I thought of Lucy, briefly.) Ella removed her shawl and hung it over the back of the chair behind her. Her skin seemed palpable to me in a way that it had never before. Now it was flesh; tumescent and yielding. It gave off heat and scent . . . vanilla, plum, apple blossom.

"It looks a bit uncomfortable down there," she said, peering at me and then shying away from the eye contact. "You can come up here . . . if you like."

Both rising, we stood face-to-face for the slightest of moments, and then I sat down on the chair. Without hesitation, though my heart was playing along with the beat, the off-beat, and any other more complexly syncopated beat on the track, I curled my arm about her waist and channeled her onto my lap. I linked my hands round her soft, pliant midriff. She felt luxurious. The song rose and broke into its full wave of melody—the drums, the swirling strings, that voice. Again she looked over her shoulder, for a second, and smiled. We both faced the laptop but really stared out into nothingness. Up this close she smelled of rich, smoky wood . . . the aromas rising from those tight crevices and hidden gullies . . . like smells from the forest of experience where the young girl loses her innocence. Neither of us acknowledged that such a position and proximity was unusual. We allowed ourselves to exist inside the assumption that it was entirely natural. Our bodies breathed together and her weight became mine. Ella placed her hands on my own, fastening their clasp tighter against her stomach.

With an unsteady and quietened voice she asked, "Would you rather kiss someone or *be* kissed by someone?" She was looking down at her shoulder so that I could see her flushed profile. Then I slid my hand around the far side of her neck, tucking it beneath the underhang of her jaw and pulling her mouth toward mine. We took gentle bites from each other's lips. Our tongues grazed, unintentionally, encouraging us both to take a full, swollen lick. Ella unlocked my grasp and placed my right hand on her bare leg. Still arching round to kiss me she began guiding it up the smooth strip of her inside thigh, her dress hitching upward as my hand drew farther in, nearer and nearer, her legs parting. She gave a slight jump and sigh—a high, breathless "huh"—when I hit against her crotch. I quickly removed my hand, but when she started to kiss me harder I placed it back again, this time firmer and more direct. She pressed her forehead against mine, eyes closed, mouth agape, moving her hips in harmony with the motion of my hand and rolling her head back and around. *You thrill me and thrill me and thrill me.* My other hand dropped from her neck to her breasts. She took it and forced it inside the cup of her bra, lending me her full cushiony swell. I traced the Braille of her viscera. She read so differently from Lucy. She became warmer and slick . . . more fragrant.

We got up from the chair and she led me to her elfin grot, getting amongst the pillows and cool sheets. We trawled each other's bodies for every inch of history. I dug after what I had always imagined and came up with even more. She stroked my outlines in perfect synchrony until I was febrile in her hands, willingly guided elsewhere.

We collapsed into each other and died a thousand deaths, to find ourselves breathlessly alive in wrapped arms and legs . . .

When I withdrew and shifted over to the edge of the bed I was confronted by a menacing ring of rubber squeezing the base of my sorry cock. The condom had ruptured, like one of those paper hoops that circus performers pounce through. I held it in dismay as it shriveled in my sticky palm, staring up at me in all its gunky matter-of-factness— *gotcha!* I looked over my shoulder to see Ella snug under the duvet, smiling.

"You okay?" she asked.

"Yeah, course."

The music in this bar is too distracting and the image quickly fades. Ella is looking at me, as though she has seen the memory too. I can't tell if it is the recollection or the strawberries-and-cream vodka that is making me feel nauseous, but her knowing gaze is making it exponentially worse. I pull out my phone and pretend that I'm writing a text. It's not even turned on.

Do you ever wake in the night? Ever wake in the night grappling with the a.m. light? Early-morning hours blink through smudged eyes to no one, and then someone.

It comes as a jolt. Irrational fears magnified to the nth degree manhandle your feeble body, doped as it is on gooey sleep and warm saliva. They pummel you in the stomach and wrench your heart up to your throat: what if she's pregnant? What if I never get a job? What if I've got a disease? A bloody STI . . . what if I die? Oh god, what if I die?

Obscene hypotheses terrorize your fuzzy head. Shaking to the core with syncopated terrors you fling the duvet and gasp after strangled air. The water on the bedside table tastes of chlorine and your hot flush is swelling. It comes like this, entirely uninvited yet somehow willed—self-inflicted. You fall and fall into the oblivion of your sunken stomach. Sick to the pit. Perhaps it's the absence of light. Maybe it's the immediate panic of knowing you're meant to be doing something else: sleeping. You're meant to be sleeping, and you're running out of time. You've been caught waking on the job, and no one can bail you out except yourself.

Do you ever wake in the night, to fetch a glimpse of the abyss?

★

I'm in one of those clothes shops. You know, the ones where everything is built slightly too small, slightly too tight. It's called "Other," or some such nonsense, a hot mess of check, Burberry, tartan, and dayglo. Low-cut tops and skinny jeans for your metro scenester, simple tees and pumps for the middle-aged tragedy. The male shop assistants have designer stubble diarrheaed all over their pimply mugs and lightning fringes prepped by girlfriend's/sister's/mum's hair straighteners. It's all rather scene.

So I'm in one of those clothes shops: a teenager with his bag-laden mum (footing the bill) holds a luminous yellow shirt up against himself, the design of a tropical lizard's guts chundered all over the front; a semi-beefcake winces his way unnaturally toward the mirrors in some testicle-squelching skinny jeans, trying to convince himself that they look *stylish*; runts with fancy scarves and pointy shoes clog the aisles, picking up items and putting them down in the wrong places.

I'm in a changing cubicle, trying on a paisley shirt, going for the retro mod look, though I'm not quite feeling it. I adopt different facial expressions (a smile, a pout, a brood) to see if it makes any difference. I talk to myself, feigning conversation, to see how well I'd socialize in it. Bell-end. I fold my arms. I put my hands in my pockets. I turn and look over my shoulder from behind. I do a little dance to see how it would hold up in a club. Not bad. Tucked or untucked? I opt for the former. I test it buttoned to the top and then buttoned a few down to show off the chest hair. Then I start *really* undoing it to see how well it—

I am confronted by a nightmare myriad of mes. The eight cubicles forming a square around me are all open and empty, baring their glass insides. Each mirror catches a reflection of my reflection, refracting me into disarray, an infinite prism of images. Eliot-to-the-power-of-$n$, but utterly powerless.

The now familiar pram glides in beside me . . . I watch its approach in the mirror. I can see the baby's face getting closer, magnifying in front of my very eyes. I want to ignore it . . . make it go away. I ram my fingers into my ears as it starts to talk, and go, "La-la-la-la-la. La-la-la-la-la. La— can I get

some attention around here
please?"
it says.

"Won't you leave me
alone?

I could say the same.

I don't understand what

I want from you?
Who said this was all
about you? You've got
quite the Ego on you, haven't

I?"

A troubling sense of jubilance comes over me. I feel ecstatic in a profoundly muddling way, captivated by the recurring image. And then I begin to notice more changes in the babe's appearance. The face is getting fatter, the hair less consistent, and patches of scattered stubble are starting to pierce through the nicked skin. He's morphing into something altogether other. A hole burns its way through the white blanket that is wrapped around his paunch. Beneath this I catch a glimpse of a deep, complicated purple.

"Don't worry.
It's just an imaginary stage.

That's easy for

me to say? I disagree.
Does it look like I'm
finding this easy?

No. Not all.
What's happening to you?"

We watch each other in silence, slowly fading into the end credits of awakening.

I think Ella's pissed.

The girls got well hooked on those shots and kept going back for more. Now they're dragging us onto the makeshift dance floor for our cardiovascular warm-up.

It's like Milton's hell around here, minus the artfulness: groaning limbs and moaning throbs, sliding all over each other in abject toil. It's as stifling as a morning hug from your grandma. The music has been raised to new heights of senselessness—beyond perception and out of reach. It shuffles and swells, operating on a wavelength hostile to our fuzzy antennae.

There are some bastards in the middle dancing with flair, busting out panache. They're actually impressive. We turn our backs on them. No one wants to see that.

A reveling clown, all arms and legs, slops some of his J.D. and Coke down my back as our prancing bodies collide. He hasn't even noticed and continues on with his rhythmic convulsions, those tribal dances of time immemorial. I arch my back and shift fitfully, waiting for the spillage to be neutralized by lashings of spinal sweat. Careening round to locate the root of my discomfort, I spot Ella with that stylish player from before; the one who was giving her the "oi oi love" when we first got here. She appears trapped, politely dancing but wanting to escape. She's alone in a crowd of rampant male attention, wriggling for invasive eyes.

Her pursuer puts his hands on her hips and she brushes them away. Ella seems to give me a pleading glimmer. And then he starts kissing her neck. I'm not having this.

"Do you wanna fuck off?" I say to him, squaring up while Ella steps aside.

"Huh?"

"I said, do you wanna fuck off?"

"I can't hear you, boss."

This is kind of embarrassing . . . really takes the wind out of my bravado.

"I said you're a cunt." He'll be glad he can't hear that one.

"Oh yeah? The fuck you gonna do, pretty boy?" Oh Christ . . . selective hearing. Good question too, if we're being honest. I hadn't really thought that far ahead and, frankly, I'm new at this.

Ella's looking at me with troubled eyes, so I full-fist the guy in the ear.

Now, I went for the ear because I'm not totally committed. I figured the jaw would be too dangerous (can't that kill someone if luck isn't swinging your way?), and the nose would've just felt gross—all bony and crunchy. No, the ear was a good place to start: it's inoffensive but it stings. I can tell it hurt too, because he's now proceeding to nut me. *Thwack.*

My head is tasting all sorts of colors and special effects . . . the memory of the only other fight I've ever been in rushes to the fore: *"So let me get this straight,"* the policeman had said, post-ruckus: *"The big yellow banana was acting as peacemaker when the assailant head-butted the tomato, provoking the giant pineapple to square up to the assailant?"*

*We nodded.*

*"And then the melon throws a punch?"*

*"That's correct."*

*"Right . . ."*

*It all began when we were standing at a kebab van—those ubiquitous chariots of the student-framed nightscape—in the orange crush early hours, binged on booze (again), looking for the illogical conclusion to our night. A banana, a pineapple, a melon, a tomato, and a pair of strawberries. We'd been at a food-themed fancy dress party and constituted a cartoon hamper, dressed in full body suits. I was the banana.*

*Beer-bloated bellies yapped "FEED ME" to the dissonant tune of drunken self-certainty.*

> *Here comes the kebab van man,*
> *Driving in his kebab man van,*
> *Bringing lots of vegetables for us to eat:*
> *CHIPS CHEESE BURGER*
> *CHIPS CHEESE BURGER*
> *Come and get your veg'tables from the van.*

*Alliances form swiftly in kebab van culture, and we had wasted no time in fully committing to Abdul's on the High. Fidelity is so evanescent in this day and age, you have to take a stand.*

*"How are you, my friend?" asked Abdul. It's impossible to envy him his task, dealing exclusively as he does with slurring nocturnals.*

*"Ten on ten, mate, ten on ten."*

*"Chips cheese hummus?"*

*He had my order by heart—already. It still brings a tear to my eye every time.*

*"You know it."*

Abdul plied his trade, trunching about in the corrugated steel trailer, grease and steam sinking into every pore.

*"Salt vinegar?"*

Abdul doesn't have time for grammatical conjunctions, too stretched and awearied.

*"Absolutely."*

I retrieved the polystyrene coffin of bellyache with sincere gratitude.

*"Legend."*

There I was with Sanjay, Jack, Scott, Abi, and Ella. And this is when it all kicked off:

Some razor-edge thug, with his Burberry cap tilted almost vertical and his trackie-bs tucked into white socks like he'd come straight from the AstroTurf, spotted us from the other side of the High Street. He brought a pal with him. Real bike-chain-scrapping, White-Lightning-glued, wood-block-oaf types. The second one was fat, the first one thin. The skinny one gobbed venomously on the road. They walked like they'd got Lilt cans lodged up their arses; they had faces like written-off Vauxhall Novas; they were like broken fridges that have been dumped on the roadside.

Getting amongst us, they glared and leered, tightening their lips and jerking their heads.

*"Look, Chase,"* said the skinny one, his voice inappropriately high pitch, *"it's a Paki pineapple."* This Chase character pulled a badly acted smirk across his brick-wall face.

*"The fuck d'you say?"* blasted Sanjay, his spiky green hat almost falling off.

*"Chill, chill,"* I pleaded, as I stepped across Sanjay, arms spread out to keep him back.

*"Haha, it's a Paki fucking pineapple,"* repeated the mouthy one. I should point out that multiracialism has never really

arrived at Oxford University. Nor has multiculturalism. Sanjay
and Abdul's kebab van are about as diverse as it gets here on the
predictable student scene.

"Let's get out of here," reasoned the bright red tomato. The
strawberries looked on.

"Fancy some cream, love?" said the fatty to Abi, and then the
leery one head-butted the tomato.

It is a common misconception that hardness—brawling
flare—is directly proportionate to size. Not true. Hardness is
about 70 percent mentality, 30 percent muscle; more psychology
than biology. A disposition, if you will: you've got to want to
hurt someone and be tuned out from consequence. Just think back
to school: the rough kids were the mouthy little shits. This chump
was a prime example.

And they say you learn a lot about yourself in a fight, which
is halfway true. But you learn even more about your companions
in a multiplayer affair. No other occasion will lay their morality
and philosophy so unflinchingly bare; no other situation will
place their coordinates and factory settings under such cold-eyed
scrutiny.

The pineapple fought around my banana-blockade, flanked by
a bruised tomato that could sense a pulping.

"Fuckin university cunts," spat the head-butter.

"I'll fucking drop you," retorted the pineapple.

"Lamp the pineapple out," suggested the butter's sidekick.

A strawberry was crying.

The pineapple, particularly averse to the last directive, smacked
the head-butter with a swinging right hand. Like a foolhardy Jack
Russell, the kid still wouldn't back off; so the tomato twatted him
in the ear. This really did drop him, and his mate fled down a side
street. Tirelessly, the lippy one continued to mouth off, adorning
the chewing gum pavement with his felled body.

"I'll cut you, motherfucker. You all dead men. Believe."

"Shut the fuck up," shouted an aggravated melon.

"You best watch your backs. Motherfucking dead motherfuckers. Trust."

The pineapple and the tomato gave the talking pavement a sharp dose of foot-fire, kicking its hips and ribs with measured fall. Banana and melon pulled tomato and pineapple away and sat down on top of head-butter.

"Are you gonna shut up?"

"You is fucked. Believe. I is gonna fuck you all up."

"Well, we'll just have to sit here a while longer then," said the melon, perching on him.

"Fucking fags."

When the police car came nee-nawing to a halt, the absent sidekick miraculously reappeared: "They was caning my mate. We was minding our business and they kicked off."

One of the coppers tried to get information from the melon while the other pulled us apart. A second squad car arrived. A cluster of haggard spectators looked on, fresh from nightclubs and bars, bemused by our fruity antics.

"You started it all," I protested.

"Nah blud, it's a fuckin racist pineapple. He was dissing me innit . . ."

"Come off it. You called him a Paki . . . you're the racist."

"My mate ain't no racist . . . he's just straight-talking . . . calls a spade a spade . . . tells it like he sees it."

"Let's get them to the station."

"The fucking pineapple was cussing me out."

"I'll take these two. You take the melon and the banana and the . . . bloody hell, what am I saying?"

"What should we do about the strawberries? . . ."

Whatever experience I gleaned from that last fight—passing sharply and swiftly before my mind like a violent rejoicing—it isn't helping me in this one. *Crikey, my fore-*

*head licks with pain.* And it doesn't make any sense either—shouldn't the head butt hurt him just as much? Probably some law of physics which is over my arty-farty head. The dance floor opens its belly to us, hospitably lending room to operate and perform. I shove him backward to buy some time while I plan my next move. After much deliberation I opt for a knee in the babymaker. It's not very sportsmanlike, but I don't give a toss anymore.

While he's bent double, like he's reached a marathon finish line, some bloke (evidently his tag-team partner) comes pelting in with windmill arms and floors me good and proper. I grope about amongst smashed glass and spilled ice cubes, focalizing as best I can.

Jack enters the fray. His loyalty has pulled him this far—I'm his brother and he won't stand back and watch me take a beating—but fortunately for him the bouncers have infiltrated the war zone before he need get his hands dirty. Bouncer No. 1 (bald, black suit, wide as he is tall) hoists me from the floor while Bouncer No. 2 (bald, black suit, wide as he is tall) smothers the KO artist. (A bouncer's job description is a sinisterly gray area, you have to admit. Believing themselves to be outside of the law, they're just psychos looking for a sanctioned fight. I can feel this one relieving his unhappy marriage all over my neck and his shitty pay into my arm as he wrenches it behind my back. His colleague is ruffling the other participants up as hard as he can without it becoming full-blown assault.)

The bar whirls past me as I'm escorted most peremptorily toward the doors. Everyone stares like I'm a dead man walking, before returning to their unthinking routines.

Unloading us on their fag-butted doorstep, I think the bouncers (does the name derive from their guts?) want to see us start back up again—as though all they'd done was press pause to fetch some grub. But this is one cockfight they ain't gonna see, what with the two baddies walking off into the distance already.

The others join us outside, struggling with their hurriedly fetched coats like escapologists in rewind.

"Ah mate, that was sick!" celebrates Sanjay with a simpleton's grin, bouncing up and down.

"It's all my fault," cries Ella, sobbing into Abi's bosom.

"Another bar then?" says Jack, passing me my jacket, trying to erase the moment and move us on.

"Oh, it's all my fault."

"Sick."


Ella has stormed ahead, arms folded, head low. I jog—as coolly as I can—to catch her up. I try collecting her in with my left arm, but there's something hard and resistant about her now . . . angular and other. We continue along in a jagged embrace, her arms still folded, our hips clanging together. I thought she'd be impressed. I may've got floored, but it can't harm my cause.

"Hey, what's wrong?" She doesn't say anything, but I can see some silent tears on her cheeks reflecting the liquid amber of the streetlights. "Don't worry, it wasn't your fault," I say.

She raises her head in one orchestral sweep, confronting me with the vast upset that is splashed across her face.

"Ah, forget it, Eliot." I'm silenced. "You should stay away from me . . . I only cause trouble—"

"That's crazy," I protest. "After everything that's happened . . . after everything we've been through . . . you and me . . ."

"No . . . no, Eliot," she says, shaking her head. There's

something imploring in her voice. My hold of her shoulders loosens slightly and I hear a tight sigh of exhaustion escape from her lips. "That's not right," she cries. "Don't count on me, Eliot. Please—" She shrugs me off and walks away. I drop back to the others, utterly confused. Ella carries on ahead, shoulders trembling in the nighttime chill. The reverberating clip-clop of her high heels sounds isolated and desperate, searching for an echo to their lonely call.

I'm in a horizontal line with the gang, me on one end, Jack on the other. Jack looks across, inquiring and vulnerable. Of course he's curious, has every right to be, though he doesn't know the full story . . . not yet. I don't give him anything: just keep my chin down and shovel my hands inside my coat.

Jack runs ahead and puts his jacket over Ella's shoulders.


I know what she's talking about. Of course I do. But I grow excruciatingly self-conscious over these things. I'm a bungler. How to put it? Our "sexual *mishap*," I suppose . . .

The splitting of the condom. It caused all sorts of nuclear explosions inside of me, catalyzing chain reactions of terror, guilt, paranoia, and—dare I say it—depression. Not my finest moment. I stuttered and delayed . . . yeah, I fucked up. I didn't tell Ella at first. I should've come clean (excuse the unfortunate word selection . . . but all words are unfortunate in moments like this). If I had told her straightaway she could have done something about it . . . I realize that now and I feel terrible about it. I just needed some time . . . time to assess the options; you know, plan my move.

I bumped into Ella the day after the English Drinks

party, up in the café in Blackwell's bookshop. I was huddled over *The Intellectuals and the Masses* with a large skinny
latte (oh, how the words roll off my tongue) and a frankly
appalling almond croissant. Ella came over to say hello. I
couldn't take my eyes off her belly, spying subtly for a telling bump . . . any suggestion of my dreaded spawn. I felt
sick.

But I didn't say anything.


We continue to make our way through the dark streets of
Oxford—the byways between pubs, the channels between
clubs. Ella and Jack are still in front, but I won't interrupt;
I've had my chance.

"Would you rather," says Abi, savoring each word to
increase the suspense, "have green pubes or hair made out
of jelly?"

"Can I shave the pubes?" asks Scott, like it's a real deal
clincher.

"Of course you can't," says Abi, affronted that someone
would flout the unspoken rules so. "Ditto for the jelly
hair."

"Gotta go with the pubes, every time," says Sanjay.
"Once you've explained them away they wouldn't be that
freaky, not really, and it's not like they always have to be on
display." That puts an end to that. I'm not really engaging
with these philosophical binds, too busy watching Jack and
Ella.

"Would you rather," says Scott this time, "have a tail or
a fin?"

"Tail," replies Megan instantly. We're all surprised by
the alacrity of her response. I'd almost forgotten she was
even here.

"Kinky!" cries Abi. "I bet you'd like that, wouldn't you, Sanjay?" she says rather brazenly.

"Huh?" says Sanjay, mortified.

I tried a "would I rather" to solve my scenario with Ella at the time, but it never worked: Would I rather Ella find out for herself that she's pregnant or confront her about it? Would I rather Ella has a baby or an abortion? Would I rather Ella sleeps with someone else and thinks it's his or ask her to be my girlfriend and hope for the best? Not that these were the only possibilities of course . . . believe me, I figured out all the combinations. None of them ever sounded quite right.

I think about turning my phone back on and letting Lucy know that I'm ready to talk. But I'm not. So I don't.

Fifteen minutes later and we're still on the lookout. I turn my phone back on. It's time to toughen up.

Not quite a bar. Near a bar. En route to a bar. We're grizzled third-years at a cashpoint, forked into queues, hands at holsters, ready to draw. It's the Wild West shoot-out. This is a holdup. The great gold rush for all (hundred quid max).

A flapping breeze drags a bundle of stray hair and dust into the corner where the wall juts out to shelter the end machine. It's a twilight scene, many different nuances of gray and blue, with streaks of deep brooding purple, all conspiring toward a final black. A lonesome traveler wheels past on his rusty steed, unlit to cultivate stranger-anonymity. A crescent moon, unabashed in its teasing partiality, radiates a marvelous glow as though full-bodied.

The wall blinks green-lighted at me as I step up onto the pavement, weapon in hand, not particularly loaded. Nothing more useless than an unloaded gun, son. Give me all my money, punk. And yeah, give me a receipt too, or I'm gonna slap you silly. C'mon, c'mon, I say, shiftily looking around, side to side. I ain't got all day. It dispenses the gear. Spews its guts into my grubby hands. Feel the paper. Yeah boy, give it to me. Fifty bunse, that ought to see us through the night. All that finger-swirl dirt and journeyed bacteria. Yeah boy, give it to me. Give it to me straight.

My phone. It's ringing. The big moment. Time to rise to the occasion and deal with Lucy; time to come through in the clutch. I draw, ready to fire.

"Mum?"

"Oh, hi love."

(The rest cotton on straightaway: "Stop hogging the coke, Eliot!" shouts Sanj in the background. "Yeah, Eliot, give me the crack," follows Abi.)

"What was that?"

"I'm kind of out and about at the moment, Mum."

"That's okay, honey, I don't mind. Me and your dad were just wondering what time you want picking up tomorrow."

"Mum! Couldn't this have waited?" ("Do it faster, big boy," squeals Abi.) "I don't know . . . not too early though . . . I'm out tonight."

"Be careful, won't you, sweetie? Just one or two pints, okay?"

("Tell her I had fun with her last night, mate," says Sanj.)

"Yes, Mum."

"Have you eaten anything?"

"Mum, please."

"Okay, okay . . . you'll understand when you have kids of your own."

"Gotta go, Mum."

"Okay, go and have fun. You've earned it."

"Yeah."

"Looking forward to seeing you tomorrow."

"Yeah."

"Sorry, what time did you say, honey?"

"Eleven?"

"Okay. Love you."

"Yeah, okay. Bye."

"Bye bye."

"Bye."

I turn the phone off. Still not ready.

Fella!

I spin round. Quickest draw I ever did. Bang bang, you going down.

It's Scott and companion.

Meet my woman.

So she *is* out. Scott's younger lady.

He tells me her name. But I know her. She doesn't know me. But I know her. I've seen her WANTED sign before . . . I've seen it about . . . checked it on Mugshot. I know her name, her age, her interests, and what bikini she wore on that last holiday to the Bahamas with the girls. Yeah, I've checked you before. Noted. She's an unconscious celebrity, as we all are, to someone, to people. I must feign ignorance though, of course.

Howdy. Eliot.

Laura.

Pleased.

We've been hanging around here too long. Time to beat it. New haunt. Another bar. We're en route.


Who am I kiddi— who am I fooling? I can't run forever. I've got to face up to what happened if I'm ever going to make any progress here.

A week or so after English Drinks, after it all went down, I told Ella about the busted condom. Straight off she wanted to know why I hadn't owned up when it happened.

"I fucked up?"

We left it at that. Ella wasn't nearly as pissed as I thought she would be. In fact, she barely reacted at all. She must've done a pregnancy test that very night, because the next day she told me the result as we walked over to the English faculty for a lecture on "Shakespeare and the Metaphysics of the Scene." It was positive. I turned around and went back to my room. She carried on to the lecture.

Ella got her two referrals for the abortion. I was amazed by how quickly she managed to sort it all out. Personally, I would've spent a few weeks bricking it, hoping the problem might just go away. Not Ella: she was calm and level-headed. At least at first she was.

She attended her initial appointment at the clinic without telling me. That was when she would've been administered mifepristone. I looked it up on the Internet: it makes the lining of the womb inhospitable; it makes the lining of the womb inhospitable for the egg; it makes the lining of the womb inhospitable for the fertilized egg.

Ella asked me if I'd mind going with her to the second appointment. With chemicals inimical to life coursing through her blood—through her invaded and examined body—she didn't want to be alone, and I was desperate to help.

The receptionist at the clinic was a daunting figure, with stern countenance and remorseless austerity. She looked like she wanted me dead: *You bastard . . . couldn't just keep it in your lousy pants, could you . . . creep . . . woman hater . . . murderer . . . filthy fucking lump of knob cheese.* Her judgments were severe and I laid them thick on my heart. She sucked on a hard-boiled sweet—a humbug perhaps—and abruptly answered phone calls in a monotone drawl, obstinately filling her space behind the counter. *Is this sorrowful or tiresome for you?* I wanted to bellow. But it must be tough, being one of life's gatekeepers; a raw gig, admitting us as three and sending us away as two; shells of our former selves.

We took our seats. To my left was a stack of tattered magazines not up to the task of helping me forget. Just ahead was a notice board with an advert for "volunteer twins": a local doctor was writing a book on the joyous phenomenon of twin birth . . . the double gift of life . . . the reminder of which seemed doubly cruel and doubly inappropriate. Next to this, facing us, was a mirror. I had found myself sobbing that morning in front of a different mirror, brushing my teeth in my college bedroom. The evidence now confronted me, encoded into my face with its puffed skin and strained eyes, the painterly reds and blues of despair smudged all over my pitiful canvas. Ella looked stronger, though more vacant. Her usual color had dissipated but her raw beauty remained, intensified, perhaps, by life's brutal doings. Her long blonde hair fell majestically across her face, and her eyes affected a preternatural draw. I was weak in comparison. The reflection revealed two helpless amateurs, meeting life on its own terms for the first time and tensed for the fallout. We had been forced into the cold role of conspirators, not lovers. Love was the missing virtue that could redeem us and make everything okay. I tortured myself by fleshing out the little being whose passport into the world we were destroying. We were failing him (always a him to me), this defenseless foreigner whose inclusion we would bar. I took Ella's hand in mine.

When the doctor called for Ella she asked me to stay in the waiting room. I guess it was enough to know that I was nearby. There, on my own, I began to cry: molten tears of guilt and shame. I swallowed it back as best I could, my chin a quivering wreck, my eyes burning and stinging. I thought of the discoveries my parents must have made, finding me in their hands with all my podgy reality and utter neediness. How we must've grown together, entwining our roots and absorbing one another: the times I bathed with Dad, gradually recognizing our physical parity; Mum using her soap-lathered hands to enclose and wash my own, my mischievous digits, in front of the telly, a fragrant towel hanging ready over her shoulder; Dad pushing me along on my first bike in the empty playground, Christmas Day, and letting go without me knowing; Mum crying when they dropped me off in Oxford. (In the memory I call after her, "Mimi! Mimi!," but I'm not sure why. What could it augur?) Marching through my head, it all came to me like a home movie, warping and wobbling. And here *we* were, denying such affirmation— each conception so unlikely and singular, against all odds, but in some cases just not right.

The moment of termination. That was when my own unarguable being smashed me to pieces. I had never felt so real.

Ella came out empty . . . a frail cage . . . yet still so much stronger than I. The second pill was having its wicked way, working its insidious influence deep in her core. Her womb's lining was disintegrating and taking our witless mistake with it. I rose from the chair and put my arms around her as she wept into my neck, bracing herself for certain pain and the hard bloody evidence of the little stranger that we would never know.


There. I've done it. At the very least made a start. But I don't want to linger, not right now.

We've made it to another bar. Let's call it Bar No. 2. Fingers crossed we won't get kicked out of this one. Sanjay

splits a pack of salt and vinegar like a book and places it in
the middle of the table. We all take dibs, some more liberal
than others. They sting my fingers a bit from where I've
dug out the skin, the pinked excavations of anxiety. My
throbbing head murmurs reminders about the fight.

"I'm gonna get like totally destroyed?" advertises Sanjay,
swigging his lager.

"I'm like literally getting off my tits?" supports Abi. All
for one and one for all.

Both of these sentences rise in pitch at their tail ends,
almost modulating into questions. Their status is problem-
atized: seemingly indicative in content, but loosening into
something more subjunctive, the destabilizing intonation
flickering between statement and conjecture. Maybe we're
just the great Metaphysicals of our time, using language to
occupy multiple states of being; negatively capable. That's
George Herbert in front of me with his lucky Fred Perry
and pint of Stella, and there's a feminine John Donne, on
my left, large rosé, out on the pull. I guess I'd have to be
Milton.

Or maybe we're just twats.

How gloriously haggard we seem. I can't tell if the drink
brings us to life or puts us to sleep. But the teleology is
clear: *get fucked*.

We keep taking until less and less remains, each leaving
our greasy traces of fingerprints and crumbs. We're like
cubs around a carcass, exchanging subtle glimpses and
twinkles. Our innocence is threadbare, experience setting
its claws in with hideous commitment. We're phased, the
lot of us.

We are stocked with another round, building turrets
and moats of glass about us for fortification, yet my gullet
is on autopilot, letting things in without check.

"Any decisions on where we're headed tonight?"

"Scrot Lounge?"

"Nah."

"Pulse?"

"Definitely not."

"Radius?"

"Shit on a Friday."

"C'mon, it's gotta be Filth. It wouldn't be right otherwise."

"We couldn't have it any other way."

"Yeah, Filth."

"Filth it is then."

"Filth."

Abi yawns. It spreads from mouth to mouth. A compliment perhaps: we're staying awake for each other. It doesn't get more caring than that.

Ella takes the final crisp. The packet glistens on the table, beneath the spotlight, its remaindered specks inviting licked fingers. There's nothing real left for us. We've used it all up. I interrogate the wrinkled surface with swipes and prods, but it's futile. It's done.

So we just yawn and sip, shrug and sigh. The momentary lull will pass and we'll soon be back on it.


"Mate, can I talk to you about something?" says Jack, pulling me to the side as the others head to the bar for yet another restock.

"Yeah, okay," I say, uncertainly. This sudden proposition, unexpected and mysterious, makes me curious, as though he's beating me to my own duties for the night: *I'm* the one who should be doing all the talking here.

We sneak off to a dark alcove where a fitted, curving

sofa awaits. A tropical fish tank is indented in the wall above, glowing green, blue, and yellow. We slide across the leather upholstery and settle in. The clamor of the music isn't going to help.

"What's up?"

Jack's staring at his pint glass, distractedly adjusting its position on the table. "Mate." He takes a gulp, gearing himself up.

"Everything okay?" My stomach is rapidly suggesting that worry might be a suitable reaction.

"I want to ask your advice about something . . . but you've gotta swear you'll keep it to yourself."

"Of course. I'm hurt you'd even ask."

"Ah mate." We both swig our beers, impending candor being a pressure we handle with apprehension. "It's about Ella."

Great. Our unacknowledged specialist topic.

"Oh yeah?" I say, nervously.

"I feel like such a knob revealing this . . . I've kept it quiet for so long."

I'm terrified he's going to tell me something that could throw a spanner in my night; that he might reveal more knowledge of me and Ella than I suspect of him. I'm already prepping myself with wormy alibis and explanations.

"I think I got her pregnant . . . last year."

I sink into the seat, as though an invisible hand is pressing down on my head, but quickly straighten up. I've gone either deathly pale or bright red.

"What makes you think that?" I ask. I'm mirroring him now, anxiously repositioning my glass.

"I found a letter from an abortion clinic lying on her desk . . . ages ago."

"No, you're probably mistaken, mate. I mean, you don't think Ella's ever got into a situation like that, do you?"

"Well, it was a couple of weeks after . . . ah mate. I can't."

"After what?" I press him.

"After Joel Shaw's house party . . ."

Joel Shaw's house party. The memory comes fast, all the details and sensations condensed into a flash: Jack and I caught a bus on the High Street, outside Queen's College, a chill, wintry pre-Christmas night, and were swept off down the Cowley Road.

I remember the party vividly because it was the night after Ella and I got it on, and I was still sourcing the courage to come clean (there I go again!) about the condom. I had resolved to tell her that night, banking on alcohol as the much-needed conversational aid: confidence booster, news softener, memory wiper, etc. I was also agitated by the prospect of a repeat performance, as though Ella might be looking to consolidate something more long-term with further sexual activity.

Jack and I stood outside a dingy terraced house, brandishing Sainsbury's bags filled with six-packs of lager: experienced second-years; journeyed; wizened. Dry thuds of music and muffled shouts sounded from within.

"Let's just have a good night, yeah?" said Jack.

I opened the door and we were swept over by heat, marijuana, and noise, all operating in force fields of rapturous energy.

"Boys!" shrieked Abi, greeting us with temptress cuddles, the booze having gone expressly to her head.

This house was rammed fast-tight. A mixture of familiars and strangers laced the corridor, leaning against the dented walls with chemistry-class concoctions in their hands.

"Alriiiight," said Jack approvingly, jerking his head and strutting like a proud cock. "It's popping up in here."

We fed our way through the kitchen, which looked and smelled like the insides of a broken-down dishwasher, and slung open the fridge. It was about as cool as an armpit in there but would have to do. Removing other people's lagers to make room for our own, we safeguarded the gear. Then we took one each (from someone else's stash, of course) and scuzzed them open, real warm and furry.

"Living room?"

"Sure."

People sat about on the floor or leaned against walls, a chosen few taking sofa, chairs, and beanbags, the music buzzing from a stereo on some makeshift shelves.

"S'up motherfuckers," said Jack to no one in particular, seamlessly passing into party mode.

Our fellow partiers supped from a haphazard assortment of vessels: wine in chewed baby beaker, vodka from jam jar, measuring jug sambuca. Ella and Sanjay were sat in a corner, below a dying spider-plant and a Top Hunks calendar.

"S'up bitches."

"Holla."

Ella was wearing a thin bohemian dress (purple), ending halfway up the thigh, with a small vintage bomber jacket of scuffed black leather. Her toned crossed legs meandered from beneath the svelte cut of her frock. I stared at her shimmering cheeks and gravity-blessed eyes. Again I examined her figure, searching for an increase in breast size or an unnerving hump, *any* sign of transformation. I wondered if she had felt sick that morning, having read about this kind of thing in Agony Aunt columns in Lucy's magazines. She looked dangerous . . . like she had something inadvisable lined up. But she didn't seem comfortable. I couldn't look her in the eye. Something had changed.

Grinning to himself, Jack pulled a pack of cards from his rump pocket and turned to face the center of the room, ever the master of the revels.

"Ring of Fire?"

This proposal was met with a general murmur and rumble, a few keen beans leaping in affirmation. Twenty minutes later, sitting round a low-slung coffee table in the middle of the room, a group of about ten of us was engaged in a game of Ring of Fire, all changing color from the paint-stripping, budget bacchanalia on offer. The much-feared "Dirty Pint" stood frothing in the middle of a shell-shocked circle of cards, filled to the brim with menace and cruelty—a mixture of reds, whites, beers, ciders, tequila, brandy, apple sours, raw egg, whipped cream, and a corn chip floating precariously on top.

I already knew I was doomed as I lined my selection up. The game: whoever leaves a chink in the circle after drawing their card—a gap no matter how small—has to consume the Dirty Pint (plus a range of other supplementary rules and obligations depending on the specific card you draw, of course). With half the deck gone, I was screwed. Carefully teasing out a seven of clubs I haplessly revealed a millimeter of tabletop for all to see.

"He who dares break the Ring of Fire must answer to the Dirty Pint!" bellowed Jack, a touch overexcited.

"DIRTY PINT! DIRTY PINT!" chanted his trashed comrades.

"For fuck's sake."

With shamefaced defeat dripping down my chin I chugged back the toxic defreshment. My body shuddered:

*Why are you doing this to me . . . to us?* Physical pleas for
mercy: recoils; cringes; heaves. I wanted to die.

"You're an absolute leg end," congratulated Jack, pat-
ting me on the back.

"Cheers," I said, fighting through the bile that was now
lining my throat. And then I saw Ella sitting alone in the
corner, drink in hand. I knew I had to be the man and take
control of the situation . . . tell her the truth and look after
her . . . maybe suggest escorting her home so that we
could talk things through properly . . .

Cut to an hour later: I was steaming. Oh boy, was I gone.
I sat on the end of a bed upstairs with Ella, who was duti-
fully looking after me. There were a few other magic-eye
masks in there, lounging and stretching across duvet and
carpet. I hugged a tin of Fosters to my chest, clinking and
crunching it with understated pinches. Ella twirled a glass
of iridescent rosé.

"See, thing is, Ella, you're, like, the greatest."

"You're so drunk."

"Like, forget that. I like really mean it. You're, like, so
like special to me. I like really, like, like you." I was bolster-
ing myself for revelation, also trying to justify my involve-
ment.

She gave me a modest smile.

"You, like, like all the same things as me. I can actually,
like, talk to you about literature and shit. I've never had
that before." Maybe this kind of gambit would soften her
up. It was a long shot, but I meant it—so why not?

Ella rustled her hair and looked at me searchingly. She
had begun the evening rather distant and preoccupied, but
my endearing stupidity seemed to be lifting a load . . . as
though I was providing some relief with my pathetically
teenage ways.

"I know. Yes, that's good, isn't it?" She swigged her drink. "Look, Eliot . . . can I tell you something?"

"Of course!" We shifted about on the bed, preparing ourselves for candor. Once again, someone was beating me to disclosure. For a moment I entertained the impossibility that *she* was about to reveal the split condom to *me*, and apologize for keeping it quiet. ("You should've told me, Ella. I'm not mad, just disappointed.") Or maybe it was too late: she'd already given birth . . . in a day! "Hang on. I've gotta piss." I had been holding for so long, crooning and crumpling while I tried to extend the moment, but this latest turn of imagination pushed me over the edge.

"Okay, Eliot," Ella sighed and looked away.

"Sorry! People from Wellingborough have tiny bladders," I said, deferentially twisting my way from the room. "There have been scientific studies . . . something in the water. Honest." I left Ella on the bed, biting her nails.

In the midst of anonymous hairs, a sink caked in eclectic filth, a curling tube of Aquafresh, broken toilet seat, and screaming extractor fan, I released the fury. I was shaking, unsettled by the possibility of losing Ella to my dithering stupidity. I feared her anger, but worst of all I feared being relegated in her estimation. I had already lost Lucy; I couldn't process the thought of kissing Ella good-bye too. Especially now that she might finally be interested in me! I was in no state for any of this, the Dirty Pint and whatever else taking hold. Opening the bathroom door from all that spinning grime, I was met by Abi, swaying and smiling.

"Hey."

Placing a confident hand on my chest, she pushed me back into the bathroom, and with surprising dexterity turned and locked the door behind us. Even in my loose state I felt uncomfortable; vague allegiances bubbled in my bloodstream.

"I saw you in the bedroom with Ella just now," she said, impractically nuzzling my face.

"Oh?"

"You do realize that Jack likes Ella, don't you?"

"Errr, yeah, we all like her, don't we?" I replied, arching backward.

"No, as in he fancies her. Be careful is all I'm saying . . . things could get complicated."

"What?"

"Yeah, he told me earlier tonight. That doesn't bother you though, does it, Eliot?"

"Huh?"

Yanking me forward by the belt buckle, fingertips grazing the underside at the top of my boxers, Abi's lips confronted mine. These lips—thinner than Lucy's, less understanding than Ella's—contracted my own to two minutes' hard labor. She tasted of cold Malibu and Coke. While taking gouges from each other's mouths I thought of Ella waiting in the bedroom, growing increasingly impatient.

Fumbling behind my back after the toilet lid (the pesky seat sliding loose), Abi steered me to our station. Straddling me front on, she slipped out of her top, revealing a chest that was fuller than I had ever suspected of her. Well, you kept them a secret, didn't you? As she clutched after my belt and fly, unraveling me at the seams, I couldn't help thinking of all the past occupiers of that same seat, with their clenched buttocks and grinding teeth. Next I had visions of Leopold Bloom dropping a roundhouse dump, which in turn reminded me of the essay I had to write that week, which also in turn gave my erection the sharp sensation of a downward tug. And, by the look of things, I was going to be needing that stiffy right about now, because Abi's commandeering hand was delving into my pants, kneading balls of dough. It was remarkable really, how she managed to cling on to me, bury her tongue down my throat, *and* deliver a thorough handjob, all at the same time. I mean, I was genuinely astonished.

Whether I put it there, she put it there, or it was guided involuntarily by the gods, I soon found my own hand clamped tight in the crotch of her jeans, on the fleshy side. There was little room to operate, my mitt held firmly in place by uncooperative denim. Nevertheless, I started to wriggle my fingers about, freeing up a bit of space, and just hoping for the best. Fumbling in the recesses, I bore the aspect of a man rummaging for loose change. Abi seemed to be enjoying herself all the same. I had to work through spells of severe hand cramp, what with the non-user-friendly positioning, but I think the alcohol helped massively on that front.

"Bite my neck . . . bite my neck?" were the only words she said the whole time.

It was an odd exchange, just sort of rubbing and prodding each other in jagged unison; nothing more than a play of surfaces. At one point I thought her cavewoman industriousness was going to start a fire on my cock. Throughout I puzzled over her breasts that were not Lucy's and the rumpled torso that was not Ella's. It was a wank with a question mark at its end.

And guilt. I felt guilt, like a dull pain throbbing at the back of my throat. I couldn't tell if that was for Lucy or Ella. I think it was for both. But I wasn't going to let up. Increasingly, climax became something I needed, hurtling toward it ferociously, the solution of primal rapture.

I came all over Abi's hand, but mainly up the bottom inside of my shirt and along the ridge of my boxers. Standing up and re-dressing I was snared in all sorts of hygiene hazards, matted and glued against myself. There was no post-match small talk: no "What are you thinking about?," no tender spooning, no "I love you," no playful nose pinches. When Abi opened the bathroom door I was exposed for all to see, hopping around with my hands down my pants, belt and trousers flapping, a motley to the view.

There in the doorway was Ella, framed in her moment of hurt and shock. I could feel the air fleeing from her zero-shaped mouth. She bolted, and I didn't have the guts to follow—

"You know," continues Jack, "the party where Abi gave you a shiner?"

"Cheers."

"Sorry."

"And it was a handjob, by the way."

"A blowjob *and* a handjob?"

"No! Just a handjob."

"Bilateral?"

"Keep focused."

"Sorry. My bad. There I go avoiding it again!" He stares at his feet and takes a deep breath.

"So, Joel Shaw's party?" I say, somewhat impatiently.

"Well, I slept with Ella that night. We went home together and one thing led to another, as they say."

"Hang on, you slept . . . but . . ."

"Yeah, we got it on. We were both hammered."

"Oh, right."

Jack takes a slurp from his beer.

"Did you ever confront her about the abortion, uh, thing, whatever it was?" I ask.

"God, no."

"Good, good."

"What do you mean, good?"

"Well, you know, it was probably just a misunderstanding and it would've been embarrassing for you, wouldn't it?"

"But it's tormented me ever since. Why else would she have a letter?"

"Did you read it?"

"No, I just caught the top of it before she came in."

"So why didn't you ever bring it up with her?"

"Well, because I wasn't sure if I *had* got her pregnant. Plus, as time went on, I figured that if she had been pregnant, she'd obviously dealt with it, so why create all that awkwardness for nothing?"

"I guess it is quite bad for you not to have said *anything*."

Jack drops his head and sighs in regret.

"But understandable in some ways." I pat him on the back. "You wore a condom though, right?"

"I don't remember. We were so drunk . . . I always do, but I can't be absolutely sure."

"Well, it's all in the past now. And let's be rational about this—you probably did wear protection, you're just not sure . . . and even if you didn't, it doesn't mean you got her pregnant. For a start, doesn't she have to be ovulating and shit?"

"I guess . . . Does she? I'm not really sure how it all works . . . are you?"

"Err . . . And let's say she *did* have an abortion—how do you know she wasn't . . . sleeping with anyone else?"

"I'm almost positive she wasn't. At least I hope she wasn't. I would've been crushed if she had . . . I mean, I was crazy about her."

I nod silently. We lift our pints to unsmiling mouths and stare ahead into nothing, disconnected. "Maybe you did get her pregnant and maybe she did have an abortion, but—"

"What if she didn't have the abortion?"

"What! You think she's got a little baby hidden away in a room with *your* face on it? Fuck my life!"

"I know, I know!"

"How long ago was this anyhow?"

"Nearly a year, I guess."

"Well, she would've been looking pretty pregs just a couple months back, wouldn't she!"

"Okay, okay, she hasn't had a baby . . . of course not. I would've known, for sure. We all would. It's just the paranoia . . . it really fucks with your brain. But let's say she was pregnant and did have an abortion—I'm responsible, aren't I?"

I don't know what to say.

"And then after everything that happened afterward, I felt so bad . . . like I'm also responsible for, you know," Jack mutters into his pint, *"what she did"*—I start sweating at the unwanted reminder—"but obviously, after *that*, there was no way we could talk about any of this."

My head is thumping, and this is all I've got: "You wouldn't think about bringing it up with her tonight, would you?"

"I'm not sure. That's one of the reasons I wanted to talk to you."

"Mate, don't do it."

"Really?"

"Absolutely. Just don't. It isn't worth it. What's done is done. If it did happen you'll be digging loads of sad shit back up for her. And if it didn't you're gonna look like such a dick."

"You're right." He fidgets a bit, uncrossing his legs and slumping down. "It's so good to talk to you about this. I've wanted to for ages, but, well, you know . . . I felt like I couldn't."

"Mate, don't worry."

"Thanks. But, you know . . ." He stutters and swallows nervously.

I lean over and give him a man-hug.

"Fuck. I'm so glad to have you . . . and shit. I really appreciate it . . . bruv."

"No worries. I feel the same about you . . . mate. I'm always here for you . . . and that."

We both chug the rest of our beers. Jack hawks for extra manly measure.

"Just one thing," I say. "I *definitely* wouldn't tell Ella about any of this."

"You're right. I don't want to ruin our last night."

"Good lad."

★

Sitting in a cinema. I'm watching some superhero flick, not really my cup of tea. It drags and drones with the occasional special-effects thrill rocking my popcorn-peppered gut. I slouch in the aisle seat for leg room and easy pee flee access.

The place is full of couples. You've got to question the logic of the cinema date: getting dressed to the nines to sit in a dark room where you can't comfortably look at one another, let alone talk. Ideal for the three-year relationship that's barely hanging on, oh sure; stupid for the fourteen-year-old desperadoes that form the unsilent majority in here.

The picture changes. All of a sudden I'm watching myself in the waiting room at the clinic, fidgeting and burying my head in my hands. I close my eyes to escape it, but the same film is projected onto the back of my eyelids.

"You're making things really<br>difficult for me.

I'm sorry."

The babe's pram has appeared in the aisle. He's clutching a super-super-size Fanta and he's got a bowl of dripping-cheese nachos resting on his paunch. He is nearly bald, just a scraggly ring of hair running round his head, and the bags beneath his eyes have almost hidden his cheeks. The white blanket is now sodden and seeped in dark stains. It clings to his body like an extra layer of skin. The baby's eyes well up and I can hear him sobbing over the movie.

"I am jealous of everything<br>whose beauty does not die.<br>Every moment that passes<br>takes something from me,<br>and gives something to it.<br>It's all

my fault."

The picture on the screen changes again. Now I am confronted by a medium shot of Jack and Ella locked in an embrace. And then the image flicks—for a split second—to a long shot of the horrible scene that I've been burying this whole time: the last night of second year. I jump with shock. This is one memory I can't hide from forever.

The pram disappears.

I'm leaning forward onto the bar, trying to grab someone's, anyone's, attention. I play the game. Firstly, having spotted an opening and slotted my way pathetically in (sideways initially, then straightening up with hand on bar and prizing elbows), I've made sure that I'm someway toward central. If you line up in the wings, it's all over; you'll never get served, just like the wreck at the end there who has been waiting since 1986. His arms are glued on to the corner at the farthest point of the bar. He doesn't even muster a lift of the eyebrows or a point of the finger. This one's given up on life, invisible to the barmen, rushed off their feet.

Secondly, I make certain to establish eye contact with one of the almighty concoctors as they crush ice and splash our spirits. Once identified, I'm placed on the hallowed waiting list.

Thirdly, I make elaborate and experimental noises of disgust when anyone who hasn't waited as long as me, who hasn't done the time (fucking newcomers), gets served first. But it's hard when you're not stacked or over six feet tall. My average frame is average in so many averagely interwoven ways that, in this kind of setting, I'm as inconspicuous as room temperature. The rest is just con-

centration. Focus. Don't allow anyone or anything to steal
your—

"Boo!" Ella.

"Oh, hey." (The guy next to me gets served.)

"What are you getting?"

"Pint," I reply.

She wriggles in until she's level with me at the bar.

"How about you? My shout," I offer.

"What can I get you?" says the barman, going straight
for Ella.

"Vodka and Coke, and a pint of . . . ?" (she looks at me
inquiringly).

"Stella. Thanks," I say with more than a twist of bitter-
ness.

"And a pint of Stella please" (it has to be relayed by Ella.
He's just not interested in helping me out here. I puff my
chest and fold my arms).

That taken care of, we retreat to a high circular table
with two vacant bar stools.

"How's Lucy?"

I choke ever so slightly on my first pull of the pint. Ella
sips her drink, eyes cast down.

"Errr, she's fine I guess . . . I think . . . thanks."

Ella nods but seems miles away. She's gone pale.

"Are you okay?" I ask.

"Yeah, yeah, I'm fine," she says. "You've been a good
friend to me, Eliot. I hope you know that." She reaches out
to touch my arm but changes her mind, steering her eyes
away instead and looking at the table. She seems slightly
embarrassed. "A really good friend."

All I've wanted to do tonight is tell Ella that I think I need
her as *more* than a friend. I want to make a decision for
once. If I dive in now it might change her direction: "Ella—"

"SHOTS!" shout Sanjay and Abi, off-loading a cluster of tequilas onto the table, the others gathering round, seemingly out of nowhere. Christ, we've been ambushed. Everyone is grinning, except for me and Ella. There's a pile of sliced lemons and a cracked saltshaker in front of us. Words are unnecessary. It's like clockwork. I absentmindedly lick the fleshy hinge between thumb and forefinger and hold it out for Sanjay to sprinkle on the salt. He seasons me to good effect. Ella prepares herself resignedly, watching me the while.

"Salute," we shout, clinking our glasses in a merry round.

The salt makes me gag and the whiff of the tequila has me heaving before it's even past my lips. I glug it back though and chomp on the lemon, my eyes watering: they're furious with me. We all do that breathing-through-clenched-teeth jag and shake our heads farcically. I shudder. Ella jumps up and rushes to the toilet.

"Lightweight?" declares Abi.

My chin and hands are real sticky and I brush the excess salt against my soggy jeans. I think I'm going to retch but I find a way of swallowing it down. Megan looks disastrously white and I reckon I might have gone a psychedelic shade of green. That'll soon pass though. Our time in this joint is drawing to a close. Soon we'll be *club*: Filth. Maybe it's the change we all need.

Why are things turning out so much more complicated than I had anticipated? And why is it *Lucy* I can't escape from? She's still on my mind, despite everything else. Any kind of ordeal and my thoughts instantly turn to her. She's like a security blanket to which I've always felt I could go back. But after what she's told me tonight—my phone is

still off, biding me time—I'm not sure I even have that anymore . . .

Maybe I should admit that this kind of nostalgic return
has never worked. You can only run and hide for so long. I
remember one occasion, visiting home for a couple of
nights . . . if I could just get near to her again it might help
me to forget . . .

"It's lovely to see you," said Mum, fixing me a cuppa.
Dad had picked me up from the bus station, laden with
dirty washing and books that weren't going to get read. I
needed to get away from Oxford—those nightmare spires,
all that clamoring ambition, and knowledge of real loss. I
needed out. I didn't tell my parents about what happened
with Ella. Never have. I doubt they were suspicious of anything, my home self typically being a moody fuck anyway.

"Hmmph." An affirmative grunt from me, but affirmative all the same.

"Very unexpected. That's always the best though! I do
like a surprise." Mum settled on the opposite side of the
kitchen table, hugging her mug with both hands. She smiled
and shrugged her shoulders in an intimation of coziness.

"Have you got any plans?" asked Dad, hanging his car
keys on the purposely fitted hook over by the pantry
(where he has an individual hook for each key: car key,
house key, Mum's car key, Mum's house key, a vacant one
for my house key, the garage key, and the window key).
His domestic pedantry grated on me, embroiled as I was in
my internal melodrama of vertiginous grays and blues,
languishing in thick, treacly angst.

"Hmmph."

"Huh?"

"I said yes, okay? For god's sake."

"Well, that's nice then."

"Yeah, that sounds lovely," said Mum. Dad continued to rummage about the kitchen, filling his special trough-sized cup (the holy chalice; won't take his tea from anything else) with the dregs of the teapot. "So what exactly are your plans?"

"Look, I'm feeling a bit jaded," I said, getting up from the table. *Jaded?* Dad was thinking. I could tell from his chevron-flexed brow: *jaded?* . . . that's got to be a twenty-first-century thing . . . kids didn't feel *jaded* when I was growing up . . . probably an American import. "I think I'll just go to my room if that's alright." As I passed through the kitchen door I turned and added, "Oh, Lucy might be coming over tonight." I had found myself dropping her a text on the bus home. The message's themes were complex and unclear (friendship? melancholy? hope? homesickness?), its structure haphazard, the imagery muddled, the tone inconsistent, the delivery unreliable. But she said she would try to pop over.

"Lucy?" I heard Dad saying as I made my way through the living room to the stairs. "Are they courting again?"

"People don't *court* anymore," I hollered from the bottom of the staircase. "This isn't Renaissance fucking England," I added, beginning my stomping ascent.

"*What* England?" I could hear at a murmur. "Well, we courted, didn't we?"

"Yes love, we did."

I thought I was dreaming when I heard Lucy's distant voice floating up the stairs and in through the crack beneath the door like a magical elixir come to show me a hidden order. I had fallen into a deliciously insistent doze, *Rabbit, Run* lying across my chest, fanned and foxed, fully dressed atop crisp, childhood sheets. I awoke, shrugging off my doughy coating with a squirm and a yawn, the noises from below growing more authentic and convincing. Nostalgia found its perfect embodiment in my curling limbs, yearning as they were for this presence that I could not see, could not taste, feel, or smell. I thought, for a moment, that I was trapped in one of those sticky dreams where the object of your desire is unreachable, held at bay by some inexplicable perversion of physics or biology: you run but you don't move; you shout but make no sound; you jump and sink; swim and drown. It was her laugh that finally clinched the reality of the scene—so inimitable and singular; irrefutable proof of her positive being. Dad could always procure this from Lucy with one of his terrible jokes, wheezing and shaking himself into a shock of pink like a chameleon, just grateful for a sympathetic audience, so used to eye-rolling son and wife. But it was precisely this that tickled Lucy so much—Dad's self-satisfaction contrasted by our utter despair—and her kindly responses were more than enough to make him adore her. As I thought, I could now hear Dad's squeal coming through the floorboards, having probably off-loaded the one about Quasimodo and the prostitute or the hippy penguin in a bar. I reshuffled my pillow-hair in the mirror and made for the stairs.

"Yeah, I think it's the right decision," Lucy was saying, standing in front of my doting parents in the center of the living room. Dad put his arm around Mum, inspired by the sense of youthful love that Lucy had come to symbolize for them. "Just have to wait and see, I guess."

"No, that's great, Lucy," said Dad. "Exciting times, eh?"

She saw me appearing on the staircase behind my parents and hesitated for a second. "Hopefully. There's one that I've applied for at the County Council which I've got an interview for next week. I'm quite nervous about it actually."

"Oh, don't be," said Mum. "What more could they pos-

sibly want?" Lucy smiled modestly. Mum and Dad looked
as though they were having to restrain themselves from
showering her with hugs and kisses.

I brought myself further into view. "Hey."

"Hi," Lucy replied, calmly.

"I do love your hair, Lucy," said Mum, pleased to be saying the kinds of things she imagined she would say to a
daughter. "Have you changed it since we last saw you?"

"Yeah, I've grown it out a bit."

"Isn't it lovely, Eliot?" asked Mum.

"So how are you two anyway?" said Lucy, keen to dis-
oblige me of an answer.

"Oh, we're fine," said Dad. "Nothing much changes
here. This one keeps us on our toes," he added, nodding
toward me. I'm not sure exactly what this meant, but figured that it was nothing more than an automatic response,
filed away in his conversational repertoire ever since I had
been a little boy. A silence fell over us, awkward for me and
Lucy, but not so for Mum and Dad who could happily have
stood staring at the two of us for hours.

"Well, I'll call around in the next couple of weeks and let
you know how the job applications are going," said Lucy.
"You can show me those old photos you were telling me
about, Haley." It always came as a surprise to hear Lucy use
my parents' first names, complicating vague notions of age
and hierarchy that were vestiges of my eternal adolescence.

"That would be lovely."

"Do you want a drink or anything?" I asked, attempting
to move things along.

"No, I'm okay thanks."

Sensing the shift in procedure my parents funneled off
to the kitchen, leaving the two of us alone. I led Lucy
upstairs to the privacy of my room, as I had so many times

before, this time the motives more oblique. She filled its tiny space with her blossomy scent and I burst the luxuriant familiarity against my palate fine. But it was a familiarity that could not be grasped, guarded and bubble-wrapped by less hospitable dynamics. It was an unfamiliar familiarity. She was wearing a blue denim jacket with sleeves rolled back and the collar partly up. She kept the jacket on the entire time. She didn't even sit down for the first five minutes, just pacing while I sat upright against the headboard of my bed. Was this what it meant to be estranged?

"Shall I put some music on?"

"I don't mind," she said, by which she meant no. "Oh, before I forget, I've got your book." From her bag she pulled out the copy of *Under the Net* I had given her that time in the café. "I wasn't sure if I'd ever have a chance to give this back," she said, going over to my bookshelf and carefully sliding it in.

"Oh, thanks. I had forgotten all about that . . . you could've kept it. I don't suppose you got round to reading it?" I added, more as an afterthought than a genuine question.

"Yeah, I really enjoyed it," she said, finally settling down on the far corner of the bed.

"Oh."

"I liked Jake, the narrator. He was so funny and vain. Kinda reminded me of someone," she said sassily, entirely without menace. It made me feel more comfortable.

"So what was this about job applications?" I asked, intrigued by the conversation I had interrupted.

"Well, I've dropped out of uni. So I guess I'm looking for jobs now." She didn't look at me as she said this; we weren't even facing the same direction.

"What?" I exclaimed, unable to hide my surprise.

"Yeah, I didn't enroll for my second-term modules."
Lucy's tone was rueful, but as though she feared my judgments more than actually regretting her decision. "It's not for me, Eliot. I don't know, I should never have gone. I think I was worried what you would think if I didn't. I couldn't imagine you wanting to be with me if I never went to university. But that's kind of irrelevant now, I guess."

"Lucy, that's so untrue. I wouldn't have cared. But why didn't you tell me? That must've been ages ago now!"

"Because we're not together anymore, Eliot!" she said, a sudden injection of exasperation tightening her voice. "Sorry. I have to move on . . . carry on with my life."

"So what are you going to do?"

"Well, I've applied for a load of jobs . . . I'm staying at Mum and Dad's while I send my CV out and do interviews and that. I guess I'll rent with some friends when something comes up." I wanted to tell her how impressed I was that she had made such a strong decision. In some ways I knew that she was going to overtake me . . . grow up faster . . . a job, a place to live . . . she'd want someone to share it all with. Instead, I began to panic: what was I trying to achieve by having her over?

"How about you? I bet it's getting hard now, isn't it?"

"Oh, you know. The usual." The silences seemed weighty, as though they could have shifted the drawers or splintered the shelves. Ella and the abortion were becoming impossible to forget. I felt a burning need for revelation . . . to be honest with Lucy, even though it made no sense to. She was fiddling with her car keys, applying extra pressure—a reminder that she might up and leave at any moment. I moved down the bed and sat by her side.

"Hey," I said (which was ridiculous, considering that we'd already spent ten minutes together).

"Hey," she echoed. I placed an arm over her shoulder. Was this going back in time? In some ways, but not the ones I had hoped for. I felt infantilized. There we were, surrounded by posters I had Blu-tacked to my wall before my balls had even dropped: Michael Jordan, Shaquille O'Neal, Aerosmith, Beavis and Butthead. Embarrassing. My oldest teddy bear, which I usually hid when Lucy visited, was flat out on top of the TV like a defeated drinker, arms open, just desperate for a hug. There was the retro Sega Master System, the decaying sports-day medals, the china hippopotamus with all my dusty pennies in its belly. More pressing was the fact that we were sitting on my wanking bench, the bed bolstered up about six inches by all the used Kleenex stuffed underneath. It was like going back to a vivid time of skidmarks and wet dreams, cheap deodorant and youthful saltiness. But it wasn't a return . . . more a retrogression. And there was certainly no sense of return with Lucy. She was no longer the girl who'd roll around with me, giggling as I greedily tickled her lithe body . . . the girl who would list to the minutest detail every single thing she had done with her day. She wasn't the girl who said things like "You've got such a pretty brain" or "You're so lucky I love you." And she certainly wasn't the girl I could kiss at will—

"Eliot . . . don't."

"I'm sorry. You're right."

I tried to kiss her again. For a moment, this time, her lips grazed mine back. And then we were apart. Subtle tears meandered down her face like slow-motion shooting stars, each millimeter of their lengthening tails a measurement of lost history. The reminder that there was genuine feeling behind her defensiveness made me reel. I was astir with sudden guilt and self-loathing.

"Eliot, what are you doing?"

I had no answer to give. Why can't I stop hurting the people I love?

"I should go."

"Please don't."

"I should never have come."

"So why did you?"

"I don't know."

We hugged a hard, icy hug.

"Please . . ."

Lucy got up to leave, tears still making channels down her cheeks.

My parents were in the living room watching the TV. I didn't want them to notice Lucy's emotional display, so I snuck her through as inconspicuously as possible. I walked in front with haste and didn't say anything as we momentarily blocked their line of vision. They fidgeted, uncertain about what was happening or what to say. Lucy didn't pause at the front door, just letting herself out and slipping away. I followed a couple of feet behind, all the way to her battered car, parked on the corner. Holding the driver-side door I told her that I loved her and kissed her on the cheek.

Then she drove off.

I remained on the corner, barefoot, hands in pockets, folding under the knowledge that she would be driving all the way home through reality-bending tears.


Ella hasn't reappeared yet. Everyone else is over at the bar, eyeing up additional drinks with looks of beautiful boredom. Jack and I are left alone. He gives me a sidelong glance, the trace of a smile recognizable beneath the hood of his pointed noise. I want to laugh. I feel extraordinarily tense, but all I want to do is laugh. Jack's smile grows and we both find ourselves chuckling.

"Ah mate," he says, shoulders humming.

"Hah, I know," I say, the laughs unwinding as I rub my eyes and stretch my arms. "Shiiiit." I pat Jack on the shoulder. He's the best mate I've got and it finally feels like we might be back as a duo. Am I going to ruin it all before the night's over?

"Ha." His smile gradually irons out as reality reimposes itself. "Mate."

I'm glad to be sitting. There's so much crap in my system now that a sudden lethargy comes over me, filling my limbs with liquid fish and chips. Standing up will create all sorts of problems.

"It's such a relief," he says, filling his small chest to maximum capacity and letting it out. "You know, opening up to you earlier. I've gotta say, I really appreciate having you here for me . . . They say you make one or two friends for life at uni, and I guess it's true."

"Mate, don't mention it, you've always done the same for me."

He thinks about this. "Thing is, I feel like I haven't been there for Ella, despite everything. Now that I've spoken to you I feel like I really should be open with her. You know, tell her that I know what happened and that she shouldn't have had to shoulder the burden this whole time—"

"If it even happened," I interrupt. I really do not want this conversation. I wish he'd just drop it and lighten up . . . leave the angst to me; I've got it covered.

"Whatever . . . but, realistically, I am the only person who can share the burden of it—"

"If it even . . ."

Jack frowns at me.

"And if I don't set things right now we could end up

drifting apart as a result . . . and then she *will* be left to deal with it all . . . forever! Just imagine how she must be feeling . . . Fuck! I feel like shit about this."

He's right, but it's *me* who should be saying it. "Just listen to yourself," I begin, to stem his drunken outpour. "I'm sorry, mate, but that's a bit melodramatic. Nothing happened! You're being so paranoid. And even if it did, it's a bit late now, so just let sleeping dogs lie."

"Do you really think?" he replies, looking puzzled.

Is it any wonder that things have been complicated between me and Ella this past year? Just look at how it's weighing on Jack. How do you come to terms with something like that? There are no terms for the unborn . . . But all this unexpected stuff with Jack is making everything so much worse.

"Yes," I say decisively. "You need to man up. Seriously, mate, just let it go."


Ella reappears from the toilets, a gliding saint of distortions. Every context is hers, readjusting to her presence and poise: this bar, our conversation, my night. She sees the others at the bar and with a heavy heart I watch her make her way over. But contingency plays its incalculable part when she scans to her left, nothing but a whim, where Jack and I remain. Her face reads quiet alarm before softening into an unconvincing smile. She wishes I hadn't seen her, or that she hadn't seen us, and continues on to the bar.


This is it—the last stand in the bar before the finale; the warm-up for the crunch; the final push toward the main event: *club*. The adrenaline starts to pump; the skin begins to prickle. I long for the baying of the gladiatorial arena . . . awaiting . . . electric. I anticipate it with all my body. This is it, pal. Now we're *really* going somewhere.

After nailing consecutive Jägerbombs, we're colonizing the dance floor in our farewell bid to the *via media* establishment. It's so cramped in here, what with the bar area and the dance space merging into one, that we can't help but grind each other, gyrating and bouncing in a frenetic sweat swap-shop. Our personal clump has its internal dynamics, like a multicelled organism in constant flux. There's Megan and Sanjay, congealing and splitting, congealing and splitting, sometimes face-to-face, sometimes spooning. Then there's Jack, secreting energy and pumping it around to the rest of us. He gives Ella a spin and hooks an arm over her shoulder. He seems to have taken my advice to heart and Ella looks like she's finally starting to relax. Scott participates with pointing fingers and a pained expression of sudden self-consciousness. Need I say that we are now officially off our tits? Abi's fucked and she's granting me a boundless amount of attention. It's logistically impossible not to lavish each other with intimate respect. And now that I have accepted my bona-fide hammeredom, I amiably greet her rebounding loins.

Packed this tight, all gropes are permissible . . . mainly because no one can see. And so I think *fuck it* when Abi reverses into me and, reaching behind, pulls me up close by the rim of my jeans. It feels nice—the undulating curvature of her sides and soft torso as I steal my hands round to the front. Things can't get any worse right now, so why not? She dry-humps me to the beat, raising and lowering her ass over my crotch in perfect rhythm. There's no point pretending that she can't feel me harden, so I allow my cock free rein, stabbing it into her bum and spreading it around as far as the dance will allow. And she isn't pretending either when she reaches round (continuing the dance as she goes) and grabs it with devilish lust. As we bump and grind amongst the rest of the ensemble, Abi delves her exploratory mitt right inside and down my trousers. I look around, a moment of hesitation, but nevertheless breathe in and arch my back to give her easier access into my pants. She continues to face forward, away from me, while the exalted movements of the mass carry on—

A sudden memory of a college formal dinner, the last night of second year . . . Up on high table the Fellows and the Dons, the Principal, the Dean, the honorary guests and the oily Chaplain lay it on and spare not. Before these bluff talking heads stands a veritable fare of cheeses and truffles, figs and jellies, grapes and mints, rammed in the grand dining hall, all wood and portraiture. Their cheeks bulge like whoopee cushions, glowing fiercely jocular in the candlelight, blustering flatulent tsunamis from their mouths and other more hidden orifices. Watch these great bears as they pass the port to the left and masterfully refrain from taking the nose off the Stilton. See them in their sweat-glued tuxedos and gowns, dropping crumbs and tweaking the grapes. Oh, how smug and snug are these crazed hyenas in their after-dinner loathing, wretchedly bumbling and bellyaching their way through the evening, indulging in accepted hatreds. Oh, how they scoff those crackers and then, filled to the brim, scoff at the outside world. What a jolly occasion, all rumbles and booms; knowing jokes and greasy back slaps; gluttonous retching and snobbish assent . . .

Tightfisted, Abi administers staccato pumps. Her confident pole-dance has me squirming with pleasure, going all gooey in the middle, like the ground is falling away from me—

Me and Jack sat rammed against the wall, behind a long table on a long bench, farther down the hall. Another year of Oxford about to end . . . something worth celebrating. It was there, keeping his voice on the down-low, that he told me he loved Ella; how he was crazed for her; how he'd do anything for her, and any other cliché that needed fulfilling. His crisp tuxedo accentuated his earnestness while my more ruffled version added to my sense of being a fraud. He was so proud of the conviction of his feelings and I was frustrated by the muddiness of my own. I had loved Lucy, I thought, and I loved Ella, I think, and I was twisted into a stubborn knot of confusion by the idea of Jack making a move. He seemed glad to have confided in me . . . I had been chosen and trusted . . .

Abi pounds at it for half a song. I feel clammy in her palm and I run my fingers all over her body, squeezing her hips, sliding my hand up her top to her yielding belly—

Most of the college's tutors were at the formal and Dylan came down the bar afterward. Everyone was already pissed from the wine and port provided with the meal, but Dylan insisted on buying the English crew a round of drinks. Ella declined the vodka and Coke he got for her and left to sit with Jack, Sanj, Scott, and Abi—I took the spare drink off his hands. I thought it was quite rude of her, but Dylan didn't seem to mind. Like everything else, I put it down to alcohol. I remained standing to one side with Dylan, lapping up his conversation and beverages. I was always terribly impressed by whatever he had to say, as well as flattered that he would bother to say it to me. I couldn't help but feel uncomfortable though when he started ranting about Dr. Snow: "Polly's the fittest in the faculty, isn't she?"

"Stop winding me up! You're such a ball breaker." I

knew he was just trying to set me on edge, and the sadistic grin was confirmation enough.

"Hah, don't think I don't hear what all you hormone-addled undergrads say about her."

"As if!" I pleaded my innocence.

"Don't worry, don't worry. There's not much to choose from, is there, so a young buxom tutor like Polly is bound to attract attention." I noticed that Ella was watching us from the table. She seemed on edge, standing out from all the bustle and bodies of the constricted college bar like an aching hologram. I turned my back so that I wasn't facing her, but I could feel her stare clawing at the back of my head.

"She's not all that anyway. Trust me . . . I know!" With that Dylan excused himself and sauntered off to the bathroom. After a brace of astonished sips I rejoined the gang.

Ella was missing.

"Where's Ella?"

"I dunno," answered Abi. "She just disappeared."

"Oh." I looked to Jack for some information—I figured he'd be keeping an eye, considering what he'd told me earlier.

"She's left her purse," he said. "I'll go check if she's in her room . . ."

Abi is disengaging and turning to face me. What the fuck am I doing? I don't want any of this. I think Jack has noticed something, because he's looking at me strangely, but that's probably just the lighting. And we seem to have caught Ella's attention too, though clearly she doesn't know: she almost looks happy, relieved even, and it would've killed her if she had seen . . . what was occurring in my pants just now. Sanjay jutters over and shouts in my ear—

I lagged behind Jack by thirty seconds or so, having pulled into the toilets at the foot of Ella's staircase for a quick pit-stop. Her bedroom was three floors up and I was still fiddling with the button on my trousers when I pushed open the expectant door.

Great flashes of unreality projected onto the screen at the back of my eyes. I don't know what I had been anticipating, but it emphatically was not this: the dancing figure, there, in the center of the room, bouncing inadequately on hot-coal tiptoes that vaguely kissed the floor with each downward plunge, straining to slacken the dressing-gown cord hanging from the light fixture, about to give. She was pulled taut, in desperate need of unspooling.

"I've got you, I've got you," shouted Jack, sourcing the pitch and air from some uncharted depth. I was petrified, frozen in the sickening moment. Ella groped and fumbled at the cord with sloppy hands, complicating the knot against her best efforts; her lips a gorgeous pastel blue, her eyes popping stunning violence. Jack had wrapped his arms around her hips and was lifting her from the ground so that her hair scuffed the crack-stained ceiling. She could never have killed herself, the light hanging so low that she was only ever an inch or two from the ground. Her tugs brought the fixture free from its hold, collapsing her and Jack into a knot on the floor.

Jack sat her up and held her tightly in the suddenly darkened room, fearing that she might try something else. She began to cry over his shoulder as she surrendered into his solid body, her eyes settling on me, there in the doorway. But I felt like I wasn't there at all; as though she could see straight through me. Jack whispered desperate comforts and carefully stroked her hair . . .

"Ready for Filth?" says Sanj.

"Sure."

We all watch each other as this inevitable directive does the rounds, our commotions unwinding to a full stop. I can feel my body deflate as guilt and a subtle sense of sickness set in. Abi is smiling at me.

And then we're exit-bound, threading a wonky line through the ballistic mob.

# Club

I awake . . . I think. It gets harder and harder each morning. More problematic. More tiresome. I begin to stir approximately ten minutes before the alarm is due, in sickly anticipation of its blurting GBH. I cringe when it hits. A full-bodied recoil. Fuck my life.

Then (I say "then." Really I mean forty-five minutes and a severe battle of self-will later) I'm in front of the sink and mirror. I leave more of myself in the basin each time: hairs (mainly hairs), lashes, nails, and a miscellany of scum. I curse experimental curses at the thick bush on top of my head: "Get down obnoxious cunt rug," "I'll cut you motherfucker," "You're dead mate, real dead."

Next, I go nuclear on the toilet seat. It's pre-coffee though, so just a few dry explosions, opening up a wind shaft between my legs and letting it sing. I play a handful of complex notes, run through some Grade 8 scales, by which time my involuntary hard-on has gone down and I can shed the contents of my bladder. I blow my nose, provoking a final roar from my gut. That taken care of, I select some choice items from a heap of clothes on the floor, scrub my teeth, and I'm ready to roll.

I open my door and there on the landing is a black pram,

like a chariot of mourning. I wait for a familiar greeting but none is forthcoming. I look left and right for signs of delivery, half expecting a man with a clipboard asking me to *please sign here*. But, of course, no one is around.

The babe is bundled up inside, his little body rising and falling under the slow measure of heavy breath. His over-sized face is now shriveling into a grotesquely aged version of my own. His cheeks and eyes are puffed and his mouth obscenely crooked.

"Hello," I say.

He screws my eyes, watery at the seams, and shakes his head repeatedly, as if to say, *Make it stop, make it stop.*

"What's the matter?" I ask, caught off guard by the intense concern in my voice. He simply stares at me, his deep, searching gaze expressing more than words ever could. And then it hits me: the severe laceration circling his neck, quivering between crimson and scarlet.

"Who did this to you?"

He looks at me. I reach in and gently rub his earlobe between my thumb and forefinger. He leans his head in toward his shoulder to make the contact fuller.

"Okay."

I take the handle and wheel him away with me.

"I thought I told you to fuck off."

"Huh?" says Scott.

"I said I thought I told you to fuck off," repeats the bouncer, outside the doors of Filth.

"You did?"

"Is this kid taking the piss or what? Yeah, I told you to fuck off."

"Oh. What did you do that for?" asks Scott.

The bouncer scoffs and raises his eyebrows, like they're reaching up to sympathize with his bald head.

"Because you were being leery and I told you to fuck off. Now, are you going to fuck off or am I gonna have to make you fuck off with my own two hands?" He steps forward and squares up.

"When exactly did you tell him to fuck off?" I intercede, ever the voice of reason.

The long queue trailing off behind, hemmed against the wall by dented iron railings, splits into pockets of excitement and impatience: those who want to see it kick off (nearest the front of the queue) and those who are simply desperate to get in (farther back). The entrance to the club groans inarticulately before us, like a black portal into the underworld. It's a seashell of roaring waves and pounding beats. They're playing an absolute tune (with a capital T) and I want to be in there busting some moves. It's my last night of university, goddammit. The rest of the crew make their way in, pulled by the noise and the promise of flashing lights. Thanks a lot. Yeah, nice one.

"Fifteen minutes ago. Ginger lad in a pink shirt. Can't be many fitting that description."

"You'd be surprised," I say.

"Gosh, well, that wasn't me," says Scott, laughing in appeal. "We've been in the queue for the last thirty minutes," he adds, looking from me to the bouncers in affronted disbelief. The bouncer doesn't like this revelation: it dispels his cause for pissiness. "And besides, it's auburn." The backup bouncer is losing interest anyway, distracted by the dolled-up girls next in line.

"Mistaken identity," I conclude triumphantly. "Trust me, mate, this one don't do leery, d'ya know what I mean?" (For some reason I think that vamping up my hometown accent will endear me to this brick shit-house.)

Scott's unsure whether to take this as a compliment or an insult, but nods readily in agreement.

"Alright," spits the bouncer, reluctantly removing the red cordon. "Fuck off in there. But I'm warning you, if you start causing any more trouble, posh-boy" ("but . . . but") "I'll personally see to it that you *do* fuck off. Got it?"

"Thanks so much," says Scott, genuinely grateful and relieved. We pay a fiver each for the privilege to a woman behind a hole in the wall. She smiles at me (probably recognizing my excellent hair). Then we pop our coats in the raffle-prize cloakroom (two quid). We'll be lucky if we ever see them again.

I close my eyes and take a deep, dramatic breath: I've arrived.

Filth is filthy. It really is. Before the smoking ban, all you could smell in here was, well, smoke. A robust fag-screen masked all other scents and secretions. Downside was you'd wake up the next morning with a chimney sweep on top of your head and clothes that stank like your nan's kitchen. These days the olfactory experience is far more nuanced in Filth. There's nowhere for those pesky tangs to hide. Our noses are set upon by a palimpsest of farts, piss, sambuca, hair spray, armpits, vomit, perfume, shit, roll-ons, body spray, menstruation, lager, sweat, sex, and fear. It's vast and stifling, all at once. Welcome to the great Filth Sensorium.

This is liberty, my friend: I can let a huge one rip with no suspicion attached whatsoever. No one hears and it's so packed it could've been anyone. In fact, I'm pretty sure Scott's just let loose (all that tension from outside). He's grinning at me. Filthy sod.

"Thanks for that."

"No worries, mate."

Filth follows the panopticon design—circular, with a large dance floor in the center and several bars stretching around the perimeter. Maximum surveillance. We loiter and weigh our options.

"What happened to Laura?" I shout at Scott. "Haven't seen her since the cashpoint."

"She's in here . . . somewhere . . . with all her year." He peers over heads, a moonlight searchlight. The rest of the crew are standing at the rear of a pack of bar queuers, jostling for position. They give Scott a hero's welcome of jeers and backslaps ("They let you in then?," "You made it, old chap," "Get over here, you silly twat").

Now that some of my beer armor has worn off (what with the wait and the negotiations) I'm starting to feel guilty about Abi in that last bar. The memory creeps up on me with palsied fingers, poking and twisting. There's no way that was a good idea. I want to blame delayed reactions: when she started I was pretty stunned and wasn't too fast out of the blocks; it felt good and I didn't really have a chance to defend myself; and once she'd got going, well, it would've been rude of me to cause a scene. I couldn't embarrass the poor girl like that, could I? It would've been demoralizing. And if we're being honest, it has no significance compared to my dramas with Ella, Jack, and Lucy.

"Jägerbombs?" suggests Sanjay, full lunged. We do a hand count and demand six (Ella opting out).

"Sweet. You all got the dough?"

I have a tenner, so Jack gives me two fivers for the break, meaning that I can give Sanj one in exchange for three quid and then break Scott's fiver, by which time some complicating twenty- and fifty-pence pieces have found their way into circulation, moving perplexingly from hand to hand, my lost fiver ending up back in my possession and a twenty-pound note going to Jack (not a bad profit), Sanjay essentially paying for the entire round.

"I've got a pound?" says Abi, unhelpfully holding her handbag open to the light over the bar.

What the fuck was I thinking? Lucy's flashing through my head like an emergency signal, piercing and insistent. I can't even look at Abi . . . or Ella. I feel sick. Maybe I should hit the Men's for a tactical vom? My phone weighs my pocket knowingly.

We've nudged and leapfrogged to the front of the bar. You can see our warped reflections in the inch of spilt drink that swamps the surface. The bombs are prepped and lined up, brimming with delectable menace.

"Let's get filthy, boys and girls."

Drink more: it's the only solution.


But it doesn't solve anything. Of course it doesn't. This whole past year of university has been a complete fuckup, and here I was thinking I could fix it all tonight with one decisive act.

The beginning of my third year was tough, that last summer vacation an inexorable drag of self-loathing and lonesomeness. It was a relief to go home after the drama of Ella's suicide attempt, but relief soon shaded into sadness, and sadness amplified in solitude. I couldn't summon the nerve to contact her and see how she was, too burdened by clammy notions of responsibility and ineptitude; and it seemed best to leave Jack be for the summer, knowing his feelings, but he not knowing mine. I just read and studied, looking for solace in Milton, Keats, Wordsworth, Shelley, hoping that obsessive revision might pull me through relatively intact and leave me with at least one good thing still to play for. And I didn't see Lucy. How could I, with everything that had happened entirely unknown to her? She wouldn't have wanted to see me anyway. As the summer languished toward its close, the nights becoming crisper, the fallen apples in the garden beginning to rot, I looked forward to seeing Jack again and finally opening up. If we could share the memory of that night on more honest and intimate terms, then we might be able to put it behind us.

But it was with huge trepidation that I returned to Oxford. Dad wove our spluttering 206 around the streets outside my college, getting amongst all the Range Rovers,

Mercedes, and Rolls Royces, with their dyslexic private number plates: N1 BO55, T1 MMY, W4 NKR. They were like smug grins gurning at me from front and behind, and I wanted to smash each and every one of their teeth out. We pulled up as close to college as possible and began unloading all my stuff for a third and final time.

There was a chaos of panic-stricken freshers in the lodge, eager to impress, and haggard third-years battling back spasms to get their belongings into the college and up to their new rooms.

"No common sense," muttered Dad as a wide-eyed fresher lost control of a stack of boxes. "All the brains in the world, but not an ounce of common sense." With subtle satisfaction he lugged a sack barrow from the boot and stood it on the curb. "Right, Eliot, pile her up. Biggest and heaviest boxes on the bottom, light ones on top."

At the start of each academic year Dad became a man possessed, joyfully donning the role of Captain Practical. The car was packed tight with drill-sergeant exactitude, every inch of space maximized (boxes, suitcases, bags, suits, gown, guitar, speakers), all stacked and interlocked into a formidable Tetris block, loaded and unloaded at breakneck speed. If there was one thing he wasn't going to be outdone on it was practicality: packing, lifting, shifting. There were serious man-points to be had and Dad was no mug. The porter commented on our efficiency every year, which Dad noted as a considerable success. He watched in silent glee as the owners of the monstrous Range Rover rammed behind us faffed about with their poorly organized luggage ("Terrible packing system there, Eliot . . . Suitcase on top? Hah, elementary error. They've got a big enough bloody car!").

Sharing the load, we wheeled my things across the first quadrangle toward the staircase that was to house me for this final and most important year. With increasing fascination, Dad watched all the students lounging on the grass and chattering in clusters.

"Such privilege. They don't know how lucky they are," he said, flaunting our supreme luggage operation. "Isn't that your mate Jack?" he asked, nodding toward the far corner of the quad. I looked across and saw Jack and Ella, my stomach lurching when I realized that they were holding hands, lost within each other. I felt separated, flying solo across an alternative timestream. Jack then lifted his arm around her neck and kissed her on the forehead.

"Oh, yeah, it is."

Everything plummeted: the ground, the buildings, the sky. I wanted to turn around, load all my stuff back into the car and go home. What circumstances have conspired to cause *this*? I hurried Dad to the entrance of my stairwell. We made the ascent like a pair of Quasimodos, burdened by the vaulting ambition to do it all in one trip. My despondence wasn't lost on Dad, who probably put it down to the anxiety of beginning my last year.

The unloaded sack barrow, light to the touch, brought a lump to my throat as I wheeled it back across the quad, through the lodge, and to the car. "Right, son," said Dad, reaping me into his bear hug. "Work hard and look after yourself." Pulling me in even tighter, he spoke quietly into my ear: "It's been lovely having you home for a while. Keep your chin up." I could hear him choking up, as he did every time. His chippiness about all the wealth and grandness surrounding us was overridden by his pride for me. Secretly he longed for me to have it all myself, one day, and he'd do anything to help get me there.

"Thanks, Dad."

I stood and waved him off. The little car dwarfed by the

impressive colleges was inexpressibly touching. I was alone. Lucy was gone, home was gone, and I was quickly learning that Ella and Jack were now together and therefore doubly gone. The sense of isolation was pure and gutting. Take me home. Take me home. I wanted to cry, and easily would've done were it not for Ella and Jack strolling out of college, arm in arm.

"Oh, hey, Eliot."

My phone is back on. I'm reconnected to the invincible glue of the world; signal pulls me back into Lucy's life. I'm here for her, the distance between obliterated. I begin to dial.

But things are still so much more complicated than that. So much is beginning to make sense now . . . so much is becoming clearer . . .

The very last time that I saw Lucy was during that bleak first term of third year, and it begins with me slouching my way down George Street. Off my knockers, don't you see? Buses and demonic taxis splash past, whipping the cold 10 p.m. air into a gritty swirl. I'm hammered. Merry students emerge from pubs and bars to make their way to clubs, dragging themselves up and down the street, singing and mouthing off. I strut through the raucous gang of smokers outside the Bear, greased up like a mother. I'm licked. Oxford Uni kids don't go to the Bear. It's for locals only, who are harder than us and extremely keen to knock our collective teeth out. Doesn't make much sense to me: I go out on the piss in the Bear in Wellingborough, the exact same chain, all the time. Wouldn't think twice. No one would abuse me there. I'm just one of the locals. Why should it be any different here? But I tell you what, if some fairy students decided to show their munt faces at the Wellingborough Bear I'd go fucking ape! Anyhow, these lads do hurl something my way about my hair (which is utterly fantastic), but it falls on fucked ears. I'm fucked.

I'd been down the college bar, drinking with the crew (standard), watching Jack play the loving gent with Ella, when I decided that it would be a really great idea to surprise Lucy by turning up in Wellingborough unexpected (or uninvited, if you want to be pedantic about it). I suddenly realized how much I missed her (again), and how much simpler life had been in those early days.

There was a homeless bloke huddled in his body bag on the platform at the bus station. His shiny red setter considered me with wise, saddened eyes, faithfully resigned to its burden. I'm touched. Did I mention that I'm also fucked? (Was, am, are . . . it's all the same right now.) I slurred my ticket request like consonants were going out of fashion, but the driver soon got the picture.

"Hey," I said at Wellingborough bus station, two hours later, when Lucy picked up her phone.

"Eliot?"

"Yeah. Errrr, so guess what?"

"Eliot, it's gone eleven o'clock!"

"So what? I'm in town!"

"Why?" she said, startled, almost like a demand.

"Surprise?"

I could hear someone muttering in the background.

"Who's that?"

"Eliot, what do you want?"

"Ermm, could you come and pick me up? I'm freezing my balls off . . ." I should point out that although I was still fucked (I was fucked), the short journey had sobered me up a touch.

"No, Eliot! I wasn't expecting you."

"Oh. But it was meant to be a nice thing."

"What are you talking about? We haven't spoken in— Why on earth would it be nice?"

Good point.

"There aren't any more buses back to Oxford tonight . . . I'm at the station. Please?"

She grrred like a big cat. "Be there in ten." Then a long disgruntled beep. Romance was not in the air. So I waited nervously, deflated, but still pissed.

When she pulled up on the roadside in her tiny car, a rusty beetle scuttling about the nighttime streets, even her brakes rose to the sound of ire. I climbed into the passenger seat sheepishly baa-baaing an apologetic hello. She was careful not to turn and look at me, keen to let me realize her dissatisfaction as she pulled off and scraped us back to hers. The continuous firework display of headlamps and traffic lights bursting through the windscreen revealed flashes of a beautiful face sinking in darkness. She was defiantly switched to mute (not that she was ever the greatest conversationalist), and after drunken stabs at a few preliminaries, I thought it best to just sit tight till we got to her digs.

When we arrived Lucy turned off the ignition and picked up her phone from behind the gear stick.

"Just wait here a sec," she said.

"How come?"

"Please." She climbed out and left me shut in the car like an inconvenient dog; she didn't even wind the window down to allow me any oxygen. She was ringing someone on her mobile, but the conversation was muffled by other vehicles passing by and the steel shell of the car.

Eventually she uncaged me and led me inside. Lucy was sharing a house with three girlfriends, who I could hear wailing and screeching in the living room like dying cats over some god-awful karaoke game on the PlayStation. Lucy shuttled me straight up to her room. I was all up for introducing myself (of course I was: I was pissed), which appealed to Lucy about as much as having to see me in the first place. The lamps were already on in her room and music was playing, as though she had been expecting me all along. But, of course, she hadn't. Lucy was moony and fragrant, eyes twinkling, hair wild, all flushed from the rush and surprise of my unadvised drop-in. We were alone, subsumed by frigidity. I headed for the bed (out of instinct, I guess) and sat down. Lucy gauged this and took the chair.

I had been banking on playing it cool. Really, I had. But then I saw a gent's wallet over on the desk. I thought I recognized it from somewhere but couldn't quite figure out why. Lucy followed my gaze and then closed her eyes in regret.

"Whose is that?" I asked, as casually as I could.

"Eliot, I can't do this."

"I love you," I confessed rather unexpectedly, backed by a surging head-load of booze. Lucy's head lowered. My return odyssey home was fast descending into disaster. And here I was thinking I would take the hero's role, a veritable Hector of intent, but really just some nuisance punk Pandarus.

"Why are you doing this?" she asked, tearfully.

"Don't you love me anymore?"

"No."

Fucking bitch! I mean, don't beat around the bush or anything. I guess she had to say that though, didn't she? And why was I crying?

Yes, I started crying. Come on, I was drunk (*to be fair*).

"Don't you miss everything we used to have?" I implored.

She nodded, still looking at the floor. "Well, we can have it all back if you want, Lucy."

"No. We can't."

It was then that I began to beg, losing all sense of tact and strategy. "Please, Lucy, I fucking love you. No one can take your place. I've never moved on . . . I never will. You're killing me." Equating her with a murderer probably wasn't the best call, but these kinds of clichés have a knack for landing you up shit alley. "Please, Lucy," I struggled through the chokes and sobs. "Take me back."

"Eliot, no—"

I exploded, charging over to the wall and pounding it mercilessly with the side of my clenched fist. I screamed and bawled, tears gushing down my face. Thick saliva and phlegm filled my mouth as I fumbled my grip on the reality of the scene. It finally dawned on me that I was losing everyone I had ever cared about. "Fuck," I shrieked. "Fuck, fuck, fuck." I could feel the pain expanding through my hand despite all that alcohol working its fix. It was swelling and weeping, a gash having opened over the outer knuckle. The more I realized how much I was going to regret what I was doing, the more I lost it.

I went over to the chair to hug her, abject as shit. She didn't stop me, but she didn't put her arms around me either. She was hard, not soft like I remembered. I knelt before her, cuddling her, her arms locked at both sides. We vibrated against each other like phones turned to silent. Her hair smelled of apples and I tried to burrow. After a minute or two of tortured embrace she nudged me away. I went back to the bed and buried my swollen face in my hands.

And then I must have passed out, because I woke in the morning, on top of the covers, to find Lucy asleep on the floor, her rising and falling form barely contained by a spread-out dressing gown.

Haven't seen her since.

I should have known there and then. Of course it makes sense now: despite my incessant returns and deferrals, she has moved on.

Why shouldn't she? She's been at home for the last two years getting on with her life. What other choices did she have? I had my chance.

Rob has proposed to her. That's what she rang to tell me earlier . . . that's what she has been trying to tell me all night.

I'm dialing.

"Hello?"

"Lucy? It's me," I shout.

"Eliot? Where are you? It's so noisy."

"What are you going to say? To Rob?" I bellow even louder, competing with the music in Filth. It's nearly impossible to make out her words.

"I think I'm going to say yes."

"Why did you even tell me about this?"

"I had— I felt I owed it to— and he is your friend. At least he used to be. I feel like—"

"I can't hear you," I yell, shoving a finger into my spare ear, her voice constantly breaking up. "You feel like what?"

"—doesn't matter."

"When did all this start anyway?"

"What?"

"When did it start?"

"—seeing each other on and off— been there for me. And we're both in Wellingborough, you— I know that sounds lame, but it really counts for something."

"But he's such a cock, Lucy . . . surely you must see that?"

"—not . . . he's lovely . . . and he's calmed down a lot. His business is really starting to pick— it's focused him."

"Business? What business? Rob's a fucking Neanderthal. No, he's not even that . . . he's . . . he's . . . well, he's just a knob," I yell.

"His decorating business— getting loads of work now, things— really working for him."

"Decorating? What the fuck! What does Rob know about decorating *or* business? He doesn't know shit about . . . *shit*."

"Eliot, you can be such an arrogant— you know he did a foundation course in busin— it's what he always wanted to— got a distinction."

Why don't I know all this? Where have I been?

"So do you love him?"

"—don't know. Maybe. It's more complicated than that though, isn't it?"

"How?"

"He loves me and he wants to be with me. I care about him a lot and I'm making a life for myself here."

"But I—"

"Huh? I can't hear you, Eliot!"

"I—"

"Eliot?"


I remember a dream. It's pathetic really. First of all I was falling through space, outside of myself. I was an infinitesimal speck of dust, kicking and sprawling about the uncaring cosmos. The earth, spinning idly below me, was ridiculous and futile, yet it had warmth, it had life, it had presence— and I was excluded. I was confronted by sublimity in its purest form and all I could think about was my singleness.

And then I fell. I was at a dinner party. Ella, Jack, Scott, Abi, Sanjay, and Megan were all sat around a dining table. They had their backs to me. When I tried to call out I found that my mouth was glued shut by a sticky gel. Over the table there hung a portrait of me, distorted by cobwebs and dirt. I longed to walk over to them but couldn't raise myself from the ground, having broken every bone in my body from the lunar fall. They made a toast while I kept straining to shout, swallowed by a confused mumble of sobs.

Lucy always used to wake me from bad dreams with a delicate squeeze of the shoulder. She'd say, "You were having a nightmare," with heavy eyes, rolling toward me and burying her head in my neck. And I would say, "Thanks," staring hard at the ceiling. Her body would be warm against mine and transfer reassurance into my restless limbs. It'd only take a minute before she was quietly snoring away again, twitching contentedly in my arms.

But this time I was alone. I had to wake myself up. The crying did it. And then there was no one to hold.


Filth. People all around me, over me, on me. A spontaneous orgy or an atavistic brawl could break out with equal likelihood. Push me, pull me, tug me, grind me. I sip and I sip and I sip, to keep me going, to keep me occupied. My taste buds are blunted meager tuned-out. Filth. Bosh.

I hate admitting that Ella and Jack became an item after Ella's suicide attempt. I hate even thinking about it. I've never confronted them; never asked when or how it happened. I suppose it all came together over that last summer vacation. What really troubles me, though, is knowing that the abortion must have played a major part in Ella's suicide attempt, no matter how controlled she may have seemed at the time, and Jack was there for her when I wasn't. I pushed Ella to the brink of despair and then Jack swooped in to save her.

Guilt: I wrote an essay on the stuff once—"Modes of guilt in William Wordsworth's *The Prelude*." Not that long ago, in fact; but I only see by glimpses now. Which, in all honesty, is more than I used to. Back then I saw by snatches, which is less give than take. But I'm trying to move on. I'm trying to get out of this cycle. This year was a dark one at first, and in many ways I am relieved to be bringing it to a close, tonight. And it wasn't just the past that I was contorting myself over; the future has cast—*is* casting—an enormous shadow over my final year, from the quotidian (where to next?) to the metaphysical (who am I? *What* am I?). I find myself tripping up tenses here, stubbing my toe on the hefty curb that joins past and present, grappling with the burden of my own unnatural self.

Finals fagged my brain to a smoldering butt, stealing sleep and ramping up the blood pressure. Ella continued to raise the bar intellectually, and I tried to follow, like a pathetic jumping fish. She had won all the college prizes and one of her papers was even getting published in some obscure literary journal that was apparently a big deal. I was getting there though, my Collections results starting to hit the high sixties with the occasional seventy, and a First in Finals emerging as a realistic target. By this time I fancied that we were Dylan's and Polly's pet couple: Ella as the brightest student in our class and me the diamond in the rough. I recall this "guilty" essay, early on in the year, because it was writ-

ten for one of the very few tutorials that we had together.
We rarely shared tutes anymore—I made sure that I was
always tutored by Dylan, but Ella had switched to Polly. We
had both written on Wordsworth that week, and what with
Dylan being the boss when it comes to the old Romo, I had
an opportunity to be around her for a solid hour. I was still
coming to terms with her and Jack being, well, you-know-
what, and my newfound hermitry (around-the-clock studying and a lonesome episode of *The Sopranos* at night) meant
that such events acquired a greater significance than they
perhaps deserved. The very notions of proximity and stimulating discussion whipped up a bluster of emotions.

We met by the terra-cotta plant pots in the right-hand
corner of the quad, over by the memorial bench.

"Hey."

So you and Jack are shagging now, are you?

"Hey."

My two best friends. *You* and my best mate. *Motherfucker.*

"Shall we?"

"Sure."

We made for Dylan's room. We didn't say much on the
way, our throats clammy with mutual apprehensions. I
had a whole storehouse of punches, drop kicks and judo
chops rumbling to make it from my gut to my mouth, to
let her know what I thought of her and Jack. I just couldn't
get used to the idea. (I thought I was the one you'd always
liked? And did I mention that Lucy has no interest in me
anymore? What the fuck are you playing at, to be honest?)

Most of all I just felt like a sulky twat.

Dylan wasn't in his room when we arrived, which meant
prolonging the frigid proximity that bit longer, out on the
freezing cold staircase.

"How was your essay this week?" I asked, trying to dispel the tension.

"Oh, well, you know. Two thousand words too long and no conclusion. The usual."

Should we do a gobby passionate kiss, right now, tongues and all, like in the movies? Maybe that would clear all the shite. Here, let me lick your tonsils . . .

A chorus of sniffing and jangling keys spiraled their way toward us and Dylan eventually appeared, his forehead glistening with sweat.

"Apologies," he said as he dissected the pockets of his snazzy leather jacket, searching for the keys, wiping his nose all the while on the back of his spare hand. "So, Wordsworth," he said, once inside the room. "Good, isn't he?"

"The boy's got talent," I replied. "He'll go far."

"Absolutely," said Dylan, smirking, now poised on his red throne. The nude sketch still hung from the wall with its psychoanalytical bent, but it didn't interest me anymore.

"Nice essays this week," he said, scanning his overused eyes past them to remember what they were about (double-checking that he'd actually read them). "Especially yours, Ella, though a bit too researched. I want to hear your personal response more."

Well, how had she found the time to do all that research? Hadn't she been terminally occupied researching Jack's knob-end?

"Okay," she said despondently.

"Short and sweet, Eliot. Good. That's what I like to see."

"Cool. Thanks."

The two perpendicular sofas were draped with Eastern throws (it being of particular importance in the academic game to give off a cosmopolitan vibe), each taking the tutor's chair as their focal point. Ella and I went for a sofa each, which, admittedly, looked odd, placing us as it did several meters apart. Dylan noticed this subtle presentation of disharmony and raised an ironic smile. Such readable dynamics must be typical in a profession that deals predominantly with neurotic, sex-obsessed young adults. For three years I reckon he'd had his eye on Ella and me as potential star-crossed lovers. I've often wondered if tutors take this kind of thing into consideration when interviewing and selecting each year's intake: well, this Bolshevik from Barnsley is going to send that landed Harrovian into an absolute jizz, and this recovering heroin addict from Stowe is bound to turn out an ax murderer, which will garner great publicity for us; and that luscious Caribbean girl with the posh accent will keep *me* entertained through all the dreary morning tutes on Chaucer, as well as sending the spotty state-school chumps doolally with stiffies and wet dreams . . .

Dylan kicked us off: "Sticking with *The Prelude*, to start with, where do you think the poet is in all this? Because there's an interesting interplay between absence and presence, isn't there . . . both a temporal and experiential to and fro? Is he occupying multiple spaces or is there meant to be some kind of disjunction?"

I had learned by this stage of my academic struggle that there is no obligation whatsoever to answer the specific question in hand. The tutor can say anything and you would still begin with the same point that you'd lined up the night before. Apparently Ella and I were both rather keen that day, edging forward simultaneously and going to speak. This kind of eagerness can usually be interpreted in one of two ways: either you are incredibly engaged and bursting with things to say about the writer under discussion; or (more often the case) you have one point and one point *only* that you think might just about be worthy of vocalization. Ella and I faltered, slightly embarrassed by the awkwardness that such clumsy moments create, and with comic coordination (abashedly shaking our heads) we said, "Oh sorry, you go." But it was me who insisted on defeat, opening my palms in a permissive gesture and sitting back into the couch.

"Well, I think in my essay I used Schiller's distinction between the naïve and the sentimental . . ." Looking to me, she added, "The naïve being harmony with nature and the sentimental being an estrangement from nature, or self-consciousness, if you like." Yes, I do like that; I nodded, and began to scribble. "And I think that what we get in *The Prelude* is a series of parables about the emergence from naïve complacency into self-consciousness, of course bolstered by lots of self-pleasing myths and stories, like the boat and the willow tree, et cetera." Wow, I thought to myself, as I continued to make notes: Ella is *well* fit. Dylan was smiling, rubbing his forehead and somehow making his tiny body spread over the entire chair.

"But of course," Ella continued, "the sense of innocence cannot be reaccessed, as it were, because it's all ciphered through the *mature* poet's imagination. This might enable him to carry out deeper interpretations of the past and to understand early experience more fully—where before there was a severe deficit of understanding—but it does mean that the perceptions fundamentally aren't the same. They are the perceptions of the poet writing the poem rather than the recalled younger self. Just think of those grotesque descriptions of the baby Wordsworth as a 'dwarf Man,' and what he refers to as 'the monster birth.'"

This hits me like a wet slap across the cheek: my nightmares, our history . . . I feel giddy. I think Ella suddenly realizes too and silences herself, sinking back.

"Precisely. And doesn't he sound like a precocious little prick . . . Christ, he's a fucking shit: 'his teachers stare, the country people pray for God's good grace.' What a terror!" said Dylan. Ella and I laughed uncertainly. "You should both check out Kristeva on the 'semiotic realm.'" Dylan started talking about Kristeva's notion of language that is alive to irruptions, disruptions, and discontinuities, and how these moments of rupture represent a sense memory of the prenatal; recollections of being in the womb puncturing present through erratic language. All this talk of wombs and babies had me in a hot flush, my neck burning, my stomach whirling. Ella was the same; I could tell from the loud activity of her pen. I desperately refrained from making eye contact.

"The thing I find interesting about Wordsworth," I said with shaky voice, looking to regain control of myself, "is how often he seems to be in an anticipatory state. The world he evokes is one filled with the potential for fallenness, yet there is a sense that all the mistakes and trials are there for the healing, and therefore the end is always inscribed in the beginning. There's a knowingness to his narration, though he often proves to have got things wrong. But going back to what you were saying about language, Ella, it seems to me that language is constantly failing him . . . he is in a perpetual struggle to find a teleology that might harness all the stops and byways of his memory."

"That's why guilt is so catalytic in his poetry," she responded. "Guilt as both an experiential and an expressive thing: there's all the guilt of past sins, and the Miltonic notion of the fall, or multiple falls, but then there is also a linguistic guilt—that he can't do himself justice, can't access the pure thought or true moment of the past, and most importantly the prelapsarian innocence of his past."

"Of course the inability of language in the present to express what a feeling was in the past becomes a perfect metaphor for the child's lack of knowledge," I said. "I think the real tragedy in much of Wordsworth's poetry isn't so much his difficulty to deal with *himself* but the struggle to understand and deal with *others*; it's the unreachability of other lives, and the loneliness of observing from the outside, that really sticks. I think that's where the plaintive tone comes from, like when he sees the girl with the pitcher on her head." (I skimmed through my edition of Wordsworth.)

> "It was, in truth,
> An ordinary sight; but I should need
> Colors and words that are unknown to man
> To paint the visionary dreariness
> Which, while I looked all round for my lost guide,
> Did at that time invest the naked Pool,
> The Beacon on the lonely Eminence,
> The Woman, and her garments vexed and tossed
> By the strong wind.

How do you penetrate another life? Where is the language of true and accurate empathy?"

Fuck knows what Ella was thinking after I said all that. She looked at me pensively and seemed to be passing an unspoken message. I sometimes get the feeling that something from the past—something that might only exist subconsciously—is trying to tell me something; providing me with a glimpse of the truth, but I never know what to do with it.

I felt Ella's presence painfully, so rare and refined. I watched her with full measure: how she'd carefully interject Dylan's points with a forward shuffle and flick of the head; how she'd turn and watch me when I struggled to make a point and then start writing things down to validate me and make me feel more interesting; how she'd chew the lid on her pen, fold her legs gracefully, and smile and nod. It seemed she had two spheres only: Finals and Jack (in that particular order). I could just about make my presence felt in relation to the former, but I was utterly excluded from the latter, my friendship with Jack just a glimmer of the past, receding with each passing day.

Ella asked if she could go to the toilet and left me to handle the tutorial alone for the last few minutes. She waited for me outside and we left together.

"Started doing any revision?" I asked.

"A little bit. We still have so much new work to do though."

"Yeah, I'm not going to start quite yet."

The silences were unbearable as we descended the stairs and spilled out onto the quad. I wanted to ask her if she fancied a drink down the bar later on, but time was running out. Just as we approached the staircase to the college library and were about to fork off in different directions, I asked, "So what are you up to tonight?"

"Probably do a bit of work and then hang with Jack."

"Oh right. That's cool."

"You?"

"Just work."

We stopped and faced each other.

"Well, I'm going up to the library . . ."

"Okay, back to my room I think."

"Cool. Well, have fun . . ."

"I'll try my best. See you."

"Bye."

I strolled back to my staircase in the corner of the first

quad, just off from the porter's lodge. I chucked my lined pad and pen onto the desk and curled up on the sofa. The room was sullen, cold, and drab. After burning a few seconds in self-pitied inertia I pulled out my phone and started dialing Lucy but canceled the call.

I stand apart, watching vile bodies emerge from the toilets: bleary-eyed lads drawing up their flies and buttoning their jeans as they walk back into the club, the strobe lights slashing across their faces and shirts (phosphorescent hair, coral teeth, pearl buttons). Such a hapless male trait, the walking fasten-up. Men in pubs, bars, and clubs, vacating Gents while dressing themselves, careening and tripping over the tricky multitask, straightening backs and puffing chests to facilitate the zip. The quicker you get out of there the better. But it's more than that: a gesture of macho nonchalance, lazily, even cockily performed; a sign of just how long it takes to shut up shop. Men have a bodily assertiveness that far outweighs women's (I also watch the girls passing through the adjacent door, a comparative haven of sparkling surfaces and perfumed air, puckering freshly applied lip gloss and ruffling their hair), wearing our pushed-out paunches, shamelessly flaunting scratches and intricate rearrangements, broadcasting belches, hawking, and farting, even vamping up what could easily have been a tempered sneeze, all as a sign of masculinity. Maybe we like to confirm our being—our virility and potency—through such acts of carnal candor.

Or is it a challenge? A challenge to other men (look how brash and bold I am), a challenge to women (can you handle all of *this*?), and a challenge to ourselves (can I dress on the move, amplify bodily activity, *and* itch remote valleys and coves, all at the same time?).

A lack of transparency and so many subtexts—it's all getting too much.

I'm running out of time.

Desperate to set Jack straight, on one issue at least, I stop him as he pogos past, fresh from the toilet, and say, "Mate, can I have a word?"

"Huh?" he shouts, leaning his head into my mouth, struggling to hear me over the all-consuming din.

"Can I have a word?"

"Sure, sure."

There are some cushioned seats in one of the corners, mainly occupied by boys getting in there with tipsy girls— lots of ear whispering and "oi, cheeky" slaps of knees and arms—and we make ourselves at club.

"What's up?"

There's no delicate way around it. The less fumbling and stuttering the better, what with sound being such a limited economy in here. "I slept with Ella. She *did* have an abortion and it was because of me. I'm sorry, mate."

Jack has heard these words loud and clear, as though their significance has lifted them over the music. He stares ahead at the ground, ear still lowered to my face.

"Jack, I'm really sorry."

He takes a few seconds, all sound seeming to disappear and motion slowing down.

"Drink?" he asks, everything suddenly speeding back up to real time and filling in. But I'm really not up for it, not game, not psyched.

"Sure."

We jump up in tag-team mode and press on, picking

and poking our way through to the bar. SORRY, 'SCUSE, COMIN' THROUGH, EASY FELLA, 'SCUSE ME.

Up front we stand like leaders of the thirsty rabble. "Two sambucas," orders Jack. I feel my body recoil in anticipatory dissent: *really*? Do we *really* want this? Is this *really* what we need right now? I hate you.

We throw them back.

When I regain vision (having scrunched my eyes shut and reeled for a five-second dizzy spell), Jack is standing there looking at me, entirely composed. Straight up. Hello? He turns back to the bar.

"Same again."

"No, I—" I begin to intercede.

"Same again," he repeats, deadpan.

Okay then.

My gag reflexes are fuming with me now: you absolute cock; you complete wanker; you total great big fucking twat. I'm sorry. I'm sorry.

These also go back, fiery and polluted. Teeth clench and seethe.

Jack's staring at me. He's gone. Cold. On standby.

"Another," he says. The modality is unclear: Subjunctive? Imperative? Indicative? Certainly not optative. All options are shot.

"Jack, I've had enough."

"Another."

"Seriously, I . . ." He burns holes through my eyes, lighting up the back of my skull. Two more sambucas are requested.

We hold our weapons in a stare-out . . . his stoical stares . . . historical stares . . . hysterical stares.

"Salute."

"Salute," comes the weary echo.

And back.

"Hahahaha," roars Jack, head thrown toward the ceiling. "Oh, how we laugh!"

"Yeah," I say, my forced smile coming free from its holds and beginning to sag.

"Oh dear oh dear oh dear," he says in descending tones, like a deflating balloon. "Another," he concludes, almost aggressively.

"No, Jack."

"Oh come on, you pussy."

"I can't."

"Yes you can, you boring old shit."

"Jack—"

"You're having another, cunt."

We drink.

This one finally gets him. He squirms like a man trapped in a snare. Butchered. And this time it is me who watches, utterly desensitized to the spirit's snap and bite. Recovered, Jack gives a near-imperceptible nod and peels off. I stay back and watch him fighting his way toward the exit. It's for the best. He'll need some time for it to sink in.

I stand on the fringes of the dance pit. It leaks spews bleeds. Hades is four steps down and hugely tempting. At the foot of the descent, virtually in front of me, a scrum of lads is *brightsiding* (shirts off, aloft, windmilling). There's a lot of fancy dress on display, mostly intentional: boys in drag (rugby/rowing types); a few bedraggled superheroes (sweating by the gallon in their full body-kits); and any number of girls, basically nude, bar some choice accessories to signal their theme (wings, horns, hard hats).

I'm isolated. Everywhere I look I see Lucy, but there is

no Lucy. All the couples compressing and kissing are Lucy and the Other; all the girls shamelessly checked out by meat-hungry lads are showcase Lucys; even the voice booming from the speakers is Lucy. I'm drowning in artificial presence. But I'm isolated.

I spy a bloke desperately protecting his girlfriend. She's dancing about, a hell of a time, while he forms barriers around her, granting her exclusive space. It's her private party as he fends off all those alien bodies. But she's oblivious. He's torturously aware, her personal bodyguard, glaring and sending signals, wound tight as a wrung flannel.

Memories of nights out with Lucy. Her proud boyfriend. Her paranoid boyfriend. Every bloke (some nonexistent) would eye her up and apply the imaginary feelers. Then they would see me and retract or vindictively turn the knife. What's it like when I'm not around? What happens then? As all guys will tell you, *it's different for girls*. Men approach *them*. That's how it works. It's inevitable. Girls don't accost boys (ask any poor sod in a rut of sexual deprivation). We have to do the work and accept that some other dickhead will put in the hours in our absence. It's just different.

Lucy, as I recall, is one of those dancers who doesn't realize what she's doing. By this I mean to say that she has zero spatial awareness and a most compromised peripheral vision. She swings her hips wildly and undulates her back as though gesturing to people in her rearview mirror; only she has no rearview mirror. Countless lads get drawn into her vicinity, thinking they've been chosen, called, beckoned. A real nightmare for the acutely observant boyfriend. But this is all by the by, being of minor relevance to me now.

"Where's Laura?" asks Scott, emerging from the mob, struggling to keep his surveillance subtle.

"Haven't seen her, mate."

"I think I'll head to the toilet and do a recce," he says. He's shortly followed by Abi and Megan, who have spotted some netball friends, with Sanjay straggling alongside in pursuit of Megan.

I'm a boy apart.

This music is doing my nut. Dirty great club tunes gyrating in my face. Feels like I'm trapped in an ad for a techno compilation CD. *Thummmp thummmp, hummmp hummmp, dzzz dzzz, 'AVE IT LARGE* . . .

"It's rammed in here," notes Ella, more as something to say than a pressing observation.

"Mate, I'm sweating buckets already," I reply, contorting my body as yet another drink (JD and Coke) express-routes it down my gullet. Those sambucas are still sitting miserable and resigned in my stomach, waiting for the inexorable top-up.

Her eyes are thoughtful, her mouth delicately strained. "Eliot—"

The babe is looking directly into my eyes, searching for something inscrutable. He isn't saying anything anymore; just a blank canvas waiting for my traces—

"Eliot? Are you okay?"

"Yeah, of course."

"Okay," she says, looking at me doubtfully. "Do—"

I've got him in one of those baby holders, like a rucksack you wear on your front. He faces me and I face him, up close, my aged reflection, snug as one body. Where I go, he goes. But he isn't saying anything.

He has started getting nosebleeds. They trickle like a showerhead left slightly on. The babe never makes a peep about it, so I don't realize until I feel the liquid licking my chest. Every now and then he simply wipes his nose on me, which I like, because if you look hard enough, I swear, a subtle hint of his mischievous smile begins to dance and flicker across his face again. He's sleeping a lot too, I've noticed, and quite fitfully, his harmless balls of fist hammering at the sides of my arms.

I've taken him for a stroll in the University Parks. I thought he'd like that. Maples, birches, horse chestnuts, sycamores, cedars—they loom about us in polychromatic swarms—orange, red, purple, green, brown, gold—flush, flutter, blush. We weave through the elephantine trunks, gruff bark, dappled light pirouetting all about us, mysterious dusts floating across occasional sunbeams. The lush grass cuddles my feet and I wish he could feel it too, but I'm too frightened to put him down: I don't want him to fall or get lost. And besides, I'm pretty sure he can't walk—

"Eliot!" shouts Ella. "What's wrong with you?"

"Nothing!" I yell back, beginning to resent the feeling of being tested so—

Some apples drop about my head, bullied by an unexpected gust of wind, so I place a protective hand over the babe's crown. He is still looking at me with milky gaze, my little bundle of damage. A green thought in a green shade, I marvel to myself. Bending down I scoop a handful of the fruit, chucking the bruised ones away and selecting the fittest. I take a bite to test it and see that it is good.

"Here, matey, have some of this."

I hold it to his lips. He watches, locking me in his impossible stare. He gouges a hunk out of the shiny red ball, finally showing some life. His eyes close as he explores the rich, juicy fullness of his mouth.

And then I notice that the park is empty.

Even the sun has abandoned us of a sudden. An alien charge of agoraphobia rushes over me. We are alone in boundless solitude. I feel as though I'm unspooling, pulled in all directions, clinging desperately to the babe. You can't tear us apart.

I kiss him gently on the forehead. He's saying nothing, just watching me and waiting for my next move—

"Eliot? Are you okay?"

The room's spinning. I'm trying to yawn the nausea away but it isn't working. I can feel myself doing a color change.

"I'm gonna be sick . . ."

I'm off, swimming an angry breaststroke through the muddlesome pissheads, fighting my way to the toilets. *Fuck this*, screams my dissident stomach. *Let me out*, yelps my pounding brain. I explode into the Men's and line up a vacant cubicle, pawing after lock and seat.

Shut in, I survey the scene, down on my lousy knees. Some of the blokes in this club have hopeless aim: there's piss all over the broken toilet seat and in pools on the floor where I kneel, also splattered up the wall. This gets me choking and heaving. It goes something like this: cough, retch, cough, retch, cough, retch, belch (with a gulping noise at the end that swoops from high to low). My Adam's apple is palpitating like a frog's groggy throat . . . a toad's saggy sack . . . It's sick.

The first few splodges get their comeuppance, scatter-gunned about the pan. The sight and smell conspire to warmly invite more gut rot to the party, so I continue on with comic sound effects.

It's rather a supportive atmosphere they cultivate here in Filth; here in the Filth toilets. Not only is there the Nigerian vendor caring for my hygiene ("no spray, no lay"), but there's empathy in the adjoining cubicles. I can hear at least two other pukers around me. I feel their pain.

"No splash, no gash."

"Oh fuck," says the cubicle next to me, following a hefty hurl.

"Sanjay?"

"Freshen up for the pussy."

"Eliot?"

"Ah mate, you too?"

"Guys?" says the cubicle to the other side of me.

"Scott?"

"Yeah, it's . . ." (he pauses to retch) "me."

"Wash your finger for the minger."

"Ah" (*brrrrp*) "mmm" (*prfmff*) "mate" (long extended chunder).

"This is" (*hwock*) "bullshit."

Our staccato conversation is punctuated by vomming pyrotechnics. We've drunk beyond excess, and you can bet that we share formidable pride in this overt display of legendariness. (This must be the most I've drunk since the night I got so pissed that I woke the next morning to find, inexplicably, that I had purchased Seal's entire back-catalogue on iTunes.) We synchronize one final chuck: "*Blooorrrreeaaaww.*"

"Ah mate."

And there in the multicolored pan is all my money—a

full chunky refund. It's a fizzy remuneration, for sure, but you have to take what you can get when you're a student.

"Let's just have a good night" (*hurrumm*), "yeah?"


Blundering back into the field of play I'm overcome by an ecstatic post-vomit buzz; a strange euphoria of relief and renewal.

Welcome back to Filth, where it's getting harder and harder to run from the past . . . harder to disassociate myself from myself . . . harder to defer completion . . .

Glad I got that sick out of the way. Wooooooo, did I need that. I mean, sick is sick, but it has to be done. I feel so refreshed; a new man. I sink a Jägerbomb and grab a plastic bottle of the cheapest, nastiest beer to celebrate the fact. Things are looking up.

The music has progressed to hip-hop. A definite improvement (only when the right examples of the genre are chosen, of course). Oxford's private-school brethren act all urban in dance and attitude. It's unsurpassable entertainment. Savor it while it lasts, because the dreaded cheese hour looms.

Ella has spotted me. There are so many intervening bodies, zigzagging and colliding, American-smoothing and Argentine-tangoing, blocking her way. It's like one of those clichéd moments in a film when two lovers are separated on a bustling city street or at a busy airport, and one is desperate to get to the unaware other. Only I *am* aware, so I turn to escape. I can't handle all this. I'm not ready to tell her anything.

What have I done to Jack? I have to find him.

On my way out of the club I get my hand stamped by the semifit girl at the door to ensure reentry. She must get so much abuse from bladdered lads straining to be romantic. The blotchy black mark she impresses on my hand will still be there tomorrow morning, a confused bar code, unsure of what exactly it encodes.

The music deadens into a dull thud and the cold air gives my face a bitter, chap-lipped kiss. There's still a queue out here, though it has thinned and shortened. Packs of compulsive smokers scruff the place up. My sweat becomes tinglingly apparent. I'm worried about my best mate. Where's he gone? What's he doing? I follow the railings and bend off round the corner, swiveling my head in concerned search. I flick my collar and bury my hands in my pockets.

This is bullshit. So much for rebuilding our friendship.

We only became close again recently. It was just before Finals. I was sat in my room hunched over some scribbled lecture notes, revising, when there came a beep on my laptop. Mugshot.com: *instant message*.

> You in ur room?
> Yeh
> Can I come over?
> Sure thing.

We had barely talked all year. I couldn't face him now that he was with Ella, and he must have noticed the difference, though he never raised it. He wouldn't confront me and say, "You've changed," or "Is everything okay between the two of us?" Lads just can't pull off those kinds of conversations. The sudden distance made him awkward in turn, as though my frigidity was infectious. Maybe he put it down to the fact that we had been the only witnesses on that drastic night in Ella's room, like I wasn't able to factor it all in and return to normal. But as exams lurked nearer it became easier to justify detachment and insularity anyhow, what with revision to take care of and paranoia to nurture. Everyone was focusing their energies on work, so social drifts and adjustments were pretty standard. Jack definitely realized something was up though. I remember walking toward him in the main quad one afternoon, not knowing whether to say hi or duck my head and shiftily pass on by. I contemplated feigning a phone call, or pulling off a blinding sneeze. Once we had locked eyes, still thirty meters apart, I had no choice but to make a sheepish acknowledgment. When though? The distance toward our meeting point seemed interminable, and the quad was silent, making a long-range greeting a feasible option. And how? A quick "hey mate," or a token "alright" (no—that could be mistaken for a genuine question, in which case he would reply, and then I would be forced to respond to his reply, and so on), or maybe just a nod . . . In the end I peaked too soon, opting for a premature "hello" which he then echoed, with another ten meters of pained silence and self-consciousness until we actually passed.

So this request was sharply unexpected. It certainly set me on edge as I blasted around my room, sorting my personalized mess into depersonalized piles, changing iTunes to something subtle and cool. I felt like I was preparing for a date. I was nervous.

Bang. Jack was at the door. What could he want? A fight?

"Hey mate," I said, rather optimistically, as I opened up.

"Alright?" He took in the scene as he entered: pile upon pile of books (I had emptied the college library of all its lit crit) and furling A2 sheets plastered with messy brainstorms and quotations, spread over the wooden floor.

"Working hard then?" he said with that trembling yet accusatory tone indigenous to the frazzled Finalist. Ordinarily I would give the standard "Oh my god, I've done fuck all" sob story, but this was evidently impossible, busted amongst my intricate den of notes and folders.

"Yeah, well, you know, trying," I said. "I seem to spend more time *thinking* about revision than actually doing any though." That was pretty accurate (*to be fair*). "How's yours going?"

"Disastrously," he said. Yeah right. You're just lucky we aren't in your room. He dumped himself onto my sofa, so I lurched for the desk chair.

*So is shagging Ella all you thought it would be?* I felt like saying, small talk being impossible in this kind of situation. Instead I settled for the rather more reserved: "Cup of tea?"

"Cheers."

Jack fidgeted while I made the drinks, like he was trying to shake off a pest that had been dragging him down.

"Everything okay?"

"Ah mate."

"Ah mate?"

"Ah mate."

"I'm sorry. What happened?"

We sipped our drinks and I made haste to burn my tongue. Felt like carpet.

Ella and Jack had broken up.

"It's impossible really." He watched me cautiously between sentences, trying to judge whether it was wise to pull me back into his affairs. I wanted in, desperately. "She's a demon when it comes to work, and she's got a one-track mind now Finals are near. It hasn't been easy. She's absolutely convinced that she's going to fuck up her exams. It's ridiculous . . . I mean, you know better than me how clever she is . . . and dedicated. She reckons Dr. Fletcher has it in for her, and that she's been at a disadvantage ever since she asked to switch her tutorials over to Dr. Snow. You'd think there was a conspiracy the way she goes on about it. She gets really upset when she talks about this stuff. And it isn't just like nerdy paranoia . . . I mean she properly sobs and shit."

"I had no idea. We don't have many tutes together anymore, but from what I've heard she's doing great."

"Exactly. But she is beyond obsessive when it comes to her studies. She loses so much sleep thinking about whatever she's working on and pulling all-nighters to nail essays. I think the pressure of work had a lot to do with her suicide attempt, you know?"

I nearly choked on my tea. It was so unexpected—we had never talked about that event to each other. "Do you think?"

"Yeah. Well, that and some other stuff, but I probably shouldn't go into it all." I got the sense that he wanted to confide in me, but I was raring to move the conversation on, panicking at the thought that Ella might have told him what happened between us.

"Of course. I don't want to pry, mate. Maybe you just need to break until Finals are done."

We slurped our tea a bit more. Civilized, like.

"Maybe. I don't know. I'm not convinced. It's more than that though . . . Sometimes I think she only ended up with me because she was vulnerable. I was there when she needed someone and perhaps she wasn't thinking straight. I don't resent that . . . I understand. If anything, I feel guilty, like I took advantage or something."

"I'm sorry, man. I really am. It's hard to know what to say."

"Don't worry. I know. It's tough opening up about this as it is." We both looked down, feeling it excruciatingly unmanly to engage each other's eyes. "You really are the only person I can turn to right now."

"Cheers, bro." I cringed at this for it sounded far more

conceited than I had intended; almost knowing. "I've missed you, actually," I ventured, still looking anywhere but at Jack.

"I've missed you too . . . man."

I was getting choked up, which was ridiculous. I gave an "ah mate" to puncture the awkwardness.

"So was it mutual?" I said to the wall.

"Kinda . . . I guess," he said to the floor. "I mean, we're more like brother and sister these days." We silently nodded, as though we had collaboratively hit upon a hard-gleaned truth. "She better get a fucking First after all this." We both laughed, relieved to be sharing an emotion with which we were more accustomed. Mates again, I guess . . . in a way.

*Where is he?*

I'm never going to find Jack out here. I'm feeling clearer-headed though, the breeze having whipped some sense into me, so I wander back inside the club and loiter around the edge of the dance floor, trying to locate some familiar faces. I observe the dancers absently, writhing in their dis-possessed bodies. They shake their selves off like a dog shakes from the rain. They're all mass productions.

Someone nudges me in the back. It's Ella. "Are you okay now?"

Is Ella the one? I thought I had the answer, but now . . . Just tell her and see what happens . . .

My phone is vibrating. Instead of talking I pull it from my pocket and start squinting at the screen.

> Eliot, pls don't be mad.
> I do want to talk to you
> properly about this x x

"How's Lucy?" says Ella, perhaps affronted by the discourtesy and guessing the source of the message. "Still keeping in touch with her?"

"Oh fuck off, Ella." What does she know about it—about Lucy, about us? How could she ever understand how badly I've ruined things? "Just fuck off, would you?"

Ella swings wide and high with her flattened hand and although things seem to be running in slo-mo I don't bother to duck. I deserve it and I'm going to take it. My cheek stings with the immediate sensations of hard truth. I grab her by both arms and confront her: "Stop being such a cunt." My shout demands the attention of several people around us. There's a fleck of spittle on Ella's cheek, loathsome evidence of me losing it. The future is suddenly closing in on me, my chest tightening, my head about to implode. Where am I going? What am I going to do with myself?

"I hate you," bawls Ella, ripping herself free and running off.

I watch her disappear for a few seconds before I turn around. Spinning, I crash into a girl who is standing right behind me. She falls hard to the ground.

"Sorry," I say, bending desperately to help her up, everything moving in unexpected directions. A hand grabs me round the collar and yanks me to my feet.

"What the fuck do you think you're doing touching my girlfriend?" shouts a burly bloke with popping eyes and chunky jaw.

"I was help—"

"You're a fucking wanker, mate," he says, nose on nose. I don't say anything. I'm too shocked about everything that has happened. I'm shaking. "You're a fucking wanker." He throws me off and I stutter my way to the edge of the club.

He's right. I *am* a fucking wanker. So what? At least I can admit it.

## Eliot Lamb: Curriculum Vitae

I have significant and diverse experience in fucking things up. During my time at Oxford University, where I have recently completed a BA in Fucking Things Up, I have been able to fuck things up to a very high standard through my unwavering hard work and dedication, while still managing to consistently fuck up academically. Moreover, due to my personal drive and ambition I was able to fuck up my two best friends *and* my girlfriend almost simultaneously. I believe that this exceptional ability to balance my extracurricular and academic fucking up demonstrates strong organizational skills.

I relish working in a team, as evidenced by my aforementioned participation in the fucking up of my two best friends and girlfriend. At the same time, I am extremely confident in leadership roles, such as when I efficiently orchestrated the fucking up of said trio.

I have represented my county in fucking up for several years.

Furthermore, I have strong communication skills: I was able to fuck up my best mate by telling him clearly and concisely that I fucked and fucked up his ex-girlfriend. The subsequent calamity demonstrates my ability to construct an argument that is both cogent and authoritative. Indeed, I have been told by various people that I am highly effective at fucking things up.

With all of my experience in fucking things up, I have been able to cultivate a notable degree of self-fucked-upness, which makes me an ideal fucker-upper. I am absolutely committed to, and passionate about, fucking up and am fluent in several different types of fucking things up.

I am keen to enter the world of advanced fucking up, and am eager to fuck things up in a range of new and exciting ways.


Yes, I am a wanker, and it's time to be completely straight with myself about this . . .

Thus I sense this chapter of my life closing in toward a conclusion, and the past few weeks have been some of the most significant in getting here. I completed Finals just ten days ago and the buildup to this landmark event was intense and never to be forgotten. That is perhaps untrue: the details have already failed to remain, though the leaden sense of responsibility has stuck.

My mind, my welfare, and indeed my life entire, had been reduced to Post-it notes. They were splattered about the room (against the walls, up the side of the desk, above my bed) like shot-out bits of brain. They carried quotations which I had strained to learn and have since more leisurely forgotten. Revision doesn't suit me. It requires extended concentration and an airtight memory, and I have neither of these. I have the retention of a fork in a bowl of soup and the attention span of a knob. I like to tell myself that I have ADHD but it's yet to be clinically verified. Everyone's ADHD these days. The Internet and TV have programmed us this way. It's evolution, though I don't have the necessary time, concentration, or tools to prove this. Twenty-first-century condition. (Note: apply for large postgraduate grant to carry out fairly in-depth study of this.)

I did try hard though. I badly wanted a First and I knew that this meant a certain amount of total devotion. I drew up one of those revision timetables that grossly overestimates the human capacity and—when you fail to keep up with it—makes you feel like a no-good slacker. Each morning my alarm grated that much more, increasing and increasing with exponential severity. It was especially soul-crushing when it signaled nothing more than a date with Jeff Chaucer or an early-morning workout with the Middle Scots poets.

Revision fertilized thoughts of Lucy and Ella like shit on a field of crops. I was Milton's Adam, for instance, eating chocolate-caramel digestives in the Garden of Eden with my Lucy-Eve. We'd take our fill of love and love's disport, wet with the solace of sin. And then, with postlapsarian vigor, a cry of "Sex me here." And I would obey this Lady, in my head, over on the bed. And then, back on my feet, walking around the room, throwing a baseball up and down, I would recite, "Let us go then, you and I, when Ella's legs are spread out against the sky."

My wanking schedule quadrupled over the revision period. I could always find time for this, the ultimate distraction. No sweat. There was the painfully bladdered wake-up wank, the manic morning rush-hour wank, the corpulent post-lunch wank, the traditional wank-then-nap afternoon wank, the limp dessert wank, the steamy shower wank, and the fantastical knockout nightcap wank. Arm cramp, bollock ache, and bell-end friction burn were constant afflictions, but so much less painful than the eighteenth-century sentimental novel. That said, there were many sentimental wanks (over Lucy), and sociability was never far away (the frustrating Jack-and-Ella combo insisting on guest appearances: oh fuck off . . . get the hell out of here). Lucy or Ella would always claim the dénouement and end credits, of course, me being a loyal kind of guy. Unfortunately my "ADHD" even managed to infect my wanking—my subject rarely holding a position, a scenario, or even a face, for more than a second at a time. Sad to admit, I became a dour master at the limp tug, reaching dull orgasms without even getting it up—just shaking it from the wrist like I was throwing dice. This virtually always ended in sorry throbs of guilt (revision revision revision) and a grimy self-loathing (she's not yours). Try all that eight times a day with impenetrable literary quotations tramping through your head. Now *that's* what I call hard work. If I get my First I won't have anyone saying it's undeserved.

I go to the bar and reload. I need it more than ever.

Call it what you will (drunk, pissed, fucked, hammered, lashed, steaming, destroyed, blottoed, pie-eyed, wankered, off your tits, lubed, mullered, paralytic), but I like to think of it as transcendence. I'm nothing less than a spiritual ideal walking around with sticky tequila stubble and warm, fuzzy bottles of Bud. The consumption levels tonight have been abnormally high (which is the norm) and we're veering toward an entirely other plane of consciousness. Time for an outer-body experience, don't you think? I unzip myself from the mouth down and climb on out. I float up to the vaulting heights of the twenty-foot ceiling and take it all in from a cosmic perspective. Deep.

Filth is at capacity. It fluctuates like a lapping tongue, curling and twisting; its innumerable force fields work in concentricity, sending shock waves back and forth, side to side, around and around. Steam rises from the surface like heat off some mythical beast. The punters seem so insignificant, locked in their paltry games of sexual auctioneering and mindless clowning. I watch this grotesque globule of performance from afar with profound disinterest.

Who am I? Where do I fit into all this? I see an eighteen-year-old (baggier jeans, higher buttoned shirt, fresher face) prancing about, an irrepressible little first-year. Me? Eliot the kid in miracle world, leaping and swimming from station to station. Me? It's his first night here and he's hurling drinks down his gullet to get things off to an appropriate start. Me? He is religious in the attention he pays to a wide-eyed Ella. Me? He knocks about ecstatically with his hoped-for reflection, Jack. Me? He reeks of relief and contentedness. Me? He misses Lucy, his new girl-friend from back home. Definitely me. How inconsequential this all seems.

Dear lover, who art thou? O bold lover, where art thou? I struggle to find the language. Shall I compare thee . . . oh stop it, stop it. Enough. Enough; a nought; the noughties.

We are not an age kitted out for the telling of true love, hardwired for fripperies and drivel instead.

No, but we *are* capable of love, if we can just get over ourselves for a second.

Is this love? Who am I to judge.

Is this a failed love letter? Doesn't even come close.

I come back down to earth. I'm hemmed in by animal shapes and horror-show masks. A girl with a spotty face and dirty teeth pins me back—"Nice hair! Haha! How d'ya get it like that?" A gluey Neanderthal with corrugated neck pushes me aside as he plods into the pit, throwing me at a terrifying stranger who wants to dance up close and personal. Her face is in mine: eyes shot, pupils swollen black holes, mouth twisted, cheeks mushy. I slide away, dragged helplessly by the filthy, murky slipstreams, farther into the pit. It opens its fishy gob to receive me.

Down in the belly of the beast I knock heads with various stumbling blocks, sticking to dripping hairdos, swiped by hyper elbows. Can someone please take me to lost property so I can reclaim my identity? I feel utterly stripped in here, menaced by clattering bodies, stuck in *The Triumph of Death*: swarms snapping their gnashers, blurring limbs shoving me about, splashed all over in anonymous sweat. Despite all the intimacy and mutual palpitations, there is zero sense of oneness. We are monads, every bugger stagnating in a little bubble of *me*. Part of me wants to skip about with a huge fuck-off needle, popping them all and singing, "Let's all just be outside ourselves." But then I don't want nobody getting up inside my bubble, no thank you. I want to be left to myself.

"Eliot!"

Thank fuck for that. Everyone is together, right in the heart of the dance floor. Come in, come in, say their smiley emoticon faces and flailing arms.

"Where you been, you tosser?" We're all dancing, together, each to his or her own ability.

"Looking for you. Looking for you."

And here we are. Friends renewed just in time for the end credits. The last night of uni. The final dance.

This is it. Fittingly, an absolute tune comes on. We make t-shapes with our bodies to acknowledge the fact: Sanj a capital T, laying his arm horizontally across his head, me a lowercase t, stretching my arms out to the side like a cross, and Scott (the most restrained alphabetizer of the three) raising a forefinger and laying his other hand on top in a baby t, or *time out* sign. So, as you can see, although we vary in opinion on the degree of the tuneage, we nevertheless agree that it is indeed a tune. (The artist? Some American rapper. The tune? Some American rap song.) Tune.

We sing the chorus together (utter babble), arms around each other, occasionally forming a ring, beaming like imbeciles. We bloody love it. If I think about what the moment signifies for more than a few seconds (if I *really* think about it), I get teary (it's just sweat in the eyes, mate). Wrapped in our devotional circle, arms locked around waists and shoulders like a rugby team doing the motivational pre-match squeeze, we look into each other's faces: Sanjay, Megan, Abi, Scott, Laura (how'd she get in here?), and Ella. Jack is a gaping absence and the recognition makes me feel sick an instant. Ella is next to me in the circle. I'm sorry for what's happened and give her a tender squeeze to let her know. Her body gives to mine and lets me know that she's still there. I lower my head and rest it on her crown. We feel like a unit again . . . for once. There's a tired euphoria shared by all. Sheer will and emotion have eked out this space for communion amongst the shapeless ruck of pissheads. So this is what you call a happy ending.

And the bonds disintegrate.

We've had our moment.

Now is the time for the majority of the group to meet their conclusions and wave reluctant good-byes. Scott's leaving with Laura, his young love (better things to be doing); Sanjay and Megan are pulling each other, propelled by all the emotion on display and the irresistible force of the "lucky" shirt (she may have a boyfriend but we all think he's a cock anyway, so who cares?); and Abi's struck lucky with some sporty stranger (she'll be spending the night at his). Ella and I are left quite conveniently alone. I take her hand—she feels warm and soft, tired, ready for final gentleness—and lead her out from the mob to the club's outer limits. We hit a booth.

She looks at me intently, by which I mean to say she looks at me with intent. Eros or philia? But this is no time for joking. As Rob would say, it's time to put our dicks on the table.

"I'm sorry I've been so cold to you all year," she says. Well, I wasn't expecting that. Maybe I should run with this: And so you should be, you evil ice queen; you fucking bitch actually. No, that's so far off the mark it doesn't even hold up as interior monologue.

"You've got nothing to be sorry about," I say, rather impressed by the gallant maturity I'm demonstrating.

Ella stirs the ice cubes in her drink with a chewed straw, whipping the contents into a whirlpool. "Things got so horrible . . . so complicated." She pauses as a thought visibly shudders through her body. "I know this is going to sound awful, but in some ways I can't wait for all this to end; to get away from Oxford and everybody here—not you and Jack," she adds hastily. "You two have been such good friends to me. I owe you a lot." I muster all the effort I can to perform a small nod. "It's just been a shitty time in my life. I guess I need to move on."

"Oh." I don't know what to say, so I shift over and put both arms around her. She latches an arm up and over mine and holds on, round and pliant. We sink into each other, enticed by our own delicacy.

Slowly we pull apart, but I keep one arm around her and she continues to lean in. Buoyed by the physical intimacy and the torrents of alcohol tampering with my nervous system, I decide to chance something and just see what happens.

"Am I more than a friend to you, Ella?" I ask. "I guess what I mean is, could you ever see us being . . ." I pause, trying to think of a better phrase . . . something more qualifying and emotive. But it's no longer a question I even want to ask. It's only because it's been stuck in my head all night that it's taking on a force of its own, demanding vocalization. No. This isn't right.

Ella is looking at me: her eyes swimming with punctuation marks that I can't make head or tail of. Her mouth lends no assistance: no upward or downward curve; no opening or bite of lip; just level and secretive. "What did you say?" she shouts, her brow subtly creasing. "It's so loud in here!"

"Nothing," I reply. "No, it doesn't matter."

I'm getting tearful: alcohol, end of an era, wasted opportunities. The intimacy is starting to affect Ella too. We hug tightly, our faces finding their way to each other through the arms and over the shoulders. Forehead on forehead, hand in hand, we look down as though we're inspecting each other's noses. I think we are beginning to smile.

This hold with Ella feels like an eternity, each second stretching itself into abstracted minutes and hours. Tucked in the neat proximity of our hug I am forced images of Lucy, reminders of heavy love. Maybe I've got everything wrong. Ella begins squeezing me tighter, as if to stop her frame from trembling. I feel as though I'm checking back into the womb. I've got my return ticket and excess baggage. It's a moist and salty embrace, one of my hands tucked beneath the soft underhang of her jaw, cheek against cheek, lips drawn into uncompromising vicinities.

Jack stands before us, suddenly nicking the corner of my eye. We unfurl, like he's corroding the joints of our hold.

"Jack!" I jump to my feet, simply to insist on our separateness, but Jack mistakes it for confrontation. He pushes me hard and I fall straight back down on my arse, next to Ella. I go to stand up again, which comes across as further provocation, so Jack assists, grabbing my collar double-fisted and yanking me from the seat.

"What the fuck's with you?" I know what's with him . . . what's with all of us: booze.

"You just couldn't keep your filthy hands off, could you?"

"It's not like that," I appeal, although my temper is starting to rear its sleepy head. I don't like being pushed around, no matter what the context.

"You absolute cunt." Jack delivers a feeble blow to my stomach.

"Jack!" screams Ella (not that this can be heard much over the totality of the music).

Jack pushes me again, so I punch him halfheartedly on the nose. He's bleeding. He then catches me on the cheekbone with a raw, naked fist. Forget returning to the womb, this is like being born all over again: pulled about, kicking and screaming, thumping with anguish, sticky in effluence. I don't want no part of this . . . but if you ain't gonna give me no choice . . .

We start scrapping like only best mates can: sloppy and passionately ineffectual; almost farcical. It's a vulgar exhibition of love and affection. We grapple and grope at each other's faces, not really wanting to close a fist or do any serious damage. We've caused quite a commotion and word has got to the bouncers, their bald heads intuiting a change in Filth's spatio-thermal equilibrium. Send in the heavies. I feel a third hand exploring my jugular with intent to maneuver. And then I'm being shifted from an establishment for the second time tonight. That's a new PB.

"I thought I said no more trouble?" spits the bouncer in my ear, almost lifting me from the floor as he leads me by the collar. "Fuckin university shits."

O Filth, is this the farewell you deserve? Must we part on such terms? I feel scummy. And you can kiss good-bye to the coat (just as I thought).

"Now get the fuck out," says the bouncer as he gobs me onto the pavement. Jack comes flailing behind in a similar fashion, and Ella totters after.

"But we're best mates," protests Jack, as though this gives us some license.

It's freezing out here.

"Why the fuck didn't you ever tell me you'd slept with her?" demands Jack, walking alongside me, almost pushing me into the glass front of the dead Sainsbury's on our right, shut down for the night but still lit up inside.

"Why the hell do you think? What would you have done?" I vaguely nudge him away. Ella is trailing behind, arms folded, staring at her feet as though each step demands painful attention.

"And you reckon you got her pregnant? Jesus Christ, Eliot! How do you know it was you anyway? You always have been an arrogant prick."

"What did you just say?" shouts Ella, darting forward to catch us up. "Can you not talk about me like I'm not here?"

"Oh fuck off, Jack. Yes, it was me. *I* got Ella pregnant!"

"What?" shrieks Ella.

"But even if you did think it was you, how come you never once talked to her about it, hey? You were together for long enough! It obviously hasn't bothered you that much, has it, Jack?"

"Is that what this is about?" cries Ella. "Fuck me!" She laughs in humorless disbelief, looking rapidly between the two of us. "No, no, no. If it makes you feel any better, it wasn't either of you, okay?" We've all stopped. Tears are forming in her eyes. "For fuck's sake, just make up and get over yourselves." Ella squares us both in her tightening gaze. "I'm so sorry," she whispers, and then runs, leaving me and Jack to ourselves.


I've got everything so wrong. Do I understand any of this?

It's just you and me now, kid. You and you, and me and me. Ah implied listener, up in my head. Where would I be without you? It's tough in here. And for me there's no way out. But for you—

For a while I had been able to justify solitude and sacrificed relationships. Until a couple of weeks ago, Finals had practically demanded this. I ruthlessly cut all ties and shrank into myself like a cold-hearted exam killer (fortified by notes, books, printouts, photocopies, illegible annotations, highlighter pens, caffeine, power naps . . .). Strutting down the tight alley of desks and chairs in Exam Schools, a row amongst a gang of rows, my Exhibitioner's gown wafting behind me and my final paper waiting expectantly, facedown on the table like a hardened criminal slapped against a bonnet, I was ready. Once seated (five temperamental Biros laid before me and a perpetual feeling of needing a piss), the clock on the wall began its long-drawn-out gig of menacing me. It had watched me all week with threatening face as I stuttered my way through eight exams: *You're really ticking me off, mate . . . I'll give you something to be alarmed about.* Invigilators, like aged crypt-keepers, wormed around the aisles, leaving trails of skin and dandruff in their wake. Approximately three hundred pasty students ran through their pre-match warm-ups: yawns and eye rubs, nervous giggles, arms stretched skyward, knuckles cracking like cashews, nails bitten to nubs, cocky chairs swinging on hind legs, anxious legs twitching spasmodically beneath desks, brains barely functioning. Me, I play the intimidation game: I line up the BO geek just in front, to the right, and terrorize his periphery; I psyche him out good and proper. I trash talk: you going down, boy; I'm the champ; I own this paper; you ain't got shit.

That's bollocks: I simply watch the clock and then watch Ella.

She was sitting in the row to my left about four people ahead, perfectly positioned to distract me for the next three vital hours of my life.

"You have three hours to answer three questions. You may now turn over your papers and begin. Good luck," said some ordained sod in a gown.

Three essays—that's pretty steep. Three solid hours of reflection and analysis. I'm not sure I can handle that. I want to go easy on myself to be honest. Okay, one last push. Time to assay myself (god knows I've been running from it long enough) . . . I watch Ella . . . Ella's ass eh? Just look at her—nailing it she is. She leaned over her desk with supreme mastery, sailing through carefully written line after carefully written line, all the way toward a royal First.

*I'm gonna walk into the exam* (I'd told Jack in hall at break-fast that morning), *slap my cock down on the table and rag that paper right up the spine.*

*Yeah, mate* (he'd said to me), *you're gonna fuck that paper up* (a vote of confidence).

1) "Compare and contrast Lucy and Ella with special reference to—" oh come on! Jesus. Are we really going to do this? Okay. Okay then. Well, Lucy is . . . well, you know . . . and Ella is . . . yeah, exactly. Or something like that.

Is it just me or is it getting hot in here? I feel terrible. It's nearly over, I tell myself; just stick it out.

I watched Ella filling her script with gems about Philip

Sidney, Thomas Wyatt, the Metaphysical poets. Every now and then she would look up to search her memory bank and ponder a quotation. That's how she appeared to me: in quotation marks; italicized and underlined. She briefly looked over her shoulder and I buried my head to feign industriousness.

I split the page in two and title one half "Ella," the other "Lucy." Where to begin?

My mental plan remains blank. I can't distill anything from these past three years. Lucy and Ella, they just won't fit into the neat categories that I'm searching for. I can't break them down into the necessary beginning, middle, and end; I can't find the line of argument. They are incommensurable and I've given no sense of that. I've got it all wrong.

Leave it. Move on to the second question and come back.

2) "What happened to Ella?"

Now there are two ways I could approach this. I could do *The Anatomy of Melancholy*, or a bit of the old *On Love* . . . Where did we lose her? Pregnant tears of regret fall on my paper.

Why did she tell me I was responsible for the pregnancy? I know I am too drunk to think this one out straight, and I feel too numb to even begin getting angry. I need to stop simplifying. I need to grasp Ella's particularity instead of obsessing over my own. After everything she has been through . . . how work stressed her out (her high expectations and all those unnecessary insecurities about tutors and what they thought of her), her pregnancy and abortion, the guilt she must've felt about keeping everything from Jack, and I guess some guilt toward me too, and, of course, the failed suicide . . . She wants to escape Oxford,

get away from Jack and me and the feelings we evoke . . .
It's Ella who's making all the sacrifices tonight.

(But did she, in fact, tell me I was responsible? It's too
long ago now to say for sure, and the drink only bends the
memories. If it wasn't Jack, and it wasn't me, then who?
The pitcher on the head smashes! No . . . it can't be . . .
can it? I can't bear to think about that. Just move on . . .
move on . . .)

3) "Write an essay on one of the following: yourself;
you; oneself; I; Eliot."

*The Anatomy of Me*? Oh fuck off.

"Time's up. Please put down your pens."


Ejected from Filth, we stand like fallen angels in the artificial dazzle and dynamo glare of Abdul's kebab van. We've
caught Ella up. We are both too stunned to begin an inqui-
sition though. What would be the point? What could questions and accusations achieve now?

This wasn't how I expected it to end. The blood on Jack's
face has congealed. It looks more like the fake stuff you get
from the party shop. He could pass for fancy dress. We
stand apart at small distances suggestive of dejection and
despondence. Our eyes leak vapid blues and greens under
the orange light. We're a misery lineup: Jack, with hands in
pockets, looks at the pavement, feet anxiously tapping and
swiping; Ella, with arms folded for warmth, for comfort,
Jack's coat over her shoulders, stares forlornly into nothing
like someone lost at sea, given up on rescue; I stand phone
in hand, subtly spying from body to body, scrunching and
spreading my empty mitt, starting to throb from the punch,
cold air dissipating the alcohol anesthesia.

"How are you, my friend?" asks Abdul with Middle

Eastern musicality. I put on a brave face for the momentous occasion.

"Sad, Abdul." He nods to say he knew as much. "It's our last night, mate. Most likely our last ever Abdul's." He looks at each of us in turn, passing us over with thoughtful eyes. Hopefully he mistakes our sulky haggardness for appropriate solemnity. Genuine feeling. Respect.

I think I see a tear filling in his eye. "Nah, you'll be back, my friend," he says. I close my eyes and give a series of slow nods.

"Chips cheese hummus?"

"You know me too well." He has the others' orders down too—Jack: chips chicken (burger sauce); Ella: pitta salad hummus.

Standing here on this frozen spot, I can feel our paths slowly uncrossing. There are no words. I smear my nose on the back of my aching hand. Ella looks washed up; she has coldened and vacated her body. There is emptiness behind those eyes. Jack and I are too confused to open our mouths; too lost to venture thought or commentary. Our uneasy glimpses and body language are mere footnotes to a much larger piece; a larger history. There needs no underscore.

The ambience is sparse, the city about to shut down into quiet repose: one or two taxis rushing past, drunken zeros drifting through like urban tumbleweed, four different kebab vans humming and buzzing either side of the road. All is a hush of swishes and far-off cries.

Abdul seals our polystyrene treasuries and wraps a piece of kitchen towel round each.

"On the van," he says with a sniff and a twinkle in his eye, tapping the last box on top. We know not to resist. Respect the van.

"Cheers, Abdul."

"Yeah, cheers, Abdul. You're a fookin legend."

"Don't mention it, my friends," he says from up high in his pulpit. He gives us his blessing. "You've earned it." We watch him appreciatively until the moment is ruined by some pissed pissheads, uncompromising in their belligerence. Abdul goes back to work. Plies his trade. See you, pal.

Our communications are in the process of terminal severance as we turn off the High Street and onto Radcliffe Square—that site which once brimmed with potential and promise—for the last ever time. Behind my drunken windows and the dense black of the night, the Radcliffe Camera is but a watery outline. I can tell that Ella is crying. I want to put an arm around her. But I can't. Jack does.

I'm sending Lucy a text. I know it's a terrible idea—wait till tomorrow when I'm sober, right? But I've got to run with this sense of urgency; it's something I haven't felt for so long. It's a simple text, though the grammar is all over the shop: I ask if I can pop round at the weekend. I know what I need to say to her. She'll be tucked up in bed, the message waiting for her in the morning. And then the phone goes away for the final time tonight.

We reach college and turn into the lodge. The all-night porter clocks us. His watch blinks 3.30 a.m. at him. What I'd give to be young again, he's thinking. Don't do it, mate. It's not all it's cracked up to be.

In the quadrangle we know we have to go different ways. It's like a movie or made-for-TV drama—the emotion is at that high a pitch. A real tearjerker.

Jack carries on, heading for his room and the relief of unconsciousness.

"Jack," I say, stopped still. I'm surprised myself. He turns back. My best mate for the last three years.

"Yeah?"

But I've got nothing.

"Night, Jack," says Ella, softly, in recompense for me.

"Yeah, see ya then." He goes.

This leaves me and Ella. I feel like a dried-up window plant. I could snap at a touch.

She steps into my zone, her foggy breath warm against my face; my face that ducks and glances like a featherweight. She touches my arm.

"Good night, Eliot."

"Night."

I awake this morning to kiss the dawn with bated breath. Molten garlic and eggy beer.

I've finished uni.

Everything around me colludes to do me harm—the sunlight slicing through the open curtains, the noise of students and parents vacating the college for summer, memories of Filth, and the rancid smell of my self. Most of all, knowledge of my self. *This* conspires to ruin me.

Mum and Dad are coming to pick me up. Hazy plans stretch before me like dim asphalt; like soul-baring macadam. I tip my room upside down and place it all in boxes and suitcases, disordered but momentarily contained.

University: done. But what next?

Dad's just rung. They've parked up on Catte Street. He'll be out there now, off-loading the sack barrow onto the pavement in front of Mum, plotting the best formations and most effective combinations, as he drops one of the back seats and moves all his car tools to make room. He's already given me some prep on the phone: suitcases first, then big boxes, then smaller boxes, and then the rest.

Mum gives me a hug when I appear with the first load, all sweaty and doped. I can picture her smiling over my shoulder as I give her a squeeze and make a kissing noise. Then Dad puts a tight grip on my shoulder and draws me into an awkward embrace, the power and heft all coming from him, less reluctant. Before I can say "Alright, Dad," he's headfirst in the boot, legs dangling over the edge, ramming the suitcase into its specially designated corner.

"Need a hand packing any last bits away, love?"

"No thanks, Mum. All done." I take the sack barrow and start wheeling it toward the porter's lodge. In the windscreen, on top of the dashboard, I see that Dad has placed a piece of A4, on which is scrawled: *Traffic Warden— Unloading from Hollywell College. My son is an Oxford student. Ten minutes.*

"Won't be a sec."

The second suitcase goes in, the boxes of books, the box of DVDs, a box of folders and ring binders, a guitar. Clutching some final bags I lock my door for the last time and go to hand the key to the porter.

"Mate," a voice calls as I'm leaving the college gates. I turn to see Jack jogging over from the direction of the quad. "You all packed?"

"Yeah, Mum and Dad are in the car ready to go."

"Ah, cool." We look at each other inquiringly, like we're testing the ground all over again. "So, I was thinking . . . why don't you just come traveling with me and Scott? I mean, we're not going for a while, so it isn't too late." Jack's hair is startled into erratic tufts and clumps, his eyes bleary, just out of bed. "And you haven't got any immediate plans, have you? Might be what you need."

It's a tempting offer: Wellingborough or the world? Job-hunting or traveling? Home-mates or Jack and Scott? They're no-brainers.

New people or Lucy?

"I can't. There's stuff I need to take care of back home."

Jack nods, resigned. "Oh, okay . . . no worries, bro. If you change your mind . . . Good luck and that."

"Cheers, Jack."

Walking toward my parents' car I can see the giant domed library in the background . . . the library that had loomed over me with such dwarfing intention . . . I turn my back on it.

Tucked in the car at last, a guitar jabbing the back of my head, the lid of a box threatening to take my scalp, Dad rustled a bag of humbugs.

"No thanks."

"The Saints game is on the telly this afternoon . . . should get back in time," he said.

"Oh yeah?" I said. "Sounds good."

The formidable colleges began to recede through the window as we pulled away. I saw the shadows of many partings.

"Got any plans for the weekend?" asked Mum, turning in her seat to get a good look . . . her little boy returning to the nest.

"Maybe. We'll see." Mum nodded. I shifted and squinted, the sun blazing inconsiderately across my face.

I hope so.

★

One final dream. I had it last night after we got back from Filth.

He holds a mirror to myself.

"Looking sharp."

The pram is on the other side of the room but I don't

want to go over and look in. I can't handle a nightmare right now.

"Emotional," he snuffles, our eyes misting up.

"Don't," I say, preening my excellent mane. "Let's not get teary already. There's a long night ahead of us."

"True. You're going to have to keep an eye on me." I see the pram in the mirror, a few meters behind. Rejected shirts lie crumpled on the floor and aftershave permeates the air.

I'm meeting the lads at the King's Arms in twenty; the last night of uni. Pub, bar, club. Standard.

My phone vibrates against the desk, the first of the night. It bears compulsive fingerprints of waxing cream.

"It's beginning."

"Yeah."

I just don't know if . . .

The babe is crying.

"What's wrong?" I say, ignoring the phone.

It's the future. That's what's on our minds. The future, with all its misinformation and lies. It doesn't seem too hospitable from where we are.

"Where do we go from here?"

"Don't worry," I say. "It's all going to be okay."

"Are you sure?"

"Yes. I've got you now. Don't worry."

I gaze at myself in the mirror through obscured eyes. I want to cry.

"Don't worry," I say, finally walking over to the pram and reaching inside.

But there's nothing there. It's empty.

Ah mate.